TOWN IN A SWEET PICKLE

This Large Print Book carries the
Seal of Approval of N.A.V.H.

Town in a Sweet Pickle

B. B. Haywood

WHEELER PUBLISHING
A part of Gale, Cengage Learning

GALE
CENGAGE Learning·

Farmington Hills, Mich • San Francisco • New York • Waterville, Maine
Meriden, Conn • Mason, Ohio • Chicago

GALE
CENGAGE Learning·

Copyright © 2015 by Robert R. Feeman and Beth Ann Feeman.
A Candy Holliday Murder Mystery.
Wheeler Publishing, a part of Gale, Cengage Learning.

LIBRARY OF CONGRESS CATALOGING-IN-PUBLICATION DATA

Haywood, B. B.
  Town in a sweet pickle / by B. B. Haywood. — Large print edition.
    pages cm. — (A Candy Holliday murder mystery) (Wheeler Publishing large print cozy mystery)
  ISBN 978-1-4104-8089-7 (softcover) — ISBN 1-4104-8089-5 (softcover)
  1. Holliday, Candy (Fictitious character)—Fiction. 2. Large type books.
  I. Title.
PS3608.A9874T735 2014
813'.6—dc23   2015013802

Published in 2015 by arrangement with The Berkley Publishing Group, an imprint of Penguin Publishing Group, a division of Penguin Random House LLC

Printed in the United States of America
1 2 3 4 5   19 18 17 16 15

For Emily

AUTHOR'S NOTE

Many of the places, businesses, and events that occur in Cape Willington, Maine, are based on real-world New England counterparts. Zeke's General Store in Cape Willington, for instance, is loosely based on Zeb's General Store in North Conway, New Hampshire, a favorite summer vacation stop. The Monterey General Store in Monterey, Massachusetts, also provided inspiration for sections of this novel. A heartfelt thanks to those who have helped out in various ways over the past year, including Ellie, Frank and Lenora, and Bob and Irene. Mary A. Cook read and commented on an early draft of the manuscript, and once again proofed the completed version in record time. Thanks to Joel and Terry for the music, and to Russ, Debi, and Jeff for the good company. If anyone should happen to see Brian Drost (Brian Jr., that is) driving a baby blue pickup truck around

Montana, be sure to say hello. As always, a big thank-you to the fans, as well as to friends and family, including James, Noah, and Mat. For more information about the Candy Holliday Murder Mysteries and Cape Willington, Maine, visit hollidaysblue berryacres.com.

PROLOGUE

The attack came from behind, without warning.

Later, she would grudgingly admit it was partially her own fault, since she'd likely antagonized the nanny goat by appearing out of nowhere, rushing into the place like a madwoman, and then beeping the horn incessantly as the animal meandered across the driveway right in front of her, obviously holding her up on purpose. Critters could be territorial — just like her, in some ways. And ornery, like their owners. This one was both.

She'd completely ignored the goat as she climbed out of her Suburban, hurried up the concrete steps, and rapped at Sally Ann's side door. No one home, an annoying detail. But at least the woman had left out the pickle jar. It sat near Wanda's feet, on the top corner of the steps.

Something was wrong, though. From

where she stood, looking down, Wanda knew right away that Sally Ann had left out the wrong jar. The label was much too professional, and a different color entirely. Sally Ann's labels were cream-colored and handmade, somewhat crudely, with few embellishments and black spidery letters, a sort of angled cursive scrawl that looked like it might have been written by someone living in the 1800s. Often the labels were stained or creased because they'd been mishandled or applied too hastily. But they were easily recognizable, and everyone around town could identify a jar of pickles made by Sally Ann Longfellow.

The label on this jar, however, was better designed, and the writing on it much more legible. It had a light green background, with dark green lettering in an attractive, folksy font outlined in black. And it had unique entwined copper-colored embellishments at the four corners. It didn't look like Sally Ann's work, or her taste in design.

At first Wanda was confused. Why would Sally Ann leave out the wrong jar? They'd discussed this. Judging was about to begin. Wanda was in a hurry, and she was doing the other woman a favor, stopping by on her way to the event.

Was Sally Ann using someone else's

pickles? A mystery entry?

She squinted in the bright light, focusing on the name written across the top of the label. She could just make out the words:

Sweet Pickle Deli.

Wanda's head jerked back in surprise as her eyes widened.

"It can't be," she muttered to herself.

She blinked several times. This couldn't be true. It must be a fake, an imposter.

But if it was genuine — an actual jar of pickles from the Sweet Pickle Deli — then it was indeed a rare find.

But what was Sally Ann doing with it? Where had the jar come from? Had she been hoarding it all this time? And why put it out on the stoop, instead of a jar of her own pickles?

A flash of irritation swept though Wanda.

She's throwing in a ringer, Wanda thought. *What is she up to?*

I should just disqualify her right now.

But maybe she'd just read the label wrong. Perhaps she'd been mistaken.

She had to get a better look at it.

She bent over slightly, and stopped. She didn't want to lean over too far, she realized. She had on a new outfit today, an orange, beige, and rust-toned ensemble designed to herald the imminent arrival of autumn. The beige pants were more form-fitting than she preferred, but they'd been too nice to pass up when she'd found them at that new boutique on Ocean Avenue. She didn't want to stretch them to their limit, which wasn't very far, so instead of bending over further, she climbed back down the steps and came around the side of the stoop, where she could view the jar at something closer to eye level.

Once back on solid ground, she was foolish enough to turn her back on the goat as she leaned in to get a better look at the label.

Unfortunately, that exposed her to the attack.

Seeing an opportunity for retribution, or perhaps just because she was in a cranky mood, the irascible animal lowered her head, darted forward, and butted Wanda squarely in the rear end.

It was a clean shot but not a vicious one, meant to be a statement, more an act of irritation than aggression. But Wanda was so engrossed in studying the label that the unexpected bump caught her completely unawares. It had just enough force to send her teetering forward, throwing her off balance.

With a startled squawk of surprise, Wanda Boyle went down face-first onto the dry, tightly cropped grass, her arms splattering out to her sides, red hair flying.

An *oomph* of air escaped from her lungs as she landed hard on her chest and stomach. Her eyes, heavily outlined in mascara, squeezed tightly shut, and her mouth, adorned with a deep shade of orange lipstick called Autumn Sunset, drew into a tight line, pursed against the grass and dirt into which she'd fallen.

Her whole body rocked and settled. For a moment all was silent, until she blew out another breath on purpose, sputtering her lips to clear them of debris as her eyes flew open and her expression darkened.

She lifted her head and twisted about, focusing in on the four-legged critter standing behind her. She eyed the animal defiantly.

"Cleopatra," Wanda said in an accusatory, barely controlled tone, "I thought we talked about this. No head-butting. How'd you get loose anyway? You're in a lot of trouble, young lady!"

Wanda lifted an arm and brushed several strands of red hair out of her face as she took a moment to mentally assess her condition. No shooting pains. No broken bones. Nothing appeared to be severely damaged.

Other than her pride.

Her gaze shifted, head turning in both directions, back and forth, to determine if anyone had spotted her in such a compromising position — lying in the dirt, flat on her stomach, at the hands of a grumpy nanny goat, no less. If someone saw her like this, it would be around town in hours, if not minutes. She'd be a laughingstock for weeks. She might never live it down.

But today she lucked out. The street and surrounding yards were thankfully vacant. No cars whizzing by. No one walking past with a dog. No one staring out a window, catching sight of her by surprise.

Convinced she hadn't been seen and confident she wasn't hurt, Wanda pushed herself up on her side, got an arm under her, and managed to sit up. She took a moment to collect herself before she struggled shakily to her feet.

Looking down, she saw dirt down her front and grass stains on her knees. Her new outfit was ruined.

She eyed the goat again with a venomous gaze. "Just great," she growled. "What'd you do that for? I was just trying to get a good look at that pickle jar."

And, of course, that explained it right there.

The goat was after the pickles.

Cleopatra let out an obstinate bleat, laid back her ears, and swung her bony head toward the house. Then, in a burst of activity, she clattered up the steps to the top of the stoop, gave the jar a vicious knock with her nose, and sent it tumbling. It landed with a heavy *thunk!* on each step, moving faster and faster, arcing higher and higher, until it smacked onto the concrete walkway at an awkward angle and cracked open like an eggshell.

Wanda let out a howl of disbelief as a second goat named Guinevere, attracted by the noise, poked her head around the side of the building, spotted the fresh pickles suddenly available for consumption, and trotted forward. At the same time, Cleopatra triumphantly descended the steps to claim her prize.

Both goats reached the broken jar at the same time as Wanda watched in dismay. If these really were pickles from the Sweet Pickle Deli, there was no way she was going to let a couple of goats steal them from her grasp. Her brow fell in determination as she started forward as well, swinging her big arms and zeroing in on the broken pickle jar.

The goats saw her coming and moved quickly, lowering their heads and sniffing at the contents. After a few moments Guinevere drew back her head, snorted, and turned, angling away. She obviously wasn't interested in pickles. But Cleopatra wasn't as choosy. She slurped up first one into her mouth, and then another.

Wanda was horrified. "Leave those alone! Do you know what those *are*?"

She crossed the distance quickly and reached out with one hand, pushing the goat back. At the same time, she swung down her other hand and managed to carefully pluck a single whole pickle off the ground. But the goat would not be deterred, and as Wanda watched, the animal shifted around and quickly gobbled up all that remained.

Wanda was beside herself with regret. "Do you know what you've *done*? You just destroyed the best pickles ever made!"

The goat raised her head, gave Wanda a satisfied look, and started moving away, still chewing on her gourmet meal.

Wanda let out a huff. "Well, that's just great. Wait 'til Sally Ann hears about this. You'll be in the doghouse for weeks. Or goathouse. Or whatever." She wagged a finger at Cleopatra's retreating backside. "You're in a lot of trouble, you . . . you old goat!"

But Cleopatra paid her no nevermind. She had managed to snag what she was after.

With a sigh of disappointment, Wanda looked down at the pickle she held in her hand. At least she'd been able to salvage one of them.

She studied it for a moment, almost romantically. It looked relatively free of dirt and glass shards. And it smelled so delicious. She ran a finger across it, cleaning off a few small bits of debris, and hesitated. *Should I?* she thought.

"Oh, what the hell."

With a shrug, she lifted it to her mouth and took several big, crunchy bites, savoring each one. She hadn't had one of these pickles in years, and didn't care if she'd pulled it from the bottom of a cesspool. They were the dreamiest she'd ever eaten. And this one was no different. A perfect crispness, exquisite flavor, just a hint of tartness, and . . . something else.

Wanda sensed a burning sensation in her stomach. "What the . . . ?"

She felt a rumble down below, and a moment later the pickle threatened to come back up on her. "What . . . ?"

She heard a shuffling sound nearby and looked over. Cleopatra was walking funny. Her legs were wobbly. The nanny goat turned around to look back at Wanda with forlorn eyes, and then suddenly collapsed in a heap.

"Oh my god." It took a few moments for Wanda to register what she was seeing. She looked down at the half-eaten pickle in horror. "Oh, no."

She started spitting heavily, trying to get all the pickle juice and bits out of her mouth as the burning sensation in her stomach grew. Panic rising, she made a mad dash to her Suburban, where she'd left her phone. She yanked open the door, snatched the phone from its cubby in the center console, and frantically began to dial.

From the *Cape Crier*
Cape Willington, Maine
September 18th Edition

THE CAPE CRUSADER
by Wanda Boyle
Community Correspondent

Guess Who's Turning 200?
Here's a big hint: Look no further than the newspaper you're now holding in your hands. Yes, it's true! The *Cape Crier* is turning 200 years old! Who would've thought we'd be around this long! (We did, of course!) Founded in 1815 by budding journalist and world explorer Harvey Alexander Pruitt, the first issue (a one-pager) was published on Friday, Oct. 6th that year, and the *Crier* has been a mainstay of our beloved village ever since. In celebration of this momentous event, current interim managing editor Candy Holliday, as well as the paper's community correspondent (that would be yours truly!) have planned a number of special events, including the upcoming community cook-off contest (see below). More details to follow as we approach the unveiling of the

Crier's Special Bicentennial Edition in early October!

Calling All Cooks!
With all the excellent cooks we have around town, you can bet the competition will be fierce at the Cape Willington Community Cook-off, which takes place from 3 to 5 P.M. on Friday, Sept. 25th at the high school gymnasium. Part of the *Crier*'s bicentennial celebration, the cook-off is the first of its kind locally. All amateur cooks are welcome to enter, though time is tight, so call us immediately if you'd like to be involved. You can enter your own dish in any of seven categories, including breads, jams and preserves, homemade cheese and yogurt, pickled foods, pies, cookies, and candies and other desserts. An impressive lineup of judges, including popular cookbook author Julia von Fleming, will sample the entries and pick their favorites, which will be announced in the paper's upcoming Bicentennial Edition. So dig through your old recipes, pick out the best one, and fire up the oven!

Let's Put Some Food By
While we're on the subject of food, a

number of innovative villagers will be pickling more than pigs' feet on Thursday night before the cook-off contest. Calling themselves the Putting Food By Society, the group advocates self-sufficient living, and will be joining with the owners of Zeke's General Store to offer food preservation demos in and around the store from 4 to 7 P.M. The emphasis will be on canning and pickling local produce. Headed by Edna Bakersfield and Isabella Corinne, the group also includes Melody Barnes and Elsie Lingholt, all of whom will pitch in on the demonstrations. So what are you waiting for! Learn from the experts! Harvest season has arrived, and it's time to put some food by for the up-coming winter. For more information, visit www.puttingfoodbycapewillington.com.

Show Us Your Photos!

We're starting a new section in the *Crier* called "Photos from Cape Willington." Send us photos of yourself, your family, friends, pets, events, the weather, Tony the tourist, anything! We're interested in seeing everyday life here in Cape Willington. We'll print some of the photos in the paper, and put others on our website and Pinterest! Send your photos to cape crier@gmail.com. It's a great way to celebrate life the way it should be here in our beautiful village!

Vintage Treasures
The Pruitt Public Library, in conjunction with the Cape Willington Historical Society, is celebrating Harvest Season with a two-month-long exhibit titled, "Vintage Harvest." On exhibit will be vintage treasures, all having to do with harvest time in Maine. Among other items, you can view antique blueberry rakes, antique mason jars and canning equipment, garden tools, and the largest collection of antique seed packets in Down East Maine. It's well worth your time, so be sure to stop by. The exhibit will be open during regular library hours.

You Heard It Here First!
Pat O'Connor, who works at Melody's Cafe, tells us one of her tourist customers was so thrilled to be buying one of Melody's pies, she quipped, "This pie is so precious, I am going to buckle it into

the backseat of my car!" Now that's inspiring, but what will she do with her kids? . . . Did you know Lisa Taylor has a new car, and it has an impressive moniker? She calls her latest ride the New Moon Nitrogen Storm! That's a pretty big name for such a little car! She dubbed her old car Silver Moon, and decided to name its replacement New Moon to start a new chapter. "Nitrogen" refers to the nitrogen in the car's tires, and "Storm" perfectly describes its storm gray exterior color. So keep a lookout on the roads. A Nitrogen Storm just might be headed your direction! . . . While scouring our local beaches for the annual fall beach cleanup, Jim Harrison found an old blue glass bottle. On closer inspection, he saw a tiny piece of paper inside. After a tedious ordeal (a story for another time!), he got the note out of the bottle. It was dated 1964 and read, "Let everyone know that Elizabeth loves Eugene." Who Elizabeth and Eugene are, and where the bottle was thrown into the sea, remains another Cape Willington mystery!

Official Judicious F. P. Bosworth sightings for the first two weeks of September:

Visible: 2 days
Invisible: 12 days

Judicious, are you underground waiting to be harvested? Dig yourself out and join the events around town!

ONE

Candy Holliday checked her watch for what seemed like the hundredth time and glanced back at the main set of double doors that led out of the gymnasium. The doors were propped open, allowing in muted sunlight and a brisk fall breeze as a few people wandered in and out of the busy, buzzing venue. Candy's eyes flicked from one person to another in quick succession as she scanned their faces and outfits, tapping her right foot rapidly without even knowing she was doing it.

There was Edna Bakersfield of the Putting Food By Society, with Elvira Tremble from the Cape Willington Heritage Protection League, conversing softly as they came through the doors. There went Trudy Watkins, who ran Zeke's General Store with her husband, Richard. He was probably keeping an eye on the place, which is why she was here alone today. In walked Mason

Flint, chairman of the town's board of selectmen, talking on his cell phone. And Marjorie Coffin scrambled in carrying a cardboard box, probably filled with a few last-minute entries.

As Candy's gaze swept the room, she noticed many other familiar faces. But none was the person she sought.

Nearly three forty-five, and still no Wanda.

Where the heck is *she?* Candy wondered with no small amount of exasperation.

Wanda had already missed the afternoon's opening remarks, which seemed totally uncharacteristic of her. She'd been looking forward to this event for months, ever since they'd started talking about it back at the beginning of the summer. She'd been involved with all the planning, and had spent the better part of the past week holed up in her windowless office, writing and rehearsing her comments, which she'd read out loud to Candy just that morning before heading over to Sally Ann Longfellow's place. She'd honed her remarks to perfection, she'd smugly told Candy at the time, and was certain they conveyed the appropriate tone for such a momentous event.

Early on in their discussions, to avoid any conflicts between the two of them, they'd decided to serve as co-hosts for the afternoon's event, and both would give opening remarks. It was Candy's suggestion that Wanda go first, since the whole event *was* essentially her idea. They'd decided that Wanda would make the general welcoming comments, introduce the judges, discuss the various food categories and tables, and lay out the afternoon's schedule. Candy would follow by thanking the contestants, volunteers, and school staff, and discussing the event's tie-ins to the upcoming "Best of Cape Willington" feature article scheduled for the special bicentennial edition.

After that, as they'd agreed, Wanda would accompany the judges during the afternoon, provide a few brief remarks about each food category, and monitor the time the judges spent at each table to ensure they'd finish on schedule. While Wanda essentially ran the show, Candy would have time to roam the hall and take on a more social role, since she was still the *Cape Crier*'s interim managing editor, and many of the town's more prominent citizens were here today serving as honorary judges. She knew it would be a good time to network, renew acquaintances, and drum up support for the paper.

At least, that's the way it was supposed to have worked.

But for some inexplicable reason, Wanda never showed. And in the end Candy had to cover for her, stepping in to deliver the entire opening presentation herself. She'd ad-libbed as best she could the remarks assigned to Wanda, and overall thought she'd done a decent job. She'd glossed over Wanda's absence, saying the other woman was unexpectedly delayed, and had to dig out her cheat sheet to remember all the food categories and table assignments. But in the end it had worked out fine, and no one seemed to notice that anything was wrong.

The three official judges — Colin Trevor Jones, Julia von Fleming, and Herr Georg Wolfsburger — were now on their second table, the one devoted to jams and preserves. They'd spent fifteen minutes at the first table, as planned. The event was on schedule. So far, so good.

Still, Candy felt a little off-balance. This wasn't how she'd expected to spend her afternoon. There were opportunities she was missing. But it couldn't be helped.

If Wanda would just show up. . . .

Candy wasn't really angry. If anything, she was disappointed at the thought that Wanda had missed so much of an event she'd looked forward to for months.

Not for the first time, Candy wondered if

something had happened to the other woman. She tried not to let her mind dwell on that thought, lest she start worrying. She had long ago learned not to jump to conclusions, so she wasn't about to start now.

Still, Wanda's absence was very peculiar. Candy had tried calling her several times, but all the calls went straight to voice mail. So she'd left a few quick messages, asking Wanda to return the call as soon as she could and wondering what had delayed her. But so far she'd heard nothing.

And it was time to move on.

After a final glance at the double doors, just to make sure Wanda hadn't showed up in the last few seconds, Candy brushed back her honey-colored hair and collected her thoughts as she made her way through the crowd to the microphone. When she reached it, she flicked it on, cleared her throat, and called for everyone's attention.

"It's three forty-five and time for our official judges to make their way to Table Three, which is our homemade cheese and yogurt table," she said pleasantly into the mic. "Again, we ask that all honorary judges please allow the official judges sole access to this table while they're sampling the entries. We invite the honorary judges to focus their attention on the other tables around the room. There are still plenty of samples available at Tables One and Two, devoted to homemade breads, preserves, and jams, so you won't want to miss those. Again, the official judges have fifteen minutes to sample the entries and formulate their opinions. We do hope all of you are enjoying your afternoon and this incredible food that's been prepared for us by the people of Cape Willington, and we thank you again for coming out today to support this community event."

She left it at that, flicking off the mic to a smattering of applause and hurrying over to join the judges at Table Three. But before she made it there she felt her phone buzzing in the pocket of her powder blue blazer, which she'd fished out of the back of her closet last week in anticipation of this event.

Maybe it's a message from Wanda, she hoped in the back of her mind.

And it was indeed from Wanda — just not what she expected. It was a text message, and rather ominously it read:

Sorry for delay. Will call soon. Sally Ann Longfellow is trying to kill me.

TWO

Henry "Doc" Holliday bit into a thick slice of glazed lemon blueberry bread as he stood off to one side of the packed, noisy gym. He chewed slowly, concentrating on the flavors, and then took another careful bite as his gaze swept about the place. He was still amazed he was here at all, and couldn't believe his good luck. But he wasn't about to question it.

Doc, as he often reminded himself, was just a simple blueberry farmer trying to scratch out a living from the good earth — in his case, a twenty-three-acre property called Holliday's Blueberry Acres, which he ran with his daughter, Candy. It was located not far from here, out along the coastline a few miles. The height of the blueberry-picking season was a few weeks behind them, and it had been a bountiful harvest, bringing in plenty of revenue to keep them going through the rest of the fall and the upcoming winter. But they still had plenty to do around the farm. Rightly he should be in his work clothes and boots, finishing up chores, walking the fields, and tending to the farm's vegetable gardens, which were still yielding. He should be checking on supplies and prepping the mowing gear for the tractor, and there was always plenty of paperwork and general housekeeping to get done.

Yet here he was on a Friday afternoon in late September, dressed in his Sunday best — clean chinos, a nicely pressed white shirt, a green and yellow patterned tie, a decades-old green-flecked sport coat, and comfortable brown loafers — serving as an honorary judge at one of Cape Willington's biggest events in years.

It was a simple yet prestigious assignment. He'd been asked to serve as a judge for the Cape Willington Community Cook-off, part of the newspaper's bicentennial celebration. The goal was to find the best cooks and recipes in town, and publish a list of them in an upcoming special issue. He was one of twenty honorary judges, asked by special invitation to sample various types of food submitted by the general public, and offer his opinions. All he had to do was walk around the room, visit the food tables, sample whatever he wanted, and then grade what he ate. He could eat as much as he liked, and take as long as he wanted.

And there was so much to choose from.

Yup, life was pretty darn good.

As he popped the last of the lemon blueberry bread into his mouth, Doc crumbled up the small napkin that had held the sample and tossed it into a nearby waste can. There was one task to complete before he moved on, one he'd been diligent about today. So he reached into his right coat pocket and pulled out a wad of blue scoring forms.

He carried perhaps a dozen of them, four by eight inches each, attached to a similar-sized blue translucent clipboard. On the top form he noted his name and judging number (he was Judge Number 17), entered the number associated with the entry — in this case B22 (the *B* stood for *bread,* since it was from Table One, the bread table) — and awarded it seven and a half out of ten points. In the comments section he scribbled, *"Good texture. Very lemony. Not too crumbly. Blueberries taste fresh."*

Then he removed the form from the clipboard, folded it in half, and placed it into his left coat pocket while slipping the clipboard back into the right. He'd completed several scoring forms, which he'd drop off in the proper box when he passed by it again.

He glanced up at the clock on the wall. It was approaching four P.M. The event ran from three to five. He still had plenty of time to sample lots of entries. He rubbed his hands together in anticipation and took a deep breath. "Okay, what's next?"

There were seven large display tables around the room — in many cases, several smaller tables pushed and angled together — devoted to seven food categories: breads, jams and preserves, homemade cheese and yogurt, pickled foods, pies, cookies, and candies and other desserts. A few food groups, like the breads and jams, had as many as twenty-five or thirty entries each, although most had between a dozen and fifteen or so. He'd visited most of the tables at least once, and had munched on a wide variety of samples. So far several entries stood out in his mind, including a delectable peanut brittle, some wonderful zucchini bread, and a fresh, creamy goat cheese layered thick on a cranberry wafer.

He'd been by the pie table four times already, and he was thinking of making a fifth trip before the official judges reached it. So far he'd sampled slices of blueberry, apple, peach, strawberry rhubarb, pumpkin, and even a shoofly pie heavy with molasses. He didn't want to appear too greedy, but there were several he'd missed, including a blackberry pie that looked particularly interesting, and he wanted to make sure he returned to the table while samples remained.

He'd also spent quite a bit of time at the cookie table, and the same held true. Best make another swing by there while he still had the chance.

But there were a few tables he'd largely bypassed so far, like the pickled foods, and some he'd ignored on purpose, like the candies. The last one, he'd decided, could wait until a little later on, so he didn't fill up too much on sweets — at least, not more than he already had.

Still, there was a lot of ground to cover. Best get moving. But where to head next?

He spotted his daughter with the three official judges at Table Three, so that one was closed off for now. But there was much more from which to choose.

"The pickle table," he decided with a definitive head nod, and started toward it, weaving his way through the crowd.

On the way he noticed someone waving to him from the far side of the room. His gaze shifted, and he spotted a friend of his, William "Bumpy" Brigham, standing along the opposite wall with a wide grin on his face. Bumpy was standing next to another man — a villager named Ned Winetrop, Doc realized after a few moments — and both had big smiles on their faces. They were part of the event's set-up and take-down crew, so apparently they'd hung around to observe the proceedings. Ned held up something wrapped in a napkin, and both were pointing in the direction Doc was headed. Not quite sure what they were indicating, and figuring they were just having a little fun, Doc waved back and moved on.

Once he reached the table, he found quite a bit to explore. There were a dozen and a half entries in the pickle division alone, some more or less common, like kosher dills and bread and butters, as well as less common choices like spicy and sour spears, sweet gherkins, baby garlic dills, and even hot pickles with jalapenos. He also saw several relishes, a few sauerkrauts, and other unique varieties of pickled items, including olives, peppers, carrots, green beans, and even mushrooms.

A veritable smorgasbord of pickled goodness.

But then something caught his eye, something out of place. His gaze shifted.

At one side of the table sat a fat pickle jar, clearly labeled. Doc squinted at it. He knew this was a blind tasting, with entries identified only by a number, and not the names of the people who had prepared and entered them. There was a master list somewhere, matching each number with a name, but the judges were not privy to such information, nor should they be. That would spoil the whole point of the event.

There were no other jars in sight. The rest of the samples were laid out on trays or platters, with no identifiers other than numbers.

So what was that clearly labeled pickle jar doing there?

Doc took a few steps to the side and leaned for a closer look at the label. The dark green letters, outlined in black against the light green background, were easy to make out:

Sweet Pickle Deli.

Doc tilted his head curiously. "Now what the heck is *that* doing here?" he asked no one in particular. "I haven't seen one of those jars in . . ."

He couldn't remember when exactly. Three or four years, maybe more. Ever since that old deli in town had closed down —

quite suddenly and under mysterious circumstances, he remembered.

But they'd been the best darn pickles he'd ever tasted. He'd hoarded two jars through a whole winter, long after the place had disappeared, and parsed them out slowly to himself, to make them last as long as possible. He'd missed them ever since. In fact, he could still taste them on the back of his tongue.

And here was a jar, popping up out of nowhere, right in front of him.

Yes, life was very good indeed.

Unfortunately, there appeared to be only one jar, and it looked less than full. Perhaps only four or five full pickles inside. He glanced around the table. As far as he could tell, none of the Sweet Pickle Deli pickles were laid out on sample trays. And there was no associated number.

Odd indeed. An oversight of some sort. But one he could remedy in a jiffy. These, he had no doubt, were prize-winning pickles.

He wondered if they still tasted as good as they used to.

Maybe he could sneak just one for himself.

He reached out for the jar, planning to unscrew the lid and fish one out right there and then. But before he touched the jar, another more delicate hand beat him to it.

"Here, dad, let me get those. You're not supposed to know the identity of the entries."

Doc looked up into his daughter's eyes and smiled weakly. "Well, shucks, pumpkin, looks like you beat me to them. Another few seconds and I would have snagged one."

THREE

"Good thing I came along when I did then," Candy said in a gently admonishing tone. "You know this is supposed to be a blind taste test."

"Sure, I know that," Doc replied, feeling slightly put out, "so why is there a jar with the Sweet Pickle Deli label on it sitting right out there in plain sight where judges like me can see it?"

His daughter studied the offending jar with a discerning look. "Good question. Obviously a mix-up of some sort. I'll take care of it."

"Yes, but do you know what those *are*?" Doc pressed.

"No, and neither should you. At least not right now. There are plenty of other samples around the table. Why don't you try something else while I get these set up?"

"Because I guarantee none of these other pickles, good as they might be, can match those right there." Doc jabbed a finger at the jar.

Suddenly curious, Candy picked it up and counted the pickles inside. "Not many left. Looks like someone must have dipped into it already. I'll have to save the rest of these for the official judges."

Doc frowned. "So you're not going to put them out?"

Candy whisked the jar behind the table and out of sight. "If there are any left I promise to save one for you." She glanced at her watch and looked suddenly harried. "Besides, I don't have time to fool with them right now. I've got too much going on."

"Everything okay?" Doc asked, sounding worried. He knew his daughter had taken a lot on her shoulders with this event, and he wanted it to go as smoothly as possible for her.

In response, Candy glanced around the hall. "It would be better if Wanda would just show up," she said, and shook her head. "I can't believe she's missing this. She's been looking forward to it so much."

"She still hasn't checked in?"

"I've heard from her, yes. She says she's been delayed."

"Didn't think anything could keep her

from being here," Doc said thoughtfully, remembering some of the stories he'd heard from his daughter over the past few months about Wanda's enthusiasm for the event.

"Neither did I, but something strange is going on with her."

"Strange? What do you mean?" Doc asked innocently, but he felt a slight jolt when he saw the look in his daughter's eyes as they shifted toward him momentarily and then turned away again to survey the crowd. He'd seen that look before, though only on rare occasions, and realized there was something she didn't want to tell him.

She's worried, he thought. *She's holding something back.*

Doc cleared his throat. He was hesitant to prod. Whatever it was, she'd tell him in good time — when, or if, she was ready. But he also wanted her to know, no matter what was bothering her, that she had his support. So he took a moment to organize his thoughts, and was about to say something when she turned back toward him.

"Have you seen Sally Ann Longfellow around anywhere today?" Candy asked, lowering her voice to a whisper.

"Sally Ann?" Doc's gray brows fell together and the corners of his mouth dropped into a frown. "Not lately. In fact, I haven't seen her in a few weeks, I guess. Why?" He started whispering like his daughter. "What's going on?"

Candy shook her head. "I don't know yet." She looked like she was about to say something more but held back, and there was that look again.

"Pumpkin, if you . . ."

"I know, Dad," Candy said with a smile, and she reached out to pat his hand, "and if I need someone to talk to I'll come straight to you. But I've promised myself I won't overreact, and at the moment I have more pressing matters at hand. In a few minutes I need to make another announcement and get the judges headed to the next table, which is this one right here."

"Then I guess I'd better get a move on," Doc said.

"Me too," his daughter agreed, and she headed off through the crowd in the direction of the microphone.

Before he left the table, Doc quickly surveyed the alternative pickled fare. Finding a small stack of paper plates nearby, he took one and began filling it with samples. At this point he didn't jot down any numbers; he'd have to come back once the official judges vacated the table to match the various entries to their numbers.

Although he was selective in his choices, in short time he wound up with a good assortment, including several dills and sweets, small samplings of pickled green beans and carrots, a couple of dabs of sauerkraut, and some pickled asparagus that looked particularly interesting. Then he grabbed a napkin and fork before he headed off across the room himself, leaving the table to the official judges just as his daughter began her announcement.

He tried not to worry about her, but the father part of him couldn't help it. There had been some strange happenings in town over the past five or six years, and his daughter always seemed to wind up right in the middle of them. The last time there'd been trouble, she'd almost been hit over the head with a shovel. Now he had a sixth sense that something else was about to happen, though he couldn't imagine what it might be this time.

First, Wanda's absence and "strange" behavior. Then the odd question from his daughter about Sally Ann Longfellow.

That strange look in her eyes.

And then, of course, there was that mysterious jar from the Sweet Pickle Deli.

Doc was tempted to return to the table to get another look at that jar, which his daughter must have hidden away in one of the boxes under the table, but the official judges were already moving in that direction, and following her quick announcement, Candy was re-converging on the table as well.

Doc shook his head. Best to let her handle this her way.

Still, it was frustrating to think that one of those pickles had almost been in his grasp.

He heard someone call his name from across the hall and looked around. It was his friend Bumpy Brigham again, still standing beside Ned Winetrop. Bumpy was motioning to him.

Curious, Doc headed in their direction, making his way past the tables and across the gym.

"Doc," Bumpy called out as he approached them, "you won't believe what Ned found."

Ned gave his friend a sideways glance. In a low voice, he said, "Quiet, would ya? We don't want everyone to know about this."

"Know about what?" Doc asked as he reached them.

"Thanks to a little bird who tipped me off, I made a rare find today," Ned said slyly, and he held up a paper plate he'd covered with a napkin. "Something I never thought I'd see again."

"Hope you're not getting into the samples," Doc said in a warning tone. "Those are for the judges only."

"I know, I know." Ned scrunched up his face and waved a hand dismissively. "But every once in a while you've got to break the rules a little, right?"

"Wait 'til you hear what he's found," Bumpy said enthusiastically.

Doc wasn't sure he wanted to know, but curiosity got the better of him. "So what is it?"

"Well," Ned said, grinning as he dramatically lifted aside the napkin to reveal what was underneath, "you're not going to believe this, but I found a jar of pickles from that old Sweet Pickle Deli, and I managed to snag a few for myself."

FOUR

"This is our fourth table, devoted to pickled foods," Candy said as the three official judges arrived and began to survey the offerings. "As you can see, we have quite an assortment of pickled items. The villagers have really gone all-out in this category. Again, you'll have fifteen minutes to sample the items and each choose your top three."

They knew the procedure and, nodding, fell quickly to their work, chattering quietly among themselves as they poked and prodded, searching for those items that caught the eye or nose. Candy eyed the three judges one by one. They were a good group, and showed a deep dedication to their task, despite the small-town nature of the event. And they all had good credentials. She was pleased with the judges they'd assembled, and the way they had pulled the whole event together over the past few months.

During the planning stages, Candy and

Wanda had spent quite a bit of time deciding how many judges to invite to the community cook-off contest. Candy had suggested a smaller group of professional judges with food industry experience, to give the event a certain level of prestige. Wanda leaned more toward a broader group of community leaders and prominent local citizens, which would build some goodwill and buzz around the village.

In the end, they decided to do both, settling on twenty honorary judges and three official judges, with overall voting weighed in favor of the smaller professional group. Wanda focused on choosing the twenty honorary judges, with suggestions from Candy, who turned *her* attention to the three official judges, with input from Wanda.

Over a period of several weeks during the summer, they whittled down their lists, completed them, and published the results in an August issue of the paper. As they'd hoped, the unveiling of the judges had created a town-wide buzz and weeks-long anticipation of today's event.

The eclectic group of honorary judges included prominent villagers like Chairman of the Town Council Mason Flint, Cotton Colby and Elvira Tremble of the Cape Willington Heritage Protection League, the

Reverend James P. Daisy, local shop owners Augustus "Gus" Gumm and Ralph Henry, ice cream shop employee and acclaimed local actress Lily Verte, retired police officer Finn Woodbury, and local blueberry farmer Henry Holliday, among others.

Doc's inclusion had come at Wanda's suggestion. Candy had been hesitant at first about including her father, fearing claims of nepotism, but in the end she'd decided she was probably overthinking it and agreed that he would be a good addition to the group.

So far, the reaction to the entire group of honorary judges had been entirely positive.

For the three official judges, Candy settled on the first two names fairly quickly. Colin Trevor Jones, the thirtyish dark-haired executive chef at the Lightkeeper's Inn, had been an obvious choice. Known around the region for his "classic maritime" cuisine, which emphasized dishes like crab crepes, lobster bisque, fish chowder, and French Canadian pork pie, he was a perfect anchor for the group, and brought a broad range of culinary experience to the tables.

Her next choice was trickier. Herr Georg Wolfsburger, proprietor of the Black Forest Bakery, which he ran along with his fiancée Maggie Tremont — who also happened to be Candy's best friend — had served as a judge for the town's annual Blueberry Queen beauty pageant several years ago, and allowed himself to be blackmailed into swinging his vote toward one of the contestants. After he'd been found out, he'd sworn never again to serve as a judge for an event.

Yet Candy knew he'd be the perfect judge for the cook-off contest, especially for certain categories like breads, pies, and cookies. But when she first approached him about the idea, he had flatly refused. When she pressed, he told her, not totally politely, that he preferred she not bring up the subject again.

For more than a week Candy persisted and Herr Georg declined. It was only Maggie's intervention and gentle persuasion that finally convinced him to at least talk to Candy, and when he heard the idea behind the contest, and its tie-in to the newspaper's two-hundredth anniversary, he'd finally, though somewhat reluctantly, agreed to participate — just this once, as a way to give something back to the townspeople for all their support over the years.

Typically jovial, he maintained an overall stoic appearance this afternoon, obviously taking his judging duties seriously. But the third judge was beginning to loosen him up a little with her enthusiasm and bubbly personality.

That's exactly why Candy had invited her to serve as a judge — to inject a different personality into the group. Although she wasn't a local like the other judges, Julia von Fleming was a popular cookbook author who had gained some national attention with her latest volume, *Homestyle New England Cooking,* which included a large section devoted to Maine recipes. Candy had reviewed it a few months ago for a newspaper article and found herself using it in her kitchen at home. Some of the recipes, she'd found, had been quite good.

According to her author bio, Julia von Fleming lived in neighboring New Hampshire, so Candy sent her an e-mail one day, and Julia had responded. They'd been corresponding ever since. When Candy mentioned in an e-mail a while back that she was looking for judges for a cook-off contest, Julia had expressed an interest. After hearing the details of the event and its community-based theme, she'd agreed to serve as an official judge. And so far she'd been a wonderful addition to the group, bringing knowledge of homemade New England foods, including jams, pies, and pickled items, to the contest.

Julia now eyed the table with intense curiosity, as if plotting her moves. She was a middle-aged woman, probably closer to fifty than forty, with fluffed-up black hair in a loose short cut and dangling silver earrings in the shape of tulips. Her heart-shaped face was somewhat puffy and pale, which made the dark red lipstick she wore more noticeable, and her dark brown eyes were heavily ringed with mascara to make them stand out as well.

Not that she needed much help standing out. She was a vibrant woman, full of energy and attitude, who excelled at making herself the center of attention and had a sharp laugh that could cut through just about any conversation or surrounding ambient noise.

But now, as she turned toward Candy, she took great pains to keep her voice as low as possible.

"Is the rumor I've heard true?" she asked in a conspiratorial tone.

"Rumor?" Candy asked, doing her best to keep her voice from spiking, and failing. Concerned Julia was going to ask her about Wanda, or Sally Ann Longfellow, she said hesitantly, "What rumor?"

But Julia didn't ask about Wanda or Sally Ann. Instead, she said, "I've heard you have some pickles from the Sweet Pickle Deli."

"Oh! That!" Candy couldn't help but feel a little relieved. "Yes, they're around here somewhere. But they're not out on the table."

Julia looked aghast. "They're not? But that's a travesty, my dear! An affront to foodies everywhere! Why haven't you put them out?"

Candy stooped and retrieved the jar from a box on the floor she'd set it inside. As she rose, jar in hand, she said, "Well, because it's an anonymous tasting. You're not supposed to know where the samples come from."

"We'll make an exception this one time," Julia said, leaning toward her and lowering her voice again. "I've got to try one of them. Consider it . . . research. I've heard so much about them over the years."

"What have you heard?" Candy asked, looking up curiously as she set the jar on the table and, with some effort, unscrewed the lid.

"Probably the same thing you have — that they're the best pickles anyone has ever made." She glanced across the table, toward the far end, where Herr Georg and Colin Trevor Jones stood with their heads together, talking quietly. She turned back

53

toward Candy. "How many do you have?"

"Unfortunately, that's part of the problem," Candy said. "Someone has already snitched a few of them."

Julia looked horrified. "How many are left? Enough for the judges?"

"Barely."

"But no extras?"

"Perhaps one or two, although I can always cut them into smaller slices." Candy looked around for a plate and fork. She found them nearby and speared one of the pickles with the fork, lifting it out.

Julia couldn't help herself. She leaned in for a sniff, using a waving motion of her hand to direct the scent toward her nose. "They smell simply divine!"

"Do they?" Candy asked, and she leaned in closer and sniffed as well.

"Hey, what have you got there?" Herr Georg called from across the table.

Candy looked over. Instinctively, she turned the jar so the label was pointing away from the other two judges. "Just a late entry," she told him. "I'll have it set out for you in a few moments."

"But there is so much here already," Herr Georg said, waving his hand magnanimously across the table. "We barely know where to begin as it is."

Julia turned toward the German baker with a bit of a pout. "But, Georg, you simply *must* try these pickles. They are heaven sent! You've never tasted anything like them in your life."

"Then I suppose I must!" Herr Georg said, giving in way too easily. "How could I ever refuse such a beautiful woman?"

"Now, Herr Georg, you're engaged," Candy reminded him. "Where is Maggie anyway?"

"She's still closing up the shop," the baker said with a red face, properly chastised, "but she should be along shortly."

"If she hears about these pickles, she'll want one for herself," Candy said, "but there just aren't enough to go around."

Feeling a little annoyed, she glanced around the room, her eyes searching. "I just wish I knew who got into them."

FIVE

Doc's eyes widened. He knew immediately where those pickles had come from. "You took them from that jar on the table!" he said, his voice rising as he pointed back the way he'd come.

"Now, now, Doc, keep it down a little, would ya?" Ned motioned with his hand and glanced furtively to either side, but so far they hadn't attracted anyone's attention. His voice dropped into a harsh whisper. "I know this ain't exactly copacetic, but how could anyone in his right mind find that jar of pickles and not take one or two?"

"Or three!" Bumpy piped in jovially.

"Three? You took three of those pickles?" Doc looked down at the paper plate in Ned's hand, focusing on it for the first time, a shocked expression on his face.

"I could have taken more," Ned said, starting to sound defensive. "I left a few. I tried to be discreet."

"Discreet?" Doc blustered.

"Well, at least I didn't take the entire jar, right? Though I probably could have sold it on eBay and made a ton of money. Right?" He winked at Bumpy. "How much you figure I could get for a jar like that?"

Bumpy shrugged and gave the question some serious thought. "Fifty dollars easy. Maybe more."

"Maybe more. Maybe a hundred." Ned looked back at Doc with a nod of his head, as if that vindicated him. "See, I could have made some money off this deal. But I didn't. I restrained myself and took only a few pickles."

"And what are you going to do with them?" Doc asked.

Now it was Ned's turn to look shocked. "What do you think I'm going to do? I'm going to eat them!" And to prove his point, he lifted one of the pickles off the paper plate and took a big bite out of one end. As he chewed, his eyes rolled up into his head in pleasure. "Hmm, pure ambrosia," he said dreamily.

"Ned, now cut that out," Doc said. "Those pickles need to go back to the table for the judges."

Ned's gaze sharpened. "If you think I'm sending these pickles back, you're crazy."

"But this isn't something you should fool around with," Doc persisted. "Those aren't yours for the taking. Someone left them there on that table with the express purpose of having them entered in this contest."

"And they're still entered," Bumpy said, flicking a finger across the hall.

Doc turned. It took him a moment to determine what Bumpy meant, but then he saw his daughter at Table Four, opening the jar of Sweet Pickle Deli pickles she'd whisked away from him a short while ago. She had found a fork and was digging out a few.

"See, they're gonna get to taste them," Ned pointed out.

Doc turned back. "Makes no difference. There are other judges around here — honorary judges, twenty of them. They should get a chance to taste those pickles too."

"Honorary judges? Like you?"

Doc was silent, since he didn't want to admit that, yes, he coveted one of those pickles.

Ned took another bite and dramatically savored it. He breathed deeply as he chewed and swallowed. "I wish I could give them back, Doc, I really do," he said finally, "but I just don't have that kind of willpower."

"Then I'll just have to take them from you," and in a sudden animated movement, Doc reached out to swipe the plate from Ned's hand.

But he wasn't quick enough. Ned saw the maneuver coming. "Sorry, Doc," he said, snatching the plate back out of Doc's reach. Some of the previous warmth had gone out of his voice. "I'm not giving them up. There's no way. They're just too good. You know what they're like, right? You remember? They're the best, right?"

"Sure are," Bumpy agreed with a nod of his head. "Never been anything like them before or since. But I agree with Doc. They gotta go back. It's the right thing to do, Ned, and you know it."

For a moment he seemed to have struck a chord. Ned's expression softened, and he looked down at the plate, as if contemplating handing it over to Doc. "Yeah, you're probably right. Guess I gotta hand them back."

But then he grinned wickedly. "Over my dead body!" And with a muffled laugh he stuffed the rest of the pickle into his mouth.

Six

Julia von Fleming scrutinized the freshly cut slice of pickle from the Sweet Pickle Deli, impaled on the tongs of a plastic fork she held in front of her. "Luscious color," she said, and sniffed it. "Tangy bouquet. Immature seed mass — obviously picked at the opportune time, when it was still young. It may have been in that jar for a while but it appears as fresh as the day it was made."

Herr Georg appeared equally impressed as he studied the slice he held up. "You're right about that. No indication of spoilage. Firm rather than mushy. As far as I can tell they're not slippery or mucky. Nothing to suggest they've gone bad. Quite the opposite, in fact. They've been well stored, that's for certain — if they're the real thing."

He sighed. "I had no idea these pickles were still around. There was a time when I'd eat one of them every day for lunch. I kept at least half a dozen jars in the pantry.

Only finished the last one a couple of years ago. They were the type I always thought I'd make, if I owned a deli instead of a bakery. . . ."

As his voice trailed off, Colin Trevor Jones glanced from the baker to Julia and back again. "They must be very special pickles. However, since we all know their origin, I suppose we can't consider them for the competition."

Julia shrugged. "That's probably true, but there's no way I'm going to pass one up. They're still worth a taste test."

"Oh, yes, I couldn't agree more," Herr Georg said.

Colin nodded, expecting just such a response. "Then which of us should have the honor of the first bite?"

"Oh, definitely the lady before the gentlemen." Herr Georg bowed to his female counterpart. "Besides, you're the one who heard the rumors the pickles were here. The first taste should be yours."

"You're very kind," Julia said, giving him a demure smile, "but I'd like to hear your opinion first."

Herr Georg waved his hand in a gesture of generosity. "Ahh, but the honor belongs to you."

As they chatted on, Candy's phone

buzzed. Her first thought was to ignore it, but realizing it might be Wanda, she pulled the phone from her blazer pocket and checked the ID on the incoming call.

It was indeed Wanda Boyle.

Candy flicked a finger across the screen and raised the phone to her ear. "Where are you?" she asked without preamble. "This thing's half-over. You're missing it."

When Wanda spoke, her tone was oddly muted. "I know. It can't be helped. I'm at the hospital."

"The *hospital*?" Candy turned away from the judges, held her hand over her other ear to block out the noise in the gym, and lowered her voice. "Wanda, what's going on? What the *heck* happened to you?"

There was a long pause on the other end of the line, as if Wanda had turned away to talk to someone — a nurse or doctor. When she spoke again, her voice was hoarse.

"It appears I've been poisoned. They don't know what type of poison yet, but apparently I got just a small dose, so it doesn't appear to be fatal. I had to have my stomach pumped and they're giving me all these antidotes — things I've never heard of, like atropine and dipotassium."

Candy was shocked. "What? How were you poisoned?"

"It was a jar of pickles," Wanda said, "sitting on the stoop at Sally Ann Longfellow's house. I won't go into the details, but I couldn't help myself. I ate one of them and it was bad. Very bad."

"But weren't those intended for the cook-off contest?" Candy asked, not completely understanding. "Why would you eat a pickle out of the jar Sally Ann left on her stoop?"

"Because I couldn't help myself, okay?" Wanda sounded a bit defensive. "It was sitting right there, right where Sally Ann left it. A jar of pickles from that old place down at the corner of Main Street, on the Loop. It must have closed down five or six years ago. That's why it was so strange to see the jar there. But they were the best pickles I ever ate."

Candy felt her stomach tighten as she began to see the connections. "What was the name of this place?"

"The Sweet Pickle Deli. You must remember it, right?"

Candy, who had moved to the blueberry farm only a few years ago and was still considered a newcomer in town, shook her head. "Vaguely. I remember Doc talking about it, but I never went in there myself."

"It doesn't matter," Wanda said dismissively, "but something strange is going on, and I thought you should know, just in case more jars show up. If you see anything like that sitting around from the Sweet Pickle Deli, whatever you do, don't let anyone eat them, because they could be poisoned like the ones I found."

But Candy never heard the last part. She was already moving.

Julia von Fleming, having acquiesced to Herr Georg's insistence, was just about to take a nibble out of her pickle when Candy dashed up to her, swatted the offending pickled cucumber out of her hand, and sent it flying. Fortunately, it didn't hit anyone, and instead landed on the gym floor with a *splat!* and skidded away.

Julia squeaked in surprise, and for a few moments the two women stood staring at each other, eyes wide.

"Sorry," Candy said finally.

"What . . . *what* was that all about?" Julia sputtered indignantly. "What's going on?"

"Um, there's been some kind of mix-up," Candy said vaguely, and turned to the other two judges. "Colin. Herr Georg. Put down those forks right away, please. I believe the pickles could be tainted."

"*Tainted!*" Julia's eyes widened. "My heavens! What's wrong with them?"

"I don't know yet. Just don't eat them

right now."

"They're not fatal, are they?" asked Herr Georg, sounding concerned as he carefully laid his fork with the pickle slice down on the table.

"I don't know yet." Candy hesitated to say more, concerned about causing a panic if word got out. She looked around at all the tables with food samples on them, and wondered if there were similar jars out there somewhere. Could something else be poisoned, some other type of food? A pie or a jar of jam? But no, she realized a moment later. Just about everything currently out on the tables had probably already been sampled by at least a few of the honorary judges. If something else was poisoned, she'd know about it.

She looked up and around at the crowd still milling among the food tables, and wondered what to do next.

Collect the rest of the pickles, absolutely. Seal the jar. Call the police.

But should she shut down the tastings? Call a halt to the proceedings? Send everyone home early?

Or would the police want to question some of them?

She knew what that last thought inferred: Someone in this gym must have brought

65

that jar of poisoned pickles in here and placed it on the table.

But was it put there by mistake, or on purpose?

And by whom?

One name popped almost immediately into her head. Could it have been put there by Sally Ann Longfellow, who had apparently left out a similar jar of poisoned pickles for Wanda to pick up?

The idea was too ludicrous to consider. Candy and Doc had known Sally Ann for years, and although she could be cantankerous and antisocial at times, she certainly was not someone who would knowingly — or willingly — poison her fellow villagers.

But if not Sally Ann, then who?

Candy scanned the room again, looking for anything or anyone suspicious, something that might give her a clue about this mysterious jar of pickles.

Then she heard shouts coming from the far side of the room.

She looked over and saw her father standing with a group of older men. One of them was lying on the floor.

"He's passed out!" she heard someone yell, and realized a moment later it was Bumpy Brigham who had spoken. "Give him some air!"

"Careful there!" another voice called. "Maybe we should elevate his legs."

"Give him some room, give him some room!"

Almost against her will, uncertain what she'd find, Candy started across the gym. As she approached the crowd along the far wall, she could hear more voices speaking over each other, offering advice and concern, trying to sort out exactly what was happening.

"He just collapsed out of the clear blue sky."

"Strangest thing I ever saw."

"He was eating something, wasn't he?"

"That's Ned Winetrop, isn't it?"

"Anyone got a pillow for the guy?"

"Is he still breathing?"

"Maybe we should call an ambulance."

"Already have."

There was quite a bit of commotion and confusion, and with all the people hovering around the prone figure, Candy couldn't quite tell what was going on. But she spotted her father and hurried to him. "Is someone hurt?"

Doc looked over and nodded. "It's Ned, all right. I warned him but I couldn't get him to stop. Probably choked on one of those darned pickles he was eating."

"Pickles? What pickles?"

"Oh," — Doc waved a hand as if he were annoyed — "he got his hands into that jar we saw sitting out on the pickled food table."

"Oh, no," Candy said, her hand going to her mouth.

"Oh, yes," Doc said. "Ned's always had a hard time resisting food. I just hope it doesn't turn out to be the death of him this time."

But in the end, much to everyone's surprise, and despite all their efforts, it was.

SEVEN

"None of it makes any sense," Candy said half an hour later. She was perched on the edge of a folding chair, where she'd finally allowed herself to settle for a few moments. She was tired and frustrated, and it showed in her voice, which cracked a bit as she spoke.

"I have no idea where those pickles came from," she said. "I have no idea who left them there. And I have no idea why they were poisoned. I don't even know how Ned Winetrop found them! This whole thing is one huge mystery."

Chief Daryl Durr of the Cape Willington Police Department sighed in commiseration, lifted his cap, and ran a hand through his steel gray hair. "I understand all that, Ms. Holliday, and we're going to get to the bottom of this, one way or another. I promise you that." He settled the cap back on his head. "I just wish you and Doc weren't smack-dab at the center of this one — again. But it is what it is."

That got Candy's attention. "Are we suspects?" she asked, trying not to let the idea rattle her.

"Just like everyone else who was here today," the chief admitted with a grim look. "Doc found the jar. Your fingerprints are all over it. And you're the one who gave the pickles to those three judges."

"Yes, but, but . . ." Candy sputtered to a stop. She couldn't think of anything to say. He was right.

Sensing her discomfort, the chief continued, "I've got the gist of your story for now, so why don't we take a break? I have a bunch of other folks I need to run down right now, but we'll talk again soon, okay? I assume you'll be sticking around here for a while longer?"

Candy checked her watch before looking up to survey the activity in the hall. They'd promised the school staff they'd be out by six P.M. It was approaching five. They had little more than an hour to clear out all the food and tables, take down the signs, put everything back the way they'd found it, and shoo everyone out of the building.

Fortunately, she noticed, some of the volunteers, like Marjorie Coffin and some of the ladies of the Cape Willington Heritage Protection League, had already started packing up the samples, while others were folding chairs, collecting discarded cups and plates, and tidying up. Still, there was a lot to do.

"I'm sure I'll be the last one out," Candy said with a heave of resignation.

The chief seemed to approve of her dedication. "That's the spirit. I always knew you were a trouper. I'll be around for a while as well, so if you think of anything else I should know, don't hesitate to contact me, okay?"

Candy nodded slowly. "Okay." She was lost in thought for a moment, but seeing he was about to start away, she spoke up again. "Chief, before you go, can I ask you a question?"

He paused and turned toward her. "Shoot."

She waved a hand toward the tables and then at the far wall. The paramedics had taken away Ned's body a short time earlier, and the area had been roped off. "Is there any chance this whole thing was just some sort of accident or misunderstanding? Maybe the pickles went bad on their own, or maybe the person who left out that jar didn't know the pickles were poisoned."

The chief shrugged. "Anything's possible, of course. We're keeping all our options open." He paused, as if hesitating to say the next words, but decided to proceed anyway. "We've talked to the people at the hospital where they took Wanda Boyle. They've confirmed it appears to be a poisoning, and seem to think the jar was tampered with in some way. We're still waiting for more details, but we're going with that assumption for the moment." He paused. "That's all I can say right now. Anything else?"

Candy thought quickly, and realized something else *was* bothering her. "Yes, one more question. If those pickles really were poisoned — which seems likely, according to your sources — and they were left out on that table by some unidentified person, do you think it was . . . well, a deliberate act? Targeting someone who was here today?"

The chief caught her inference instantly. "You're wondering if we have a homicide on our hands."

"That's exactly what I'm wondering."

Chief Durr pursed his lips as he considered how to respond. "Well, now, we're not jumping to any conclusions at the moment, Ms. Holliday, since the investigation just started. We have some other interviews to finish up here. We've talked to your father, and Bumpy Brigham, and some of those folks around Ned when he collapsed. We have a few more interviews here but we should have those wrapped up shortly. Then we'll move our operations over to the station. We have a pretty good list of everyone in attendance this afternoon, so we'll talk to them as well and piece together the events of the past few hours. When we have all the facts, we'll make our determination." He nodded firmly. "I've got all my people on this. We'll sort it out as quickly as possible. Now, if you'll excuse me." He tipped his cap, turned, and walked away.

Candy wanted to know more. She wanted to know if the police had come across any promising leads during their initial interviews. She wanted to know if they had any idea how that jar got onto Table Four in the first place. She wanted to know its connection to a deli that had closed down years earlier. She wanted to know the type of poison used. And she wanted to know if the police had any primary suspects — besides herself and Doc.

More than likely, though, no one knew the answers to any of those questions right now — except for the person who had put that jar there.

And, Candy thought, the number one

suspect in her mind right now, based on what Wanda had told her, was Sally Ann Longfellow, since the first jar of poisoned pickles had been found on her doorstep. Sally Ann had put the jar there for Wanda to pick up. And that made her the obvious suspect responsible for setting out a jar of poisoned pickles here today.

Candy wasn't quite sure what to make of that. Sally Ann had been a fixture in town for years. She lived alone out at the end of Gleason Street, where it intersected with Edgewood Drive, and stayed pretty much to herself most of the time. Her only companions were her two goats, who had caused some friction with other villagers over the years, though nothing recent that Candy could recall.

On one hand, Candy couldn't imagine Sally Ann would want to poison anyone. On the other, she could be irascible at times. Maybe she'd become upset by something Wanda had written in her community column or on her blog, and that sent her off on some murderous plot to exact revenge.

But if that was true, why be so obvious about it? She'd asked Wanda to stop by and pick up her entry into the community cook-off contest, since for some reason she couldn't make it to the event herself. If Sally Ann really did poison those pickles, why make it so obvious they came from her? Why leave the jar out on her stoop, where it could be easily connected to her? Why not be more devious and secretive, to protect herself, if she really did intend to poison someone?

And how could she have left the pickles here, if no one had seen her all day? Had she sneaked into the gym and set the jar on the table without being noticed? Candy would ask around, but that scenario seemed unlikely. It was difficult to miss Sally Ann Longfellow when she walked into a room.

Candy had told Chief Durr about her phone conversation with Wanda, and how Wanda was convinced Sally Ann was trying to kill her. The chief made careful note of that, and promised to check it out. As far as she knew, he'd already sent a couple of officers over to Sally Ann's place.

What had they found there? Candy wondered.

She was half tempted to pursue the chief and badger him with more questions, but she knew it would be a worthless endeavor. He wasn't about to tell her anything else until he was good and ready — if ever. Police weren't known for discussing the facts of an ongoing investigation with members of the general public, especially those who also happened to be with the press — and were suspects in a possible murder.

So she'd just have to find some answers herself.

Rising to her feet, she looked around the gym, which had cleared out quite a bit. But she saw her father nearby, talking to Bumpy Brigham and another friend, Finn Woodbury. Figuring it was as good a place to start as any, she headed in their direction.

They were, of course, talking about Ned.

" 'Over my dead body,' " she heard her father say as she approached. "Those were the last words to come out of his mouth. I'm sure he didn't mean them literally, but there you go. It was those darned pickles. I tried to get him to put them back, but . . ."

As his voice trailed off, Bumpy spoke up supportively. "He couldn't help himself, Doc. I know, I told him the same thing, but he just wouldn't listen. Those pickles from that deli must have had some sort of magical hold over him. He couldn't resist them." Slowly, Bumpy shook his big head. "Damn shame. Death by pickles. What a way to go."

"Any idea where they came from?" Doc asked as his daughter reached them, and he glanced over at her before directing his attention to Finn. An ex-cop, Finn often found out information before it was made public, since he had a secret source inside the Cape Willington Police Department.

But Finn just shook his head. "Far as I know, they don't have anything solid yet. They're looking for possible suspects, but it could be just about anyone who was in the building today. No one seems to know how the jar got there. There are no direct eyewitnesses — no one actually saw who put it on the table. All we know for sure right now is that Ned spotted the jar first, snitched a few pickles from it when no one was looking, and left it on the table while he retreated to the far wall. A short time later you and Candy spotted the same jar." He shrugged. "The rest you know."

It had all happened so fast, Candy thought, and been such a shock, especially after the phone call with Wanda.

Once she'd realized the pickles were probably poisoned and grasped what had happened to Ned, she'd been hesitant in her response. For a few moments she'd had no idea how to handle the situation properly. In the end, she let her instincts take over.

After Ned collapsed, she had moved quickly to collect the uneaten pickles. Using a fork and napkins to avoid touching them, she returned the tainted pickles to the jar and sealed it tight. Doc called the police, and relayed instructions back to her to keep as many people on site as possible. It was then Candy noticed how much the crowd had thinned. Many had already left. By the time she realized the person behind the poisonings was most likely among the crowd in the gym that afternoon, it was too late to do anything about it. Too late to close and lock the doors and seal everyone inside until they could figure out what had happened.

Candy had a list of all the honorary and official judges, as well as volunteers and support staff from the school, which she'd provided to the police upon their arrival. But she knew there were unaccounted-for individuals who'd been coming and going all day. She'd seen them earlier in the day as she'd been keeping an eye out for Wanda — faces in the crowd, some of whom she knew, some not. Could one of those anonymous faces have brought in the jar, perhaps in a big pocket or a purse, left it on the table at an opportune moment when nobody was looking, and then left the building before anyone noticed them?

Then there was still the issue of motive. Why?

Why poison the pickles? Why leave them out here at the cook-off contest? Who was the target?

Again, she could think of one person who might know some answers.

But where was she?

"Has anyone seen Sally Ann Longfellow today?" Candy suddenly asked the group.

Doc gave her a questioning look. "That's the second time this afternoon you've asked about Sally Ann. Is she involved in this?"

"Haven't you heard?" Finn said.

Doc hadn't, so Finn and Candy explained about the appearance of a second jar from the Sweet Pickle Deli at Sally Ann's house, and Wanda's admittance that she had eaten at least part of one of the poisoned pickles.

"You mean there are two victims?" Doc asked.

"Three, actually," Finn said quietly. "From what I've heard, Wanda's going to be okay, but apparently one of Sally Ann's goats also ate a few of those pickles. The poor critter didn't make it."

Candy's hand went to her mouth. "You don't mean . . . ?"

"That's right," Finn said. "When the police got over to Sally Ann's place, they found one live goat — and one dead one."

"Oh, no." Candy's heart skipped a beat.

"Sally Ann's going to be devastated."

"Wherever she's at," Doc added.

"Let's just hope there aren't any more of those jars around town," Finn said.

"And if there are," Bumpy added ominously, "let's hope someone finds them fast — or there just might be a few more deaths before the day is out."

EIGHT

Georgia McFee stared at the jar in wonderment. She couldn't imagine where it came from, or who left it for her. She'd found it just minutes ago in, of all places, her mailbox out by the main road. Why someone would put it in there, and not just bring it up to the house, was beyond her. But she'd managed to find it eventually.

The mail usually didn't come until late in the afternoon, so she rarely walked down to the end of the lane before then. Sometimes she even postponed the walk until after suppertime. She didn't get much mail these days. A few bills, insurance and bank statements, cards from friends and family on holidays and on her birthday. That sort of thing, plus the regular junk mail, which often kept her entertained for a few minutes until she dumped it in the trash can.

Her daughters usually just called when they had family news, and she had an old computer with e-mail, making it easy to keep in touch with friends. It wasn't her birthday and the holidays were still months away, so she wasn't in a hurry to get down to the end of the lane, since she wasn't expecting anything special today.

But sometime just after four she thought she heard Ollie, the postman, beep his horn a couple of times while he pulled up beside her mailbox, and she thought he might have called out to her, though of course she couldn't make out the words this far away. She looked out the kitchen window and thought she saw him waving. She waved back but didn't think he saw her. He beeped again and drove off.

"Well, I wonder what that was all about?" she said to herself.

Maybe something important was in the mail.

But again, if it was important, why not just bring it up to the house, which he'd done before?

She sighed. "Best see what's going on," she said, and pulled her walking stick from the corner by the front door before heading outside.

She soon discovered what all the fuss was about. Someone had left a jar of pickles in her mailbox. Ollie had probably frowned at that — federal use only, that sort of thing. She pulled the jar out and turned it over in her hands.

The label quickly revealed itself:

Sweet Pickle Deli.

"Well, I'll be," she said. "Where did you come from?"

Her first thought was that Ollie had left it — maybe as a gift of some sort. But why would he have given her a jar of pickles from a deli that closed down years ago?

Maybe someone else left it, she thought, and that's what Ollie had been trying to tell her by beeping his horn: Someone had come by sometime during the day and put the jar in the mailbox for her.

Suddenly she looked up and around, as if the person who left it there might still be somewhere nearby. But she saw no one.

She looked again at the label with greater curiosity this time. Could this be an actual jar from the deli? Or an impostor of some sort? Why leave it here?

And, again, who would have done such a thing?

Leaning the walking stick against the side of the mailbox, she absently plucked a couple of envelopes and a flyer from inside, slid them into a side pocket of the faded pink cardigan she wore with barely a glance at them, and closed the mailbox lid. Then she took up the walking stick again with her left hand, still holding the jar in her right. She clutched it tightly to her body as she started back along the lane toward her house. She moved slowly, for she had a hard time taking her eyes off the jar. But she finally forced herself to focus on her footing, since she didn't want to trip and fall. That could be disastrous, out here all by herself.

She waited until she was back inside, seated at the small table in the front corner of the kitchen, to examine the jar more closely. The label looked relatively new, as if it had been carefully stored for years. But why leave it here, and now? Could it have anything to do with the old contest she'd won a few years back, beating that grumpy old deli owner? What was his name? Michael something? Or Morris? But no, that wasn't right. It was more exotic. Maurice. His name had been Maurice. Never Mo — she'd heard that he'd kicked a customer out of his store once for calling him Mo. It was always Maurice. And, of course, that ridiculous surname, which she felt in her bones was fake, but he'd always insisted was real.

She'd taken it as a personal challenge to beat him at his own game, since he'd been a bit of a braggart the few times she'd encountered him. For reasons she couldn't explain, she'd taken an instant dislike to the man. That rarely happened. She got along well with most people. Those she didn't, she'd lost touch with long ago. She tried not to hold on to grudges. She also tried not to be a braggart herself. But winning that long-ago contest against the arrogant owner of the *Sweet Pickle Deli* had been an especially triumphant moment for her.

But why dredge up that old memory now? Why leave a jar of pickles from that old place in her mailbox?

Of course, they'd been excellent pickles, she recalled. Certainly among the best she'd ever tasted. She'd eaten quite a few of them back then, as research, as she made adjustments to her own recipe to improve it. And she'd succeeded. But she'd also gained an enemy. Once she'd beaten him, Maurice had never acknowledged her again, or even allowed her into his deli. She never saw him after that, for one night he simply and mysteriously disappeared.

And now, again, here was a jar of his pickles.

She eyed it curiously. Could they still be as good as they once were?

There was only one way to find out.

She rose from her chair, took a fork from the silverware drawer, opened the lid on the jar of pickles with some effort, and fished one out.

NINE

A thousand questions were going through Candy's mind, but there were no real answers so far, and the random nature of what had happened today made it difficult for her to focus her thoughts.

So she started with what she knew for sure: Two jars of poisoned pickles from the Sweet Pickle Deli had been found in Cape Willington. A man and a goat were dead, and another person poisoned but still alive.

Who was behind it? And what did that person hope to achieve?

Those, Candy felt, were the two primary questions she needed to answer.

Sally Ann Longfellow remained a primary suspect, of course, but why would she want to poison someone with jars of pickles? She didn't seem like a vindictive person, although sometimes people cracked. But if she had such evil intent in mind, why make it so obvious one of the jars came from her?

Why leave one right there on her side stoop? Why place the other one on Table Four at the cook-off contest? And why use jars from the Sweet Pickle Deli? If Sally Ann really did intend to poison someone in town, it made sense that she wouldn't want to use her own jars of pickles. But why jars from that particular place?

There were other suspects, of course, but whoever was behind these acts, what had been the goal? At the least, to create a certain amount of chaos around town, Candy thought. At worst, murder. Obviously, both goals had been achieved.

And what about the target? Had it been general in nature, or someone specific?

Ned Winetrop had dipped into the jar on Table Four, unnoticed and uninvited, and paid the price. But he obviously wasn't the intended target. His involvement had been a random occurrence — something no one could have foreseen.

So if not Ned, who? Who were the pickles meant for?

Her first thought was, *It could be anyone. Anyone in town. Anyone who was here today.*

But that immediately seemed wrong to her. If that was the plan, it was a bad one. Too broad and unpredictable — although unpredictability had interfered anyway. But whoever left the jar on Table Four *could* have had a more specific target in mind.

So . . . who?

Three individuals quickly came to mind: the three official judges.

That thought struck Candy as one possibility that made sense, and she mulled it over as she turned and surveyed the remaining crowd with a more discerning eye.

The official judges were almost guaranteed to taste-test the pickles — it was part of their job here today. Maybe that's why the jar had been put out late, right before the official judges reached the table. That would have kept the honorary judges away from them, and made sure the tainted pickles were out on the table at exactly the right moment.

Of course, Candy herself had aided in that process. She remembered with a shiver that Julia von Fleming had almost bitten into one of those pickles. If anything had happened to her, Candy could have been considered an accessory to attempted murder — or worse.

As it was, she was already under suspicion. She decided she'd better figure this thing out, and fast, before both she and her father found themselves placed in handcuffs and hauled off to jail.

The gym had largely emptied out following the demise of Ned Winetrop and the subsequent halt in the afternoon's proceedings. Other than Doc, Finn, and a few others, most of the honorary judges had already left the building, though glancing out through the double doors Candy could see a few people still gathered in the parking lot outside, apparently hesitant to leave the scene just yet. They milled about or stood around in small groups, chatting with one another in lowered voices and shaking their heads in disbelief. A few were talking to police officers. Mason Flint and Elvira Tremble were both engaged in conversations with officers. Elvira looked especially animated as she pointed back toward the building and recounted her story, whatever that might be, to Officer Molly Prospect, who was dutifully writing down Elvira's comments in a notebook and occasionally prompting her with a question.

Turning her attention back inside, Candy noticed that all three of the official judges were still there, much to her surprise. She was even more surprised when she realized they were all huddled around the last of the food tables — and from what she could tell, they were still going about their business, judging the samples that remained.

Candy felt a moment of gratitude at their dedication but she also became concerned, considering what had just happened with one of the food samples. Warning signals rising, she hurried over to them.

"Herr Georg, Colin, Julia, what are you still doing here?" she asked in a hushed tone as she approached the group. "And, well, what exactly are you doing?"

Three pairs of eyes shifted toward her. Herr Georg flashed a weak smile but Julia spoke for the group. "We talked it over and decided we should go ahead and finish the taste testing, as best we could," she told Candy. "We've asked the volunteers to leave the entries on these last two tables so we could sample them. After all, wonderful townspeople prepared all these items, which deserve to be considered for the contest."

"But . . ." Candy hesitated. "But what if something else is . . . tainted."

"We talked about that," Colin said with a great deal of seriousness, "and decided it's unlikely. For one thing, that jar was an aberration. We all knew it. Because it was labeled, and wasn't properly checked in, it didn't belong in the contest anyway. We rightfully should have excluded it entirely, but, well, we got caught up in the moment."

"I'm afraid that's all my fault," Julia

confessed to Candy, giving her a contrite look. "I pestered you about those pickles and bent the rules a little. It was an unregistered jar and should have stayed in that box, where you'd put it."

"As far as we can tell," Herr Georg continued, "everything else out here on the tables has been registered, and can be traced to a specific person, so we don't expect any more problems."

"We've asked a couple of the volunteers to re-verify all the samples for us," Colin added, "just to make sure they're legitimate."

Candy nodded her approval. "Good thinking."

"So, you see, we decided as a group there wasn't much risk in finishing our job," Herr Georg concluded with another smile, slightly stronger this time.

It made sense. And at least it would alleviate one of her concerns — what to do about the article for the newspaper. She knew it was somewhat mercenary of her to think about filling pages at a time like this, right after someone had succumbed to a poisoned pickle practically right in front of her. But she couldn't ignore the fact that there had been a real purpose behind today's event. It had all been for the sake of an article in the paper's bicentennial edition.

She couldn't help but feel a tinge of guilt that someone had died at an event essentially held for entertainment purposes.

However, that raised another concern. Would all this cast a shadow over their planned special edition? Would readers — and subsequently advertisers — shy away due to a negative stigma?

She shook her head. She didn't want to think about that right now. Better to keep focused on a more positive outcome.

Figure out what had happened here. Solve this mystery quickly. She couldn't save Ned, but she could do the next best thing:

Find the person who had poisoned him, before anyone else died.

TEN

She knew exactly where to focus her attention next — with the people right in front of her.

She turned first to Julia von Fleming, who was taking a petite bite out of a caramel cluster. She held a napkin under her chin as daintily as possible to catch any falling crumbs. "Julia, can I ask you a question?"

Still chewing, Julia nodded as she shifted her gaze to Candy.

"Well, earlier, you said you'd heard a rumor about a jar of pickles from the Sweet Pickle Deli. I'm just wondering where you heard that."

As Julia finished chewing and swallowed, she pointed with a pinky around the room. "Just whispers," she said. "People talking."

"Anyone in particular?"

Julia thought a moment and shook her heard. "Not that I can recall. I don't know many of the people around here anyway, so

94

I don't think I could name names."

Candy accepted that answer for the moment and shifted her gaze to Herr Georg and Colin. "Did either of you hear these rumors?"

Colin just shrugged and shook his head, but Herr Georg said, "I heard some chattering. I was so focused on what I was doing that I didn't think much about it, though, until you brought out the jar."

"Right," Candy said, moving on. "Did any of you notice who put the jar there?"

All three considered the question but were soon shaking their heads. Julia said, "Personally, no, I didn't notice anything strange. A lot of the volunteers were still putting out last-minute samples on the tables, so it could have been any of them. People were coming and going all afternoon, and all the tables had other judges hovering around them. There was so much activity that it blurred out everything else." She paused and glanced at her fellow judges. "I don't want to speak for Colin and Georg, but I was so absorbed in what I was doing that I simply tuned everything else out."

"It's the only way, really, to make a fair assessment of the samples," Herr Georg agreed. "You have to concentrate on what you're doing and not allow yourself to be distracted by the activity around you."

"So there's nothing that sticks out?" Candy pressed. "Nothing that seemed out of place? Maybe something you overheard, or some sort of strange behavior from someone you might or might not know?"

Again, all three of the judges contemplated the question, but in the end, all shook their heads.

Candy wanted to ask more questions, but they seemed eager to return to their task and finish what they'd started. So she decided she'd leave them to it. She could always talk to them again later. "How much longer do you need?"

"We'll be finished here in less than ten minutes," Herr Georg told her. He paused and glanced around at the others before turning back to Candy. "Do you need our scores today? We're all a bit, well, off-kilter after what just happened. It would be nice to have the evening to collect our thoughts, review our notes, and determine the winners in each category."

Candy nodded. "I completely understand. Monday morning will be fine. That will give you the weekend. And once again, I want to thank all of you so much for doing this. We truly appreciate your time and expertise. I'm sorry it didn't turn out the way we planned, but your assistance has been invaluable today."

She gave them a smile and was about to turn away, when Julia said in a solemn tone, "They were meant for us, weren't they?"

Candy stopped and turned back to face the woman. "What's that?"

"The pickles. They were meant for us — or one of us."

Herr Georg let out a breath and shook his head. When he spoke, he did so with a frustrated tone. "Now, Ms. von Fleming, you know we can't say that for sure. Maybe it was an accident of some sort —"

"That was no accident!" Julia said, and hushed herself when she realized her tone had sharpened. In a lowered voice, she continued, "Those pickles were meant for us — for the judges!"

"But why would someone target you?" Candy asked, curious to hear what she had to say.

Colin calmly intervened. "I think we're all just a little overexcited by what happened here today. I'm not sure we should jump to any conclusions just yet."

"Here, here," piped in Herr Georg. "This is all complete speculation."

"But someone died today," Julia said, looking worried.

"And we're going to find out what happened as quickly as we can," Candy said reassuringly. "Trust me on that."

"Was it . . . *him*?" Julia asked, her gaze shifting back and forth as her voice suddenly dropped to a mere whisper.

Candy shook her head, not understanding. "Was it who?"

"You know." She waved a hand vaguely off toward town. "Maurice."

"Maurice?"

Herr Georg cleared his throat. "She's referring to Maurice Soufflé."

When Candy said she still didn't understand, the baker clarified. "That's what he called himself, at least. He was the owner of the Sweet Pickle Deli, before it closed down mysteriously one night a few years back. If you're looking for the person behind this whole thing, perhaps you should start with him."

Eleven

Who is Maurice Soufflé?

Candy pondered this new bit of information as she turned away, leaving the judges to their task. The name vaguely rang a bell. She thought her father might have mentioned him years ago, when she first moved to town, but she hadn't remembered that until now, and hadn't made the connection in her mind, since she'd been focused on the town's current residents as possible suspects behind today's events, and not a ghost from the past.

The cleanup effort was moving along quickly, and as she considered what she'd just learned, Candy jumped in to lend a hand. Working with Marjorie Coffin, she helped pack up dishes and food containers in cardboard boxes, which would be loaded into a van, taken back to the newspaper's office, and returned to their owners over the next few days, something Wanda had promised to do. They'd originally planned to donate any leftover food to the local church, for distribution to those in need, but decided that was too risky now, given the current circumstances. Instead, any leftovers would simply have to be thrown out, for safety's sake.

As they were working, Candy looked over at Marjorie. She was short and squat, with plump cheeks, a reddened face, and farmer's hands. Her long brown hair, dulled by prolonged exposure to the sun and showing streaks of gray, was pulled into a ponytail. Dressed casually in jeans, a sweater, and sneakers, she was quick and efficient in her work. She ran a farm outside of town with her husband, Pierre, and had gained a reputation around town for her jams, pies, and especially her honey.

"So, Marjorie, how many entries did you have in today's cook-off?" Candy asked, trying to ease the tension in the room with some light conversation.

"I entered a pie, of course," Marjorie replied in a high, birdlike voice. "Strawberry rhubarb. And raspberry jam, and some honeycakes."

Candy nodded. "That sounds like a good assortment." She paused. "You've been in town awhile, right?"

"Sure have," Marjorie said, still working quickly as they talked. "I was raised just up the coast. I've lived here with Pierre for almost thirty years now."

"So you probably can remember a lot of the people who came and went, right? I mean, people who lived here for a while and then moved on?"

Marjorie seemed to stiffen just a bit, as if anticipating what was to come. "Yes, I suppose so."

"Have you ever heard of someone named Maurice Soufflé?"

Marjorie stopped, her hands pausing in midair as her face tightened. "You don't think *he's* behind this, do you?"

"It's a possibility," Candy acknowledged. "What can you tell me about him?"

"We used to supply him with some of his produce, back when we did that sort of thing," Marjorie said. "He believed in using local ingredients long before it was popular. But he was also a hard man to deal with. Very difficult."

"In what way?"

Marjorie shrugged as she started moving again, filling up more boxes. "He always thought we were cheating him — shorting him on this or that, or overcharging him. He'd reweigh boxes, recount the number of flats, that sort of thing. He was a very distrustful person. But —" she hesitated. "You don't think he's back, do you?"

"Like I said, it's a possibility, but for the moment it's just conjecture."

Marjorie's face had suddenly gone pale. "Could he be the one who left that box out on my car this afternoon?"

"What box?"

Marjorie paused again, looking quite uncomfortable. "Well, it's probably nothing, really. Just my imagination getting away from me."

"Tell me what happened," Candy urged.

"I'm not sure it's that important," Marjorie said, "but after the judging started I talked to Trudy Watkins, who told me that someone had left a cardboard box on the hood of my car, so I ran out to check it. There was a note on the box, saying some last-minute entries were inside. And that's what I saw — several jars of pickled items, as far as I could tell. Well, I don't mind telling you I was a little upset. It was almost too late to get them out on the tables."

"Do you know who put it there?" Candy asked.

"No, that's just it. There was no name attached — nothing to indicate where the box came from. So I brought it inside and stashed it under one of the tables. I meant to come back later and put out some of the items but I never had a chance."

"Do you remember if one of the jars had a label on it from the Sweet Pickle Deli?"

Marjorie shook her head. "If I knew for sure I would have mentioned it to the police. But I was just in too much of a hurry. I didn't pay that much attention to the jars themselves. But, well, I suppose *I* could be the person responsible for bringing that jar in here — though it was completely unintentional."

"Is the box still around?" Candy asked.

Marjorie shook her head. "I looked for it a little while ago. Someone must have already picked it up." She bit her lip. "Do I need to tell the police about this?"

"I think it would be a good idea," Candy said, "but why don't we walk out to your car first? I'd like to have a look around. Maybe we'll find something that will tell us who left that box for you."

TWELVE

They finished packing up quickly before venturing outside together. Marjorie appeared nervous as they walked toward the parking lot, her short legs and arms pumping in her haste. "I just hope I didn't do anything wrong," she said, her voice trembling just a bit. "If I'm the one who brought that jar into the building, I'll never forgive myself."

"Even if you did, no one could hold you responsible," Candy said reassuringly. "You had no idea what was in it. Besides, like I said, it's all just conjecture at this point. No one really knows what happened yet. We're just trying to put all the pieces together."

Marjorie said nothing for several steps, then pointed. "My car is over there."

She'd driven an old Buick sedan with a large trunk and a big backseat. As they approached, she pointed toward the vehicle's wide hood. "I found the box sitting right there. Strangest thing."

Candy stopped beside the Buick and looked around. Earlier the lot had been full, but now most of the cars had cleared out. Candy surveyed the ones still parked near Marjorie's Buick but didn't recognize any of the vehicles. They could belong to anyone — even the school's faculty members or staff. It would be impossible to determine if someone who owned one of the cars had left the box for Marjorie to find.

"You said there was a note on it," Candy said, turning back to Marjorie. "Do you think it's still with the box?"

Marjorie shrugged, looking more worried by the moment. "I don't know. I have no idea where the box went or who picked it up."

"I'd really like to get my hands on it. It could be important evidence." Another thought came to her. "Was the note handwritten?"

Marjorie nodded. "With a black felt-tip pen, printed in block letters. It was very neatly done."

"Did the handwriting on the note look familiar at all?"

Marjorie said it had not.

"So just about anyone could have written it," Candy concluded.

"Do you really think any of this is important?" Marjorie asked, looking to Candy for guidance.

"I don't know for sure, but at this point we have to follow every lead."

"What should we do?"

Candy thought about that for a moment. "I think we should definitely let the police know, although I doubt there's much they can do about it at this point. But maybe you should look around the gym one more time and see if you can spot that box before they're all loaded up."

"Okay." Marjorie nodded and started off, then stopped and turned back. "Who should I talk to from the police?"

"Chief Durr, if you can find him. If not, then one of the officers who are taking statements. Here, I'll go with you."

Together, they headed back down the walkway toward the gym, but before they reached the double doors, Candy's attention was drawn to a small group of people gathered around Mason Flint. The group, which stood just outside the double doors, included Cotton Colby and Elvira Tremble, as well as the Reverend James P. Daisy of the local Unitarian church. Apparently, from the intense looks on their faces, they were discussing something of great

106

importance.

As Candy and Marjorie walked past, their voices trailed off and their eyes shifted in her direction. She couldn't help but feel they were talking about her.

She tapped Marjorie on the shoulder. "Why don't you go on ahead and look for that box? If we can find that note, we might be able to tell who left it for you."

Marjorie looked worried. "What are you going to do?"

"I'm going to talk to Mason real quick. I'll join up with you shortly and we'll go to the police together."

That seemed to reassure Marjorie a little, and with a final nod she headed the rest of the way toward the building, disappearing in through the double doors.

Candy took a deep breath and made her way over to the small group gathered around Mason. For the most part they were silent as she approached, although she noticed Elvira whisper something to Cotton, who nodded with eyes squinted and mouth drawn tight.

At the very least, Candy thought she might have to defend herself against whatever rumors those two might be spreading about her.

She nodded to each of them in turn as

she reached the group, and they nodded back. Although the Reverend Daisy seemed pleasant enough toward her, it was Mason Flint who broke the awkward silence.

"Ms. Holliday," he said with a strained expression, "we were just talking about you and your event. A rough afternoon, unfortunately."

"Yes, unfortunately." She thought of saying more but held back.

"Of course, we're all devastated by Ned's passing," Mason went on. "But from what I've learned, it sounds like some sort of fluke occurrence. A tragic mistake. Those pickles weren't intended for him, as I understand it, and he made a terrible error in judgment by eating them, against the protocol of the event. Wouldn't you agree?"

Candy was careful with her response. "It does sound like an accident, yes — at least that part of it."

Feeling emboldened by her verification, Mason continued, "Whoever left that jar on the table must have surely done so by accident as well. It would be difficult to think someone in this town could have done something so deliberate."

Candy said nothing.

"None of this might have happened had the event been better organized," Elvira

Tremble cut in, her tone sharp and accusatory. "I was just telling the chairman. These local events need to be better managed. Where was security when all this was going on? Who was in charge?"

Candy admitted that she was in charge of the event, and a security officer was on standby outside the building. "And, of course, we had volunteers such as you and Cotton helping us out," she said without a touch of sarcasm.

"Yes, well, it all seemed a rather slipshod event — the way those pickles wound up on that table without anyone noticing. I would have thought you'd keep an eye out for such things."

Candy accepted the criticism, knowing Elvira was just letting off some steam. They were all concerned, she knew, not only about the town's reputation, now that there had been another death, but for their own safety as well.

And in a way Elvira was right, Candy thought, though she didn't think it would matter much if she mentioned the fact that Wanda Boyle was supposed to run the whole show, and that Candy had stepped in when Wanda failed to make an appearance. They had indeed been shorthanded, which could have contributed to the confusion over the jar of poisoned pickles. All of that had been out of Candy's control, though, but for the moment she wasn't about to issue excuses, which might stir things up even more.

So she just let Elvira go on a little more, agreeing with the other woman as she expressed her dismay at the recent developments and her concern for their effect on the town's image, with some support from Cotton Colby.

"As you know, our group has been trying to shine a positive light on our village," Cotton said primly. "That's the main mission of the Heritage Protection League. Unfortunately, today's events did not help at all. Not at all." She shook her head in dismay.

Thankfully, the Reverend Daisy cleared his throat and spoke up on Candy's behalf. "I'm not sure this is the proper time to lay blame, Cotton, especially since we don't know all the facts." He nodded toward Candy. "The whole purpose of this event was to spotlight all the wonderful cooks we have in our community, and it was an admirable endeavor. No one could have foreseen the set of circumstances that led to Ned's death. Isn't that right, Ms. Holliday?"

Grateful for the opening, Candy said, in

as nonconfrontational a tone as possible, "Our intentions — mine and Wanda's — were only the best, of course, for the benefit of the community. But it didn't turn out the way we'd hoped."

"It certainly didn't," Elvira said, emphasizing the point with a sharp nod of her head.

Candy decided to leave it at that. She turned back to Mason. "Could I get a few minutes of your time to talk — in private?"

He nodded brusquely. "I was just on my way to my car. Walk with me." He turned to those around him. "Ladies and gentleman, I hope you'll excuse me but I have to get back to work."

As he turned away he pulled out his phone and checked it, walking at a quick pace along the sidewalk, angling toward the far side of the parking lot. Candy hurried after him.

When she caught up with him, he stopped, glanced back behind them to make sure they were out of earshot of the others, and then said to her in a tone tinged with exasperation, "Candy, would you please tell me just what the hell is going on around here? Pardon my French, but this is not what I expected to happen when I got out of bed this morning. What exactly are we dealing with here?"

She tilted her head and narrowed her gaze as she looked up at him. "What do you mean?"

"You know exactly what I mean. Despite what I said to that little group just now, there's no way that jar was left there by accident. Someone sabotaged that event, plain and simple. And I'd like to know who and why. Can you tell me why someone would want to do something like that?"

Candy let out a breath and shook her head. "I don't have any answers right now."

"Well, we'd better find some — and fast. This town is in a pickle, both literally and figuratively. You and I both know that. Given what's happened over the past few years, if I didn't know better I'd say we're being targeted by some unknown assailant, or assailants, who for whatever reason are trying to damage our reputation — or worse."

Candy was about to interject, but Mason held up his hand and continued. "The league ladies have certainly picked up on this. Everyone in town has. All these deaths and murders that have taken place over the past five or six years are not . . . natural. Not for a small village in Maine like ours. So we need to get to the bottom of this as quickly as possible. We need to figure out exactly what's going on here, and find out who's behind it."

"So you think this is all some sort of . . . conspiracy?"

Mason leaned in closer, and his voice lowered. When he spoke, his gaze sharpened and he showed lots of teeth. "Honestly, I don't know what to think. But lots of people are looking to me for answers, and since I don't have any right now, I'm looking to you. You've solved a bunch of these murder mysteries. You have some expertise with these sorts of things. You must have some theory as to whether there's a larger story going on here."

"But that's just it," Candy said. "I have lots of theories, but there's nothing I can prove — at least, not right now."

"Then get on with it," Mason said, straightening as he checked his phone again. "Solve this mystery. Find out who's behind that jar of pickles, and why it was left there. I want answers, Candy, and I want them today. If there's any way I can help, let me know."

That gave Candy the opening she was looking for. "Actually, I do need your help with something. That's why I wanted to talk to you. What can you tell me about Maurice Soufflé?"

"Maurice?" At the mention of the deli

owner's name, Mason's face tightened and his lips grew thin. "I suppose that's as good a place to start as any."

"You knew him?"

"I dealt with him a number of times, unfortunately. He was an antisocial troublemaker who never had a kind word for anyone, but he also was one of the best chefs to ever work in this town. Maybe *the* best."

"Why do you say he was antisocial?"

"Well, there was no pleasing the man, no matter how far we bent over backward to accommodate him. He was always complaining about something — his neighbors, the water pressure in his restaurant, his electricity bill, how quickly we cleared out the snow from the parking spaces in front of his shop, community interference —"

"Interference?"

Mason waved a hand impatiently. "He wanted to put some tables and chairs on the sidewalk outside his place. We told him he needed a permit for that. He disagreed and fought us for six months about it. He even brought in a lawyer from Boston. But here's the thing: The permit costs only forty-five dollars. Why not just pay it and move on? But he said it was the principle of the thing. He was the most argumentative and infuriating man I ever met. He fought that permit just for the purpose of fighting it. That's the kind of person he was."

"Did he ever get the permit?"

Mason shook his head. "Said he'd rather die than pay forty-five dollars. He called it highway robbery, if I remember correctly."

"Did he have any friends around town — any acquaintances I might talk to, any family or buddies?"

Mason thought a moment. "Not that I know of. He was a loner. But I know he made a lot of enemies while he was here."

"And who were his enemies?"

At that, Mason almost laughed. "Just about everyone in town — including, from what I've heard, your friend Maggie Tremont."

"Maggie?" That surprised Candy. "But Maggie doesn't have an enemy in the world. What would she and Maurice fight about?"

"Why don't you ask her? Ask your father? Ask just about anyone in town. They'll all tell you stories about that man."

Candy had one last question. "Do you know what happened to him?"

Mason pursed his lips. "Well, that's the damnedest thing. He just disappeared one night. Turned off the lights, locked up the restaurant, and left town. No one knows why. It was quite a mess to untangle his business affairs. We had to hire an accountant and our own lawyer to sort through all the details. If I remember correctly, he owed a lot of back taxes, as well as payments to vendors and suppliers. Eventually we had to auction off the fixtures in the restaurant to pay some of his bills, but he still owes the town. So if you happen to stumble across him, would you let him know we'd sure like payment from him? We'll even accept a check — though I doubt it would clear."

Just then his cell phone rang. He glanced at the screen and held up a finger. "Excuse me a moment. I have to take this."

He turned away as he held the phone to his ear, said "Flint here," and listened intently. Even though his face was angled away from her, she could see his complexion turn paler as he listened to the person on the other end of the line. Finally he said into the phone, "Thanks for letting me know. Keep me posted."

As he keyed off the phone he turned back to Candy. "That was Chief Durr. They've found another one."

Candy gave him a confused look. "Another what?"

"Another jar of pickles from the Sweet Pickle Deli. This one showed up in the mailbox of some elderly woman up north of Cherryfield."

"Cherryfield? But that's, what, half an hour, forty minutes from here? How did a jar of pickles get up there?"

Mason's intense gaze zeroed in on her. "That's what you have to figure out. You've done it before, and I believe you can do it again. Someone has our town — and apparently some neighboring towns — in his crosshairs, and I want to know who and why. The sooner you solve this business, the sooner we can put it behind us and get back to normal."

With that, he turned on his heels and walked to his car, once again pressing the mobile phone to his ear.

THIRTEEN

As Candy headed toward the gymnasium, a whirlwind of thoughts swept through her mind. She felt she'd learned quite a bit in a short period of time. Now she just had to make sense of it all, and figure out where it all led.

She found Mason's comments about a possible conspiracy interesting, since they echoed feelings she'd had herself over the past few years. And she'd experienced a few encounters while investigating previous murders that led her to believe certain individuals were targeting their town for unknown reasons. But what she'd told Mason was true. At this point it was all speculation, conjecture, theories. She had no proof or evidence. And how the poisoned pickles or the death of Ned Winetrop might tie into that conspiracy, she had no idea.

However, this newest revelation about a *third* jar was key, she mused. Whatever else it might mean, it seemed to establish, once and for all, that the appearance of these jars was not some random act or accident. If a jar of pickles — presumably poisoned like the others — was placed in someone's mailbox, then it was almost certainly a deliberate act.

That was one point, at least, she could more or less accept as fact.

And it could mean, as Bumpy had said earlier, that others in town might be in danger.

But who was behind it? Maurice Soufflé? Sally Ann Longfellow? Marjorie Coffin, who had brought in a box that possibly contained the tainted jar of pickles? Or someone else none of them had thought of yet?

Candy decided to assume, for the moment, that all three jars had come from the same person. The next step, she knew, was to identify the intended targets. She'd already established that the first two jars were most likely meant for someone at the cook-off, possibly one of the three official judges. But what about the one left in the mailbox at a home in Cherryfield? As far as Candy knew, it had nothing to do with the cook-off contest in Cape Willington. Its appearance complicated the whole issue, for it was an aberration, the one jar that didn't fit with the others.

Could the same person have left the jars at all three locations, Candy wondered, all on the same day within a relatively short period of time? The locations were only about half an hour apart. Mason hadn't told her exactly when the jar was found in the mailbox in Cherryfield, but Candy decided generally that yes, it was possible the same person could have placed all three jars at their various locations within a reasonable amount of time.

So who in this gym today, she wondered, had the opportunity to disappear for a few hours during the morning or early afternoon before showing up here around three?

She suspected it would be a short list, since if pressed, most people could probably prove their whereabouts earlier in the day. She certainly could. Many worked in offices or had meetings or meet ups with friends, so they all had alibis.

Who else?

Maurice Soufflé could have done it, since his whereabouts were unknown. Though he hadn't been seen around town in years, he could have returned anonymously just in time for the cook-off contest. If he had been here today, would anyone have recognized him? she wondered. Could he have disguised himself enough to wander through the crowd unnoticed, leave a jar out on the table, then make his escape without anyone knowing he'd been here?

Sure, it was possible, but the opposite could be true as well. While he might be considered a suspect in name, the truth was that he could be anywhere — across the country, living on another continent, perhaps even dead and buried somewhere. So far, other than hearsay, there was no evidence he had left out those jars.

But Sally Ann was a different story. She was local. One of the jars had been found at her home. And she'd been mysteriously absent all day. No one had seen her or knew her current whereabouts. Allegedly, Candy decided, Sally Ann had free rein to leave the jars in their various locations.

Still, it struck Candy as all wrong. She couldn't imagine any reason why Sally Ann, who had lived in Cape Willington for most of her life, would want to poison anyone with tainted pickles.

Where was she anyway?

On an impulse, before heading in through the double doors, Candy pulled out her cell phone and scrolled through her contacts to see if she had Sally Ann's phone number. When she didn't find it, she called the *Cape*

Crier instead. Betty Lynn Sparr, the newspaper's office manager and jack-of-all-trades, answered on the second ring. After conducting a quick search, Betty Lynn located Sally Ann's number, which she relayed to Candy.

Running the number through her head so she wouldn't forget it, Candy keyed off the call and then quickly tapped in Sally Ann's number. She waited as the phone on the other end rang half a dozen times, and then more. No answering machine clicked on or phone service picked up the call — she wasn't sure Sally Ann was that technologically advanced — so she couldn't leave a message. She waited a few more rings before ending the call.

Shaking her head, she walked into the gym, and almost immediately spotted Marjorie Coffin talking with Chief Durr. By the time Candy reached them, they were just finishing up.

"I appreciate the information, Ms. Coffin, and we'll look into it," the chief was saying. "If you think of anything else that might be important, please let us know immediately." He cast a questioning glance at Candy before adding, "I have to get back to the station, so you ladies can contact me there if you need to talk to me."

After he had gone, Candy turned to Marjorie. "So what did he think?"

The other woman shrugged. Softly, she said, "I couldn't tell, really. He listened to me but, well, he seemed distracted the whole time. I don't know if what I told him was important enough or not."

"Well, he has a lot on his mind right now," Candy said, "but you did the right thing in talking to him. And believe me, he listened to what you were saying. Did you have any luck finding that box you brought in, and the note?"

Marjorie shook her head and sounded almost apologetic when she spoke. "I've looked all over the place, but I can't find it anywhere. I have no idea what happened to it. It might have been packed out already, or maybe it was just thrown into the Dumpster."

"Well, don't worry yourself too much more about it," Candy said supportively. "You've done everything you can for now. If it turns up, let me know. I'll be around."

As Marjorie hurried off, Candy pondered her next move. As she saw it, she had several options. She could drive over to Sally Ann's place and see for herself what was going on there. She was certain the police had already been there, but she still might turn up a clue or two. She could run past the Black Forest Bakery and ask her friend Maggie what she knew about Maurice Soufflé and the Sweet Pickle Deli. She could head over to her office and dig into the newspaper's archives to see what she could find out about the deli and its owner. Or she could swing by the police station and see what else she could learn about the third jar of pickles and this elderly woman in Cherry-field who found the jar in her mailbox.

They were all viable options. But first, Candy decided, she had to finish up here in the gym and make sure everything was back in its place before she did anything else. After all, the event was ultimately her responsibility.

As she surveyed the gym, she thought again of Wanda. She'd entirely missed an eventful afternoon here at the gym — all of it, not just the early excitement of the contest, the setup and preparations, the introduction of the judges, the speeches, and the small-town pomp and color, but also the appearance of the mysterious jar, the sudden demise of a local resident, and now the ensuing investigation — so far the biggest news story of the year. Had Wanda been here and healthy, she would have been in her element, racing around the crowd, interviewing people, getting quotes, snapping photos, and running down the story.

On the other hand, she now had an integral role in the afternoon's events — certainly not what she wanted, but she was part of the story. Because she'd discovered the first jar of pickles and endangered her health by eating one of them, Wanda would obviously find herself on the receiving end of lots of questions and attention, especially from the police. She'd become a central point of their investigation, and it would give her a front-row seat on how the police operated in a homicide case.

Maybe she'd take some small solace from that, since it might give her an opportunity to write a few articles for the paper from an inside-the-investigation point of view.

That in itself might hold huge appeal for Wanda, who always loved to put herself at the center of attention.

Of course, she'd need time to recover first. Fortunately, it seemed she'd be all right — the poisoning wasn't terminal, at least in her case. How long would she be out? Candy wondered. How long does someone need to recover from a poisoning? A few days, at least, right?

It was something she'd have to check on, but for now she filed it away in the back of her mind.

Most of the cleanup work in the gym was completed, she was surprised to see. All of the remaining food samples, along with platters, plates, silverware, and cups, had been removed, and the tables and chairs were in the process of being folded up and stacked away. Trash barrels were being emptied, and a small crew was sweeping and mopping the floor where necessary. Everyone, including the remaining volunteers and some members of the school's janitorial staff, seemed busy and engaged.

Candy soon realized why. Scanning the room, she spotted her father, Finn, and Bumpy directing various aspects of the cleanup effort. Bumpy was helping to put away the tables and chairs, working with a few volunteers and the school's janitorial staff, while Finn was taking down signs and packing up promotional materials. And Doc was overseeing the cleanup effort, currently wielding a wide janitorial broom. Under their supervision, the work was progressing quickly and nearly finished.

Relieved, she headed across the gym toward her father, who spotted her and waved as she approached him. "There you are," he said, leaning on the top of the broom as she reached him. "We were wondering what happened to you. We thought you were already out trying to solve this latest mystery, so we decided to give you some cover and pitch in to help with the cleanup."

"Dad, that's wonderful," Candy said. "I can't tell you how much I appreciate it."

He waved it off. "It's the least we could do. You probably have a lot on your mind right now, with everything that's been going on today."

"It has been a busy day, hasn't it? Not at all what I expected." She let out a breath, dropped her head, and crossed her arms, thinking. "The truth is, this whole incident with the poisoned pickles is crazy. None of it makes much sense — at least, none that I can figure out. For one thing, there's no clear motivation, as far as I can tell. I'm having a hard time believing Sally Ann could be behind any of this, though I'm getting concerned about her disappearance today." Doc arched his eyebrows at that comment, but he kept silent as Candy went on. "Wanda Boyle is in the hospital and sidelined for a few days due to a poisoning. There's an elderly woman up in Cherryfield who received a jar, which doesn't fit the profile. And, apparently, we have a dead goat."

She shook her head, and after a few more moments looked back up at her father. "Dad, I'd like your opinion — what do *you* think happened here today?"

Doc had a quick answer. "What do I think? I think it's damned unfortunate that Ned Winetrop stuck his fingers into that pickle jar and ate something he wasn't supposed to!"

"Yes, but what about the jar itself? You were right in the middle of the activity today. You spotted that jar on the table and watched Ned as he ate a couple of those pickles. You must have some theory about who's behind this. Where did the jar on Table Four come from? Who's responsible for leaving it there?"

Doc pondered her questions for a few moments before tightening his jaw. He gave a single, subtle shake of his head. "Honestly, pumpkin, I just don't know. Logically, I guess, you could make a strong case that one of the locals at the event today, possibly one of the judges or observers, put the jar there, for whatever reason. Maybe to actually kill someone. Maybe to create some havoc around town, or maybe just to frighten people. But I don't think that's what happened. The people around here are just normal everyday folks. Maybe a bit quirky at times, and set in our ways, but not calculated murderers. They're just good people."

"I agree," Candy said. "So if not someone local, then who? Maybe someone like Maurice Soufflé?"

Doc's expression tightened. "Maurice?"

"You knew him, right? I just talked to Mason Flint. He suggested I should ask you about Maurice."

Doc nodded, and his voice took on a harder edge. "Yup, I knew him. I had a few run-ins with him, that's for sure, just like everyone else around here. He always seemed to have something against the people of this town, though I don't know why."

"From what I've heard, he sounds like a real character," Candy agreed. "But he disappeared years ago, so it seems far-fetched to consider him a suspect, doesn't it? Still, I suppose I can't rule him out, since the labels from his deli are on the jars of poisoned pickles. That links him at least in some way to today's events. But there's no real evidence to suggest he's personally involved."

"Have you talked to Finn lately?"

"Finn? Sure, just a little while ago. You were there with us, remember?"

"No, I mean recently. Within the past ten minutes or so?"

Candy shook her head. "I went outside for a while. Last I heard, Finn didn't have any new information."

"Well, that's changed. He's got some news you might be interested in."

"What kind of news?"

In response, Doc leaned the broom handle up against a wall, spoke briefly to a volunteer, and then pointed off across the room. "Why don't we talk over there?" he said to her softly.

Without another word, Candy nodded her agreement, and followed her father as he headed off across the gym, toward a spot he'd indicated along the back wall, away from the others in the room. It would allow them to talk without being overheard, she realized. Apparently her father wanted a certain amount of privacy before they continued their conversation.

Once they reached a secluded spot along the back wall, Doc glanced around a final time to make sure no one else could listen in. Satisfied, he tucked his hands into the back pockets of his chinos. Still speaking softly, he said, "There's been a development, but it hasn't been made public yet, and I don't want to create a frenzy around town," he explained, his eyes taking on a glinty appearance.

"What kind of development?"

Leaning in close, he whispered, "They've found a third jar."

"Ahh." Candy nodded. "I've heard that. Mason just told me outside."

"Did he tell you whose house it was found at?"

Candy's cornflower blue eyes grew just a little wider as her voice fell to a whisper. "No, he didn't tell me her name specifically. He said it was some elderly woman up in Cherryfield, but that's all. I was thinking of heading over to the police station to see what I can find out about her."

"Well, Finn's got all the particulars, and it just might help solve this case pronto."

"Why? What's her name?"

"Her name," Doc said, "is Georgia Mc-Fee. Now, that might not ring a bell with you, since all this happened a while ago, shortly after you moved up from Boston, but at the time it caused quite a bit of a stir around town."

"Why is that?"

"Because Georgia used to live here in Cape Willington, before she moved up to Cherryfield," Doc said, "and she was one of the fiercest enemies of none other than

Maurice Soufflé himself, owner of the Sweet Pickle Deli. That's a pretty solid piece of evidence, if you ask me."

"So you're saying he's the one who put that jar in her mailbox?"

"It makes sense, doesn't it? It's not too far-fetched to think he might have returned and had something to do with this. If you're looking for the person behind these poisoned pickles, I'd say he's a pretty good place to start."

FOURTEEN

So she had her first real suspect, and a possible motivation. Finn filled in the details a little later, though he insisted they talk elsewhere. "This is sensitive information, at least for the moment," he told her once Doc drew him into the conversation. "I need to make sure it stays between us."

Doc checked his watch. "It's almost six. We're just about finished here. Let's wrap this up and head outside."

Ten minutes later, with Bumpy in tow, they exited the building. Before she left, Candy took a few minutes to thank the remaining volunteers and school staff for their help, and after ushering out the last few stragglers and conducting a final check to make sure everything was in order, she headed out to the parking lot with Doc and the boys.

"We're supposed to meet Artie at the diner," Bumpy said as they walked toward their cars, referring to Artie Groves, the fourth member of their group.

"Where's he been all afternoon?" Candy asked. "I didn't see him at the cook-off."

Bumpy shrugged. "Tied up with his eBay business, I guess. Sales have been picking up, he says, so he's been trying to keep the momentum going. A little supplemental income never hurt anyone, especially us retirees."

They fell silent as they reached their cars. Most of the crowd had left, though there were still a few people milling about. But they soon cleared out, and Finn felt comfortable continuing the conversation about Georgia McFee. He leaned back against the side of his fairly new Ford compact car, folded his arms together, and said, "So, what has Doc told you so far?"

Candy shrugged. "Just that another jar from the Sweet Pickle Deli — a third jar — was found in the mailbox of an elderly woman in Cherryfield — this Georgia Mc-Fee. And that she used to live here in Cape Willington."

Finn nodded. "She did indeed. You probably don't remember her, since she moved out of town just about the time you moved in, and right before Maurice disappeared."

"Is that significant?" Candy asked.

"Possibly," Finn said. "But here's the thing: Georgia was one of the few people around here who didn't kowtow to Maurice. In fact, there was open animosity between the two of them, especially toward the end."

"And what caused the animosity?"

"Well, as you probably know, many folks around here thought those pickles from Maurice's deli were the best they'd ever tasted. And not just his pickles — just about everything else he made and sold in his shop. Gave him a certain prestige in town, which went right to his head. But Georgia apparently wasn't impressed by his cooking or his pompous attitude. They had a few spats when she questioned the quality of his wares, and he wound up banning her from his store. But she would have none of it. One day she just walked in and challenged him to a one-on-one contest — his pickles against hers, with an impartial panel of judges making the final decision. Of course, it was a blind taste test, like this one today. At first he refused, but she goaded him into it."

"So who won?" Candy asked.

"Well, Georgia beat him at his own game, of course, though I heard the votes were close. Maurice didn't accept the result and accused her of cheating. Georgia accused him of being a cantankerous old man, which he was. As far as I know, they never spoke again, but it stuck in Maurice's craw, I can tell you that. No one ever dared mention it to him. If you did, he'd kick you right out the door."

Candy was silent for a moment, considering what Finn had just told her. Finally she said, "And you think that's why he presumably left a jar of his pickles in her mailbox? He was getting his revenge, after all these years?"

"It's one possible scenario, isn't it?" Bumpy said.

"Yes, but . . . why now? Why wait five years to strike back at Georgia? And does that mean Maurice left these other jars around town too? That he's returned to Cape Willington with revenge and murder on his mind?"

The three men were silent. No one had answers to those questions.

So she asked another. "Were the pickles poisoned?"

"They appear to have been, yes."

"Did she eat them?"

Finn nodded. "She did."

"And?"

"Fortunately she'll live, though she had to make a trip to the hospital, like Wanda.

She's pretty shaken up, from what I've heard."

Candy whistled low. "Wow. Whoever's behind this sure means business."

"They sure do," said Doc in a low growl.

"The police are searching for Maurice now," Finn continued, "though no one knows if he's still in the state, or in New England — or if he's even still alive. Since leaving Cape Willington, it's as if he's completely fallen off the map."

"Well, someone must know where he's at," Candy said, and she was half-tempted to pull out her smart phone and do a quick Internet search right then and there. But that could wait until later. "So, if what you're implying is true," she said instead, "and Maurice Soufflé was responsible for leaving that jar of pickles in Georgia McFee's mailbox, why would he also leave one at Sally Ann Longfellow's house? Did she cross him in some way that would make him want to kill her? And why leave another one here at the cook-off contest? Again, who was his target?"

Finn shook his head as the corners of his mouth rose slightly. "I wish I had all the answers for you, Candy, but I don't. That's why I'm telling you this — because if anyone can find out the connections between those three jars of pickles, and why they were left where they were, and whether or not Maurice Soufflé is involved, it's you."

Doc nodded his agreement. "You have experience with these sorts of situations. We figured this lead about Georgia and Maurice might put you on the right track, and maybe help solve this mystery before anyone else gets hurt."

"Or dies," Finn added ominously.

Doc grunted his agreement, but the others were silent until Bumpy broke in, changing the subject. "On that note, I suggest we get moving," he said, rubbing his hands together. "I know some of you have been munching on goodies all afternoon, but I've only been able to watch from the sidelines, and I'm starving. So why don't we head over to the diner and get something to eat? After all, no one ever solved a murder mystery on an empty stomach!"

FIFTEEN

As Candy drove the few blocks to Main Street, following the vehicles of Doc and his buddies, she realized Bumpy was right about one thing. She hadn't eaten since breakfast, and then it had been only half an English muffin and a cup of gulped-down coffee, since she'd been in a rush. Like Bumpy, she hadn't had a chance to sample any of the entries that afternoon, other than a fleeting nibble or two. She'd been too busy and too distracted by the absence of Wanda and the burden of extra duties to dip into the many offerings. By all rights she should have been starving too.

But once they'd all settled into the corner booth at Duffy's Main Street Diner, where they were joined by Artie Groves, she found she had little appetite. She ordered a shrimp salad and a glass of iced tea, which Juanita the waitress brought out promptly and placed before her with a flourish, along with a cup of homemade New England clam chowder. "Fresh batch. No extra charge!" Juanita said with a quick smile as she hurried off to tend to her other customers.

Candy ate a few spoonfuls of the chowder, which was very good, rich and creamy, but just pushed the salad around her plate as her mind worked.

She had to admit, if Finn's story panned out, Maurice Soufflé, the proprietor of the Sweet Pickle Deli, was the most likely person behind the poisoned pickles, and the best lead to pursue. The name of his deli was right there on the labels. The pickles were allegedly made with his own recipe. There was now a clear line from him to one of the intended victims. Candy decided she needed to look into his background and dig around to see what else she could find out about him.

Finn told her the police had already checked the jars for fingerprints, but there'd be no immediate results, even if the jars were already on their way to the state forensics lab in Augusta, although more likely they were still squirreled away somewhere in the confines of the local police station. She knew from past experience that it could take days, even weeks, to get results back from the lab, which was often bogged down due to an overwhelming number of cases, limited resources, and an overworked staff.

So scratch that avenue of inquiry if one wanted a quick solution to the identity of the person behind the poisoned pickle jars. Candy suspected everyone in town wanted a hasty end to this case, if only to absolve all those who were at the cook-off event today with the best intentions in mind — including her. No time to wait for details on fingerprints and lab reports. She'd have to pursue a different angle.

She wished she could get a closer look at those jars right now. She'd had only a few moments with the one Doc found on Table Four, and hadn't devoted much attention to it. She regretted not taking the time to examine it more closely, although it still formed an image in her mind. Did all three jars look the same? She suddenly and desperately wanted to compare the three of them, to check for similarities and differences, or anything else that might yield a clue or two. But she knew they were out of reach. Again, for now, a dead end.

However, there were other avenues she could pursue. She hadn't heard from Wanda in a while and wondered if she should head over to the hospital. She could stop by the bakery and see if Maggie was still around, though she imagined the shop was closed by now. Or she could get started on researching Maurice Soufflé.

But within the next few minutes, two of those options were addressed. Wanda called to say she was spending the night in the hospital "for observation," but she expected she'd be released the following morning. She'd recuperate at home for a day or two but would be ready to get back to work on Monday morning.

"In fact, I'm following a possible lead right now," she said breathlessly over the phone. "Can't say much about it at this point, but there's something brewing over at the police station. I can sense it. I've got an instinct for these kinds of things."

"Just make sure you take care of your health first, before you go chasing after stories," Candy said with mild admonishment. "You had a pretty big scare. You don't want to push yourself too much right now."

"Have you heard from Sally Ann?" Wanda asked, changing the subject.

"No, have you?"

"No, and I've been trying to get hold of her all day. Maybe she's skipped town, though I have no idea where she went. I think she has a family camp somewhere

142

around Millinocket. Maybe that's where she's at."

"I just hope she's okay," Candy said. "I don't suppose they have a phone up there?"

"I don't suppose they do, but you could always check the directory to see if there are any Longfellows listed in the area."

Candy made a mental note to do that as soon as possible.

"Sally Ann can be pretty unpredictable," Wanda continued. "She doesn't adhere to any sort of timetable. Wherever she's gone, she'll be back when she gets back, I guess."

They agreed to touch base the following morning, and Candy ended the call. A few minutes later, with Bumpy hungrily eyeing her uneaten salad, her cell phone buzzed again. This time it was a text from Maggie:

Sorry we couldn't connect this afternoon. Busy at the shop all day! Headed to dinner with Georg. Stop by the shop in the morning for tea?

And in a second text she added, *Sounds like we have a lot to talk about. Whew! What a day!*

Candy texted her back, agreeing to meet her at the bakery in the morning. Mason Flint had suggested Maggie might have some information about Maurice Soufflé, but any questions Candy had for her friend would have to wait until then.

That left the final option: find out what she could about Maurice Soufflé.

No time like the present to get started.

"Dad," she said, leaning forward during a lull in the conversation around the table, "what else can you tell me about Maurice Soufflé? Do you really think he's capable of something like this? Poisoning people with bad pickles?"

Doc sighed deeply as he scratched at his neck. "Well, harsh as it might sound, I wouldn't put it past him. He was an unpredictable fellow. You always had to watch what you said around him. He was like a pistol with a hair trigger — he could go off at any time, and it didn't take much to get him riled up. But he was unpredictable in other ways too. He'd shut down his shop without warning for a day or two at a time — just disappear. There'd be people lined up by the front door in the morning, waiting for the place to open, but some days it never did. No one knew where Maurice went or what he did during those times. A day or two later he'd show up and unlock the doors at eight A.M., ready for business. You sort of had to catch him at the right time."

"So why'd you put up with him?" Candy asked.

"Because of his food," Bumpy admitted. "Best in town, no matter what anyone says."

"People came from miles around to eat at his place, and there were often lines out the door," Finn added. "There were times when that deli significantly increased foot traffic all over town, which helped out the other shop owners."

"And no one knows what happened to him?"

Doc shook his head. "When he closed the shop for the final time and disappeared, everyone assumed he would return. But he never did. That was the last we heard of him."

"What did he look like?" Candy asked. "Just in case I happen to run into him somewhere."

Finn was the first to answer her question. "Average height, five eight or so, maybe a hundred seventy pounds, something like that.

"He had a long, narrow face," Doc added. "And a moustache."

"He liked to keep his black hair slicked back," Bumpy piped in.

"Dark brown eyes," Artie contributed, "and he used to get manicures. He had nice fingernails."

"Any distinguishing features?" Candy asked.

"He had a mole," Finn said, pointing to a spot on his upper check just left of his nose, "right here. Of course, he's probably changed in appearance since we last saw him. He might have streaks of gray now. Maybe he's shaved off the moustache. But I can't imagine he's changed too much."

"And none of you saw anyone fitting his description around the gym today?" Candy asked.

"Not that I can remember," Finn said with a shake of his head, and the others agreed.

"Maybe he was in disguise," Bumpy put in.

"Maybe," Finn admitted, "but it's hard to hide that mole of his."

"What about out in the parking lot?" Candy asked, remembering Marjorie Coffin and the box of last-minute entries left on the hood of her car. "Did you see anyone suspicious out there?"

"The parking lot?" Finn asked.

She waved a hand. "Never mind. It was a long shot." She took a different approach. "When you were helping with the cleanup in the gym this afternoon, did any of you notice a box with a note attached to it?"

"What kind of note?" Doc asked, scrunching up his face.

"You know, just a . . . handwritten note . . . printed in block letters." Candy felt as if she was grasping at straws. But she tried one more time. "Did you see anyone strange there today? Anyone who didn't belong?"

This time it was Bumpy who shook his head. "I don't know, Candy. There were an awful lot of people in that gym this afternoon, doing all kinds of different jobs. It was pretty tricky to keep track of who belonged there and who didn't. I saw lots of faces I recognized, and many I didn't. No one knew *everyone* who was there."

"That's the thing," Finn said. "I agree we should focus on Maurice, and it's possible he could have slipped in and left that jar on the table, but honestly it could have been anyone who was there today. Maybe it was someone we all know, someone who *wouldn't* stick out in a crowd — a familiar face."

"Someone around town?" Doc clarified. "A villager?"

"We shouldn't rule it out just yet," Finn said. "It's a possibility, isn't it?"

"I suppose so, yes," Doc admitted, "but that means the list of suspects would include many of Cape Willington's most prominent citizens. Look who was there today: the

147

chairman of the town council, the pastor of a local church, the ladies of various leagues and societies, businesspeople and retirees. All the judges and volunteers. And me! And you guys! That's a lot of suspects!"

"I tend to agree with Finn," Candy said. "We have to consider all the possibilities, right?" On an impulse, she reached into the inside pocket of her blue blazer, which she still wore, and withdrew some of her notes from that afternoon. She quickly paged through them and pulled out the list of the official and honorary judges, as well as a list of volunteers, which she laid out flat on the table in front of her. "Could anyone on these lists have done it?"

"Let me see those," Finn said as he reached out and pulled the papers across the table toward him. The others leaned in close to have a look. But after a few moments they all shook their heads.

"We've known most of these people for years," Finn said with a frown. "Could one of them have gone off the deep end and put out those poisoned pickles? Sure, it's possible. But not likely."

"Especially the three official judges," Doc added, pointing at one of the lists. "They almost ate those pickles, so it's not likely one of them put out that jar. You can probably take them off the list of suspects."

"I suppose so," Candy said, "but we could probably take a lot of people off the list — you and Finn and Bumpy, for instance, and maybe Mason Flint, and the Reverend Daisy. We could go on and on, but where do we stop? *Someone* who was there today left out those jars, so who do we include on the list of suspects, and who do we take off?"

They were all silent for a moment, until Finn slid the papers back over to Candy and said with a grimace, "You're right. There's really no way we can effectively narrow that list."

"So we're all still considered suspects?" Doc asked.

"Not me!" Artie said. "I wasn't there!"

"Maybe we just need to step back for a few moments and take a breather," Bumpy suggested. "Sounds like we're going in circles."

But Candy wasn't ready to let go just yet. "I can't help but feel like I'm missing something," she said, glancing through the lists again. "Something's right under my nose. Something that doesn't quite fit."

"It sounds like it all goes back to that deli that used to be down on the corner," Artie said helpfully. "That seems to be at the center of everything."

"Right," Candy said, "and now there's a pizza joint there."

Suddenly she had a taste for pizza. "Maybe I should go check it out. You know, get a feel for the place, see if anything jumps out at me."

Artie turned and looked out the window behind him. "If you're walking you might want to grab an umbrella. Looks like a storm's brewing out there."

SIXTEEN

Almost from the moment she stepped out of the diner and looked down the gentle curve of Main Street, lined by darkening storefronts, she knew what had been bothering her.

She'd returned the lists to the pocket of her blazer but didn't have to refer to them again to know she was right. She *had* seen someone in the gym that afternoon — or, rather, *leaving* the gym — who wasn't on any of those lists: not a judge, volunteer, crew person, member of the school staff, or an entrant in the cook-off contest, as far as she could recall. Someone with no real reason to be there, other than curiosity about the event.

That in itself wasn't a crime, of course. But at the moment Candy was looking for anything out of the ordinary.

She remembered standing near the double doors that afternoon, watching to see who entered the gym, looking for Wanda Boyle. She'd spotted Edna Bakersfield, Elvira Tremble, and Marjorie Coffin all entering the venue, and one person — Trudy Watkins, who ran Zeke's General Store with her husband — leaving.

What time had that been? Around three forty-five, Candy decided after thinking about it. So Trudy had been there in the gym for at least a while, probably since the event's kick-off at three, apparently observing the proceedings.

Candy didn't necessarily think Trudy was the person behind the poisoned pickles, but since her name hadn't been on any of the official lists given to the police, she probably hadn't been interviewed by anyone. Maybe she'd seen something no one else had. Maybe she had some insight, some perspective, no one else did.

She'd also left the gym at a critical time. Someone had placed a cardboard box, possibly containing a jar of poisoned pickles, on the hood of Marjorie Coffin's car right around that time. Maybe Trudy had noticed something — or someone — out of the ordinary in the parking lot on her way out to her own car.

It was at least worth talking to Trudy and hearing what she had to say.

Zeke's General Store was located on Main Street, several storefronts down from the diner, but before she headed that way, Candy made a quick stop at her Jeep. The winds had picked up, pulling down colder air from the north, which chilled her, even with the blazer on. She also felt a few drops of rain, so she reached into the Jeep's backseat and pulled out an umbrella, gloves, and a burnt orange rain jacket with a hood, which she slipped on over the blazer. Then she locked up the vehicle and headed down the street.

Most of the daytime traffic had cleared out but there was still some activity downtown. The headlights of oncoming cars shone brightly, and periodic streetlights just coming on provided some additional illumination, though much of their light was drained away by the lowering sky. The approaching night gave the town a gloomy feel. As she walked, the few drops of rain became a steady drizzle. She huddled deeper into her raincoat as she continued on.

Like most of the surrounding stores, Zeke's was closed for the evening. Unlike those that surrounded it, it was a large building of wood construction, with a two-story yellow-painted facade, a wide entry porch, a peaked roof, and some Victorian architectural features that gave it a charming and inviting exterior. During the summer months it stayed open later, as did most of the stores in town, but in the off-season it closed down early at six.

Candy checked her watch. It was closer to seven now.

Still, she thought, with some luck she might find someone inside, so she stepped up onto the porch and rapped lightly at the thick window in the front door. She held her hands to either side of her face as she peered inside, protected for the moment from the oncoming rain by the porch's overhanging roof. Security lighting was on inside, and she could see part of the store. The place looked empty.

She knocked again, just in case someone was working in the back, and waited. But no one appeared.

For a moment she thought she saw a fleeting shadow, back among the aisles, and she knocked again, louder and more persistent this time. But she must have been mistaken. She'd just have to come back in the morning and talk to Trudy then.

Still, as she stepped off the porch and continued down the street, she had a strange feeling that someone was watching her. She stopped and turned back toward the store, expecting to see someone at the door, staring out at her, but again she saw no one there.

Must be my imagination, she thought with a shake of her head as she started down the street again, umbrella held over her against the worsening rain. She crossed the street in front of Gumm's Hardware Store, about halfway down the block, and walked along a darkened stretch of brick buildings where the streetlights had not yet come on.

She was almost to the southern corner of Main Street, where it intersected with the Coastal Loop, when she sensed she was being followed — or at the very least, again, closely observed.

She heard a cough somewhere behind her and a shuffling of footsteps, and turned casually to look back, but all she saw was an indistinct shadow lurking in the vicinity of a battered baby blue pickup truck parked along the curb on the opposite side of the street. As she glanced toward the shadow it seemed to shrink away, as if it didn't want to be seen.

It seemed an odd movement to Candy, and she felt the skin on her arms prickle under her jacket, but she tried not to read too much into it. As she continued on, quickening her pace just a little, she thought she heard the footsteps again. This time they sounded as if they were crossing the street to her side. She kept walking but turned to look back over her shoulder, more surreptitiously this time, and saw the shadow again, though it was still some distance behind, near the hardware store.

But by this point Candy had nearly reached the corner. After a few more steps she turned to her left and then headed into the well-lit storefront of Village Pizza, pushing her way through the front door, accompanied by a burst of wind and a few stray raindrops.

She'd been in here numerous times before but usually just dashed in and out, chatting only briefly with the staff behind the counter. She'd never paid much attention to the shop itself. She doubted she'd find anything specific related to the previous owner, but maybe someone would remember something about him.

She was greeted by the welcoming smells of tomatoes, garlic, and baking pizza crust, which perked up her senses. Tables with red-checkered tablecloths were set by the front window and along the center of the shop, with booths lit by low-hanging shaded lights along the sides. Perhaps half a dozen of the tables and booths were occupied by couples and small families. The order and pick-up counter was located in the rear of the shop, in front of the kitchen.

Just inside the door, Candy stepped off to one side and turned so she could look out the front window. She wanted to see if anyone walked past. But when, after a minute or two, she saw no one, she let out a small breath of relief and turned back toward the shop.

She'd never been in here when it was a deli but imagined the setup was similar. The pizza owners had simply co-opted the deli layout and made it their own, with red and green interior furnishings and European-inspired murals on the walls. The place had a warm, pleasant feel, and the buzz of quiet conversation put her at ease.

She headed back past the tables to the counter, where after viewing the menu written on a large white board, she ordered a slice of white pizza with ricotta and mozzarella and an iced tea. A teenaged girl behind the counter took her order. As casually as possible, Candy said, "By the way, I think I've seen you in here before. How long have you worked here?"

"Six months," the girl said.

"Do you like working here?"

The girl shrugged. "Sure, it's fine. The best part is we get free pizza if there's any left over at the end of the night."

"Sounds like a pretty good deal." Candy paused as she glanced around the shop. "So, this place has been here for what, about five years or so?"

"I don't really know," the teenaged girl said as she rang up the sale, "but that sounds about right, I guess."

Candy handed her a few dollars. "I don't suppose you were around when the deli was here?"

The girl shook her head and gave Candy her change.

"Just out of curiosity, is there anyone here who might remember the previous owner — the owner of the deli?"

The girl thought a moment. "It's possible. You might want to talk to Phil. He's the manager."

Candy brightened. "Great! Is he around?"

"He works the day shift. He'll be in tomorrow morning at eleven."

"Oh." Candy's brightening mood faded. "Okay, I guess I'll check with him then."

The girl disappeared into the back and returned with a slice of pie on a paper plate. She placed it on the counter along with a drink.

"Thanks," Candy said as she picked up the plate and cup and started away, but surprisingly the teen girl piped up, as if she'd just remembered something.

"Hey, there was one person who might have worked here back then, back when the place was a deli. She stayed on here for a while, working for Phil, but she left a few years ago. They still talk about her. I think her name was Gloria. She might remember the previous owner."

Candy nodded. "That's very helpful, thanks."

"I don't remember her last name, though," the girl continued, "but Phil might. You can ask him when you see him."

Candy slipped into an empty booth along the side wall and sat facing the front window. She'd just taken her first bite of pizza when she looked up and saw a shadowy figure pass by the front of the shop along the sidewalk, from right to left, headed down the street. The figure was tucked into what looked like a black rain jacket, and the face was hidden under a baseball cap. But she saw the glint of the figure's eyes as they flicked toward her before shifting away again.

Candy almost choked on her pizza.

She coughed several times and took a few

sips of her iced tea to help her swallow the mouthful of food, her eyes never leaving the window.

The figure quickly disappeared from view.

Candy watched and waited, but it didn't return. The rain was coming down harder now, slashing across the window, and the lights in the pizza shop flickered once but stayed on.

"Looks like it's getting rough out there," observed an elderly gentleman sitting with his wife at a nearby table.

"It sure does," Candy muttered to herself.

SEVENTEEN

Before she'd finished her slice of pizza, the shadowy figure crossed the window one more time, headed back in the opposite direction, up toward the intersection of Main Street. Again, the figure was hunkered down into the black raincoat, and Candy couldn't get a good look at the person's face, nor did the figure turn to look in the pizza shop's window this time. The head was angled down, the eyes aimed toward the sidewalk or straight ahead, until the figure again disappeared from view.

Candy wondered if she was imagining things, making herself unnecessarily worried about some harmless villager who just happened to be on one of the dark streets at the same time she was. As she dropped the paper plate and empty paper cup into a waste can, she cautioned herself against overreacting and took a few breaths to calm herself down.

But once she was back out on the street, huddled under her umbrella beyond the warm safety of the pizza shop, her uneasiness returned. Perhaps it was just the uncooperative weather, she mused, that made her feel so uncomfortable.

Or perhaps it was something else.

She'd always trusted her own instincts, and they were on edge now.

Out on the street she hesitated, trying to decide which direction to go. Finally, she turned to her right and headed up the sidewalk. But the moment she turned the corner onto Main Street, she stopped.

She sensed a presence somewhere ahead of her, in the dark shadows of the brick buildings and storefronts, which were sleek and hazy in the slashing rain. She couldn't make out anyone in particular lurking there — nothing specific stood out — but she didn't feel comfortable continuing in that direction.

So she turned and headed back in the other direction, around the corner, past the pizza shop, and down along the sidewalk toward the Lightkeeper's Inn at the village's lower end. Though the popular inn was still some distance in front of her, it was well lit and offered refuge from the driving rain — and from whoever might be lurking behind her along the dark street.

She tried to resist looking back but couldn't help taking one or two quick peeks. The sidewalk behind her looked deserted. She stuck her hand in the left pocket of her blazer and felt for her cell phone. Her hand closed reassuringly around it. She could always call 911 if she felt truly threatened. Or she could call her father, who was probably still at the diner, and ask him to meet her halfway up the street.

But she had another idea.

Tightly clutching the umbrella's handle and quickening her pace, she passed the last of the storefronts and crossed in front of a small parking lot, which occupied the space behind the inn, then angled toward the historic building's broad wraparound porch. After a dozen more paces she stepped up onto the porch and, under the shelter of the overhang, put her back against the inn's outer wall, shook out her umbrella, and looked back the way she'd come.

The sidewalk was still deserted. No shadowy figure trailing her. A few cars came down the rain-slicked road, their headlights and red taillights flashing in her eyes, brighter and dimmer as they approached and then receded into the distance.

She waited a full five minutes, just to make

sure, then walked the length of the porch and ducked into one of the inn's side doors.

She entered a short, thickly carpeted hallway, lit by antique pewter wall sconces. Again she stopped, just inside the closed door, looking out through a glass window at the rainy night. She wasn't sure why she was so spooked, but she felt a need to keep an eye out on the street. She stood there for several more minutes, watching.

And then she saw it. First, just a pair of oncoming headlights, but as the vehicle came slowly down the Coastal Loop, it began to take shape.

A pickup truck. A smaller, older one, battered and worn.

In the light of the vehicle behind it, it appeared to be light blue in color.

It was the same baby blue pickup truck she'd seen parked up on Main Street.

The truck drove down past the pizza shop and passed alongside the inn. She could see the driver silhouetted against the headlights of other vehicles, but with the windows rolled up and streaked with rain, she couldn't make out any distinctive features.

Then it was past, following the curve of the road around the front of the inn, toward the intersection with Ocean Avenue.

It finally passed out of view, though she

could see the reflected glow of its small red taillights on the wet road.

She shivered as she continued to watch the spot where she'd last seen the truck.

Her first thought was that she was indeed being followed. This seemed too deliberate, too obvious an action to be a coincidence. On the other hand, maybe she was just being paranoid. Maybe the dark, rainy night and the events that had occurred earlier in the day were causing her to overreact.

Because she was looking outside the building, she didn't see the figure approach her from behind, coming along the hallway. The rain was drumming on the porch roof, masking the sound of the person's footsteps, which were also muted by the thick carpet, so Candy didn't hear the approach.

When she felt someone tapping her lightly on the shoulder, she let out a yelp of surprise as she spun around.

Eighteen

Instinctively she raised her folded umbrella, holding it out in front of her, prepared to protect herself from what she thought was the shadowy figure, who had sneaked up behind her.

But much to her surprise, it wasn't a shadowy figure at all. Instead, she found herself looking into the inquisitive face of a fairly well-lit, easily recognizable Julia von Fleming.

Julia yelped in surprise, a spontaneous reaction to Candy's yelp. Her eyes went wide and she took a quick, sharp breath. But she recovered quickly.

"Candy, I thought that was you! Is everything okay? You look like you've just seen a ghost."

Candy's hand had gone to her chest. She could feel her heart thumping. "Julia. I didn't hear you come up behind me. You gave me quite a start."

"What are you doing here?" Julia asked, looking out the door as Candy had been doing. "Is something going on out there?"

"No, it's just . . . I was . . . just trying to get out of the storm."

Julia continued looking out the window. "Yes, it is coming down pretty heavily out there, isn't it? But they say it's going to pass during the night. Hopefully tomorrow's weather will be better for the book signing."

In addition to serving as a judge for the cook-off contest, Julia had made arrangements to stay on for the weekend, signing copies of her cookbook at the local bookstore on Saturday morning, and giving a talk on authentic New England recipes at the Pruitt Public Library on Sunday afternoon. With Candy's help, she'd managed to snag a room at the usually expensive Lightkeeper's Inn at a highly reduced rate, aided by Candy's acquaintance with innkeeper Oliver LaForce and his staff. And at Julia's suggestion, the ladies of the Cape Willington Heritage Protection League had agreed to pick up the tab for her room and board, for what they felt was a series of worthwhile cultural events.

Now that she was safely inside the building and in the company of someone she knew, Candy felt herself beginning to relax a little, as her concerns about being followed faded away. "Yes, hopefully," she said hesitantly, trying to make conversation. "We should have a good turnout. I've talked to many people who are looking forward to it." She paused, and her expression changed. "I know it was a crazy afternoon, but I can't thank you enough for helping us out today."

"But I loved doing it!" Julia admitted. "And, of course, it's good publicity for the book. These days it's all about promotion, promotion, promotion, you know. I'm just sorry it turned out the way it did — that poor man! — but I'm glad we had a chance to finish the taste tests."

"So am I," Candy said. "That was very brave of you."

Julia took the compliment easily. "Herr Georg and Colin were wonderful to work with — and very brave to finish with me, considering what happened." She shook her head. "To think I was so anxious to eat one of those pickles — and I almost did! You saved my life when you knocked it out of my hand."

"Thank goodness you didn't take a bite of it," Candy said. "I never could have lived with myself if anything had happened to you, since you came here at my request, and I practically put that pickle into your hand myself."

"Yes, well, speaking of pickles, I'm actually glad you showed up here tonight," Julia said, steering the conversation in a different direction, "because I've been thinking a lot about what happened in that gym today, and I believe I have some information that might be helpful to you. In fact, I think I might know why that pickle jar was put there in the first place."

Candy was intrigued. "Really? Why?"

"I think it was meant for someone specific."

"Who?"

"Me!" said Julia, her eyes going wide again.

"You? But why would someone target you?"

Julia looked around and lowered her voice. "Why don't we find a place to sit, and maybe order some tea or hot chocolate to warm us up, and I'll explain."

They found a cozy spot in the front lounge, next to a fireplace, which was lit with glowing embers. After they'd each ordered green tea with lemon and honey from a passing waiter, Julia pressed on.

"I have to confess, I haven't been completely forthcoming with you," she said in a low voice, so only Candy could hear, though they were almost alone in the lounge. "I've actually been to Cape Willington before, and I've tasted those pickles before, so I knew what they'd be like. That's why I wanted to try them again. Well, I *had* to try them again, to see if they were as good as I remembered. That's how much they've stuck with me over the years. I wanted to see if I could figure out the recipe he used. I thought of trying to recreate it for my next cookbook." She paused to quickly gauge Candy's reaction before going on.

Candy was uncertain of how to react to this news, but curious to hear more. "When were you here?"

"Well, this happened a few years ago. Among other jobs I had before I got started as a cookbook author, I used to write a food column anonymously for a few regional newspapers. I'd write about some of the local recipes I'd found during my travels around the region, and review restaurants around Maine, New Hampshire, and Vermont. Sort of an amateur foodie thing. I discovered the Sweet Pickle Deli while on a trip through Down East Maine, and wrote a review of it. Of course, the food was wonderful, but unfortunately I had a run-in with the owner. In the end, because of the negative experience I had there, my review wasn't very flattering."

"Ahh," Candy said, beginning to see where all this was headed.

"As I said, I wrote the column anonymously. I used the byline Yankee Food Girl, which was my pen name, until I established my own name a few years ago, started a blog, and relaunched my career in connection with the cookbook."

"So you think Maurice Soufflé found out you were the author of a negative review of his restaurant, which you wrote several years ago, and targeted you today with that jar of pickles?"

Julia nodded. "It makes sense, doesn't it? I mean, everyone knew I'd be here. Lord knows I've publicized it enough over the past few weeks, and I'm sure you have too. The event has been well-advertised. Maurice didn't know my real name, at least not when I wrote the review, but he must have figured it out somehow. Maybe he heard something about me in connection with the cook-off contest, or read one of the interviews I've given about the cookbook, or maybe he stumbled across my blog and learned of my true identity that way. I don't publicize the fact that I had a pen name, but I don't deny it either. I've posted some of those old columns on my blog lately using that byline, so maybe that's how he found out. Maybe that's why he waited until now to take his revenge. It took him that long to find out I'm the one who wrote that review."

"Maybe," Candy said. "It's certainly an intriguing possibility." She paused, thinking it through. "You said you had a run-in with him. What about?"

"About the pickle recipe, of course! I told him I wanted to interview him about it — maybe talk about how he came up with it and some of the ingredients. Of course, it was too much to hope that he'd give me the recipe outright and allow me to print it. I'd hoped to wheedle a little information from him about it, but he was a stubborn man. When he found out what I was doing, he refused to talk to me. In fact, he was quite rude to me — as, I've heard, he'd been to many of his customers."

"And what exactly did you say in your review?"

Julia shrugged as their tea arrived. "I said the food was good but the atmosphere in the shop was inhospitable. No customer should be treated the way he treated people. In the end, I told my readers to avoid the place."

"I see." Candy pondered that for a moment. It could, she thought, provide the motivation behind the appearance of the jar on the pickle table that afternoon. "Have you seen him since you were in his shop?" she asked after a few moments. "Had any contact with Maurice?"

Julia shook her head. "No, nothing like that. I had no interest in ever running into him again — although I'd still like to get my hands on that pickle recipe for my next book."

As they sipped their tea, they chatted about the deli, its owner, and pickling foods in general, as well as some of the more obscure recipes Julia had come across in her research. "Many of the most interesting ones are the centuries-old Irish and German recipes that came over from the old country as immigrants made their way to New England," she told Candy. "Some had almost been lost to time, but I managed to rescue them for the cookbook."

It was, Candy admitted, a worthy achievement, and she told Julia she was looking forward to the book signing the next morning. Then, checking her watch, she finished her tea, and sufficiently warmed, thanked Julia for the information and headed out once again into the stormy night.

Nineteen

She left by a door on the opposite side of the inn, which put her on Ocean Avenue, across from Town Park and just half a block from her office up the street. Thankfully, while she'd been inside sipping tea, the rain had lightened. But the chill wind still blew in hard gusts, sweeping off the dark churning sea to her right and swirling up the town's broad avenue. It tugged at trees opposite her in the park, some of which had just begun to turn for the fall. Their highest, thinnest branches, still full of late-summer leaves, thrashed together, adding to a building cacophony underscored by heavy waves pounding on the rough shoreline, unseen in the mist and gloom.

The rotating light atop the English Point Lighthouse, half-visible on its rocky spit of land some distance ahead of her and off slightly to her right, punctuated the night with its questing beam. Up the avenue, streetlights were aglow, and Town Park was well lit with the glow from antique street-lights.

It was not an unfriendly scene. Quite the opposite.

Still, just outside the inn, she paused on the wraparound porch, her gaze turning up along the avenue to her left and then out to the open ocean on her right. Cars drifted past, headed up and down Ocean Avenue and along the curving Coastal Loop, which followed the shoreline. But the sidewalks were now mostly deserted, even this early on a Friday evening. Tourist season was behind them, and most of the villagers had apparently opted to stay inside tonight due to the inclement weather.

She saw no sign of a baby blue pickup truck or a shadowy figure lurking in some dark alcove or behind the glistening trunk of a tree. She had things she still needed to do, and she planned to do them, but vowed to remain alert.

Pulling her rain jacket together near her neck and tucking her umbrella underneath her left arm (where she could easily reach it if she needed to use it as a weapon, if it came to that), she stepped down off the porch and started up the avenue. She walked quickly, pushed along by the strengthening wind.

As she passed the dark storefronts to her left with her hands tucked deep into her jacket pockets, she wondered if her alleged pursuer had anything to do with the poisoned pickles. Perhaps it had even been Maurice Soufflé himself, she thought. It was possible he could indeed be lurking around Cape Willington, if what several people had told her today was true. Some felt he was the one who'd left that jar of pickles in Georgia McFee's mailbox, and Julia von Fleming had gone so far as to suggest he was targeting her specifically. If she was right, it meant he had returned to their town, and may still be here somewhere.

That could all be true — but to her it seemed too big a leap in logic, because in her mind the motivations remained weak, and some just didn't make sense. If Maurice Soufflé really was behind the poisoned pickles, why put the label of his old deli on the jars, clearly linking himself to the crime? Why wait five years to take revenge on Julia, or whomever else he might have been targeting? And why be so obvious in going after people with whom he had a bad history, as in Julia's case, even more clearly pointing a finger at himself as the perpetrator?

As she walked up the street, she tried to make sense of what it all meant. There seemed to be quite a bit of evidence to suggest Maurice Soufflé was the person behind the poisoned pickles, but she could come up with several reasons to suggest otherwise. The same for Sally Ann Longfellow.

So if neither of them had put out those jars of pickles, then who?

She thought of Trudy Watkins leaving the gym, of Marjorie Coffin bringing in the box of last-minute entries, of all the judges and volunteers who had been at the cook-off contest that day. But nothing clicked in her mind.

Despite all she'd learned in the past few hours, she felt she'd made little progress in solving this mystery.

But she wouldn't let herself be defeated so easily. She just needed to keep asking questions, to keep digging for more information, and sooner or later the answers to her myriad questions would begin to reveal themselves, she thought as she reached the street-level door that led up a wooden staircase to the second-floor offices of the *Cape Crier.*

She had her key ready in her hand and made quick work of unlocking the door, stepping inside, and locking it behind her.

She stood on the lower landing just inside, looking out through the door's glass window, just to make sure a final time she wasn't being followed. But she saw no one — just a windy, rainy night.

Maybe, she thought, the day's events, along with the rain and general gloominess of the evening, had affected her judgment and perceptions. No one appeared to be pursuing her. Maybe she'd just imagined the whole thing.

Maybe.

She was only slightly reassured as she climbed the stairs, unlocked the door to the paper's second-floor suite of offices, and disabled the security alarm system before she again locked the door behind her.

She flicked on the hall lights.

The place, as she'd expected, was deserted. Sometimes, on tight deadlines, she or Wanda or Jesse Kidder, the paper's graphic designer and photographer, or one or two of the volunteers would work a few late-night hours, but rarely, if ever, on a Friday night.

"I guess I'm the only one crazy enough to work tonight," she said to herself with a mildly chiding tone.

She headed to her office and flicked on the desk light before shaking off her rain jacket and hanging it on a wall peg, along with her umbrella. Slipping into her office chair, she turned toward her computer and double-tapped the space bar, bringing the screen to life. It seemed like forever since she'd last been here, with all that had happened today, although she'd spent some time in her office that morning responding to e-mails, proofing copy, and reviewing Jesse's layouts for the next issue before heading over to the high school gym for the cook-off contest.

But she wasn't here tonight to answer e-mails or proof copy. She had other business on her mind.

She'd heard a lot of rumors, speculations, and accusations throughout the day. It was time to start separating the truth from fantasy.

The paper's digital archives would be a good place to start, she'd decided earlier. They went back nearly twenty years, giving her easy access to articles, columns, event information, interviews, sports stories, and more. For earlier editions she'd have to dig into the print library, squirreled away in a cobwebby closet somewhere, but she didn't think that would be necessary.

In short order she'd turned up half a dozen references to the deli and its owner, often in the paper's community column, which at the time was being written by a woman named Sapphire Vine. Candy and Sapphire had a long history together. Candy had helped solve the mystery behind Sapphire's murder, and had subsequently inherited her job and her research files.

Sapphire, Candy remembered, had been a community columnist and well-regarded citizen, generally cheery and upbeat in public, but she also had a dark side. Among other things, she'd been a spy and a blackmailer, and she'd kept secret files on many of the villagers.

After Sapphire's untimely death, Candy had come into possession of those files, and a few times over the years since, when she was working on a case, she'd dug into them, finding one or two clues to help her solve a mystery. But she couldn't remember if there had been a file devoted specifically to Maurice Soufflé or the Sweet Pickle Deli.

And, for better or worse, she could no longer access them. Because of their age and general uselessness, as well as the potential damage they could cause due to personal and private information they contained about many of the villagers, Candy had burned those files one evening last summer. She and her father had actually roasted marshmallows over the small bonfire. She'd never regretted her decision to destroy the files, but right now, for a few fleeting moments, she wished she had them here with her now. They might actually prove useful this time.

Candy's mind wandered for a moment. What if there had been more going on between Sapphire and Maurice than anyone knew? Could Sapphire have kept information in her files that incriminated Maurice in some way, causing him to leave town?

Was she blackmailing him for some reason, as she'd done to others to get what she wanted?

It was a tantalizing idea, but at this point nothing more than that, since any potential evidence kept in those files was gone. She was left only with Sapphire's digital trail of published columns and news items that had appeared in the paper years ago.

It didn't take Candy long to determine that Sapphire had had her own run-ins with the deli's proprietor. While in one column she praised his food, in another she poked fun at his general grumpiness, which had apparently escalated into a personal feud between the two. While overall Sapphire relied on humor and sarcasm to get her points across, at times she descended into harsher language.

It had all predated Candy's arrival in town, though, and in later columns mentions of the Sweet Pickle Deli dwindled to almost nothing, until a final series on the strange disappearance of the deli's owner.

Candy scanned the columns, looking for any other interesting tidbits, but nothing stuck out. If Sapphire had known more about Maurice Soufflé, she didn't mention it in her columns.

There were other articles as well, by other writers, going back to the deli's opening. From the dates of the issues, Candy was able to determine that the place had been open for six or seven years before it mysteriously closed. She reached for a pad and pencil and made a note to find out the specific date it closed down. And the owner's address while he was living in town, and a few other points she wanted to check.

That sparked another thought in her, and she remembered a mental note she'd made earlier, to search for the phone numbers of Longfellows living near Millinocket, in an effort to track down Sally Ann. But before she could do that, she heard a sudden banging noise that made her nearly leap out of her seat. She stopped what she was doing and sat perfectly still, her breath caught in her throat.

It sounded as if the banging had come from the lower door at the bottom of the stairs, but she couldn't be sure, given the way the sound echoed through the building.

She waited. A few moments later, she heard what sounded like a muffled shout, followed by more pounding at the door.

Rising from her seat, Candy went to the window overlooking Ocean Avenue and peered out. The avenue was still rain slicked and dimly lit. In between the patches of mist and an oncoming fog, she could see gray storefronts and sidewalks in both directions, except for the area directly beneath her, due to a ledge that jutted out from the building, blocking her view.

Besides, the lower street-level door was tucked into an alcove. If someone was pounding on that door, she wouldn't be able to see the person from here anyway.

She'd have to go down and have a look for herself.

Before she left her office, she picked up her umbrella. She had no other weapon to take with her.

If this keeps up, she thought as she headed down the hall, *I'm going to have to invest in a bigger umbrella.*

As she suspected, there was no one outside

the upper door, at the top of the staircase. The pounding came a third time, and now she was certain it was at the lower door.

She took out her keys, unlocked the door in front of her, and opened it wide. She left it open as she turned to her right, walked the short distance to the landing at the top of the stairs, and looked down. The bottom landing was lit only by a single dim bulb. A hazy light came through the lower door as well, throwing an ill-defined, elongated shadow on the lower stairs.

Someone was standing outside the door.

She froze, the hairs on her arms prickling. Her first thought was that the shadowy figure had been real, and had returned for her. She had an instinct to stay hidden, but fought it.

More than likely, she reasoned, it was just some villager who had noticed the light on in her second-floor office, and stopped by to talk to her for whatever reason.

So who was it?

Only one way to find out.

Cautiously, Candy took several steps down the staircase and dropped her head to get a better view of the door, but it was still mostly blocked from her view by the sloped ceiling above her. She caught a glimpse of black wet boots, though, and a long black raincoat.

She descended several more steps, holding tightly to the side rail.

The person outside the door saw her now and knocked heavily again. "Hey there! It's me! Let me in!"

Candy didn't budge. "Who are you?" she called back skeptically. "What do you want?"

"We have to talk."

"About what?"

Candy knew she had to get a better look at the person outside the door, so she descended again. She was halfway down the staircase now and could clearly make out the person who was again pounding on the lower door. A wide-brimmed black rain hat, clamped down heavily on the head, prevented Candy from making out the details of the person's face, which was hidden in shadow. The long black raincoat similarly disguised much of the person's physique, though Candy could clearly see it was a relatively large person, with sturdy legs and a wide stance.

"Let me in!" the figure demanded again. It spoke in a husky voice with a Maine accent, and after a few fleeting moments, Candy realized who it was.

"Speaking of the devil," she muttered to

herself with a shake of her head.

She descended the rest of the steps and looked at the figure through the window. "Sally Ann? Is that you?"

"Well, who the hell else were you expecting?" growled the other person, her voice muted through the door, and she raised the brim of her hat so Candy could clearly see the drawn, weathered face of Sally Ann Longfellow. "The boogeyman?"

TWENTY

Once they were back upstairs in her office, with both doors again safely locked behind them, Candy got straight to the point. "We've been looking for you all day. Where have you been?"

Unbuttoning her raincoat and shaking it out a little, Sally Ann stood uneasily in the center of the room, dripping and scowling. "Up in Millinocket, if you must know," she groused. "My dad has a camp on the Twin Lakes. I go up every fall to help him get his boat out of the water. One of his friends heard on the radio what happened down here and came out to tell us about it late this afternoon. I drove back as soon as I could."

"Why didn't you call?"

"No phone at the camp. No service up there. And I don't own a cell phone, anyway."

"So how long have you been here? And

why have you been following me around town tonight?"

"What do you mean? Following you? What makes you think I've been following you? I just got here."

"Wasn't that you lurking along Main Street in the shadows tonight, watching me? And driving that baby blue pickup truck?"

"I don't own a baby blue pickup truck," Sally Ann said, "and I haven't been lurking in the shadows anywhere." Her face scrunched up in annoyance. "What the heck are you talking about?"

Candy dropped into her office chair as she waved Sally Ann toward a vacant seat nearby. "I'm not sure," she said after a moment. "It's been a long day, and too much has happened. Maybe we should start at the beginning — though I'm not even really sure where *that* is."

"Then I'll start," Sally Ann said, ignoring Candy's signal to sit. She pulled off her hat and ran a hand through her matted hair, which only worsened her appearance. "I want to know why everybody's so darned concerned about where I've been all day. I want to know why the police were out at my property this afternoon. I want to know what's up with this whole pickle thing. And I want to know who killed my goat!"

She'd started out angrily enough, her voice rising, but it gave way quickly by the time she reached the end, and Candy heard the hitch in her throat. For the first time Candy had a good look at Sally Ann, and noticed how exhausted the other woman appeared. Her dark brown eyes were drooped and watery, her face pale and clammy. She teetered a bit, looking like she was about to keel over.

"Sally Ann, sit down," Candy said, as she herself rose. "I'm going to fix you a cup of hot tea. I'll be right back."

But Sally Ann waved her down. "Nah, I don't need no tea. A shot of bourbon might help."

"I'm afraid we don't have anything that strong around here," Candy said as she settled back into her chair, "though there might be a beer in the fridge."

Sally Ann shook her head. "Never mind that right now. Tell me what's been going on around this town while I was gone."

Candy put a hand to her forehead, brushing back her hair, as she took a moment to think. "Well, I guess it all started with that jar of pickles from the Sweet Pickle Deli you left out on your porch for Wanda to pick up this morning."

But Sally Ann stopped her right there,

holding up a hand as her brows came together to express her confusion. "The Sweet Pickle Deli? I didn't leave out that jar. I left out one of my own jars. There must have been a mix-up."

"Wanda specifically said she found a jar from the Sweet Pickle Deli on your porch."

"Then Wanda is mistaken," Sally Ann said adamantly.

"There's no mistake, unfortunately," Candy told her. "The police have the jar with the Sweet Pickle Deli label on it. The one sitting on your porch. The one Wanda found."

"Have you seen it?"

"Not that particular one, no. But I've seen another one just like it, at the cook-off contest."

"And those pickles were poisoned?"

Candy nodded. "Three jars have been found so far, all containing poisoned pickles. But yours was the first. That's why there was trouble out at your place." And Candy explained how Wanda had wrestled with Cleopatra for possession of the pickles, and how the goat had eventually won, though Wanda still got a taste of one of them, which sent her to the hospital.

Sally Ann listened in rapt attention, suddenly silent, as she eased back a few steps and finally lowered herself into a folding chair set against the wall opposite Candy. She appeared to have difficulty believing what she was hearing, but she focused hard on every word.

When Candy finished, Sally Ann could only shake her head in confusion. "But that's not what happened. That's not the jar I left out," she repeated, "or, maybe, not the one I intended to. Maybe" — she paused as she reached up to scratch at her damp hair — "maybe I left out the wrong one. I was in a hurry this morning, that's for sure, and I have lots of jars of pickles, including a few from that old deli. I've held on to them for years. Stashed them away in the back of my pantry, though I've kept them separate from the others, so I wouldn't mistake them for a jar of regular pickles. Wanted to make them last, you know. I had three left until I opened one of the jars last winter. Now there are only two."

"And the pickles from the jar you ate last winter didn't make you sick?"

"Sick?" Sally Ann shook her head. "They're still the best damned pickles I ever ate. They made my day, every time I ate one of them. Helped me get through a tough winter."

"And none of the pickles you've eaten in

191

the past from the other deli jars have made you sick?"

"Nope. Not in the least."

Candy pondered this latest bit of information. "Maybe the one you left out for Wanda was an aberration — just a jar of bad pickles."

Sally Ann threw up her hands. "But that's just it. I didn't leave out a jar of those deli pickles — at least I don't think I did. They're just too good to give away."

"Then why did Wanda find one on your stoop this morning?"

"I don't know. But I'm sure I left out a jar of my own pickles. That's the point, right? Wouldn't have been fair to enter a jar of professionally made pickles. In fact, I thought commercial establishments were barred from the cook-off. It was for amateur cooks. So I never would have left out a jar from that deli. I left out a jar with my own label on it."

"That's not what Wanda found, and not what Cleopatra ate," Candy reiterated.

"Then something fishy is going on," Sally Ann said, her growl returning. "I suppose that's why you've been looking for me all day, isn't it? You thought I left those poisoned pickles there for Wanda to find. And then, what, left others around town as well? You thought I was a murderer or something?"

Candy had to admit there had been some rumblings to that effect.

"Well, it just ain't true!" Sally Ann rose out of her chair indignantly. "I've been a part of this community for more than thirty years now, and I'd never do such a thing!"

"I know that, but you need to go to the police and tell them what you just told me. That's the best way to handle this."

"But I can't!" Sally Ann protested. "From what you just said, I'm the prime suspect in this mess. If I walk into that police station right now, they'll just lock me in a jail cell and throw away the key!"

"No, they won't. They need to hear what you have to say."

Sally Ann's face pulled down in thoughtfulness. After a few breaths, she said in a more controlled tone, "This is why I came to see you first, instead of going to the police. I wanted to get the real story. And now that I know where I stand, I need your help in clearing my name."

"We'll figure it out," Candy said supportively.

"I can't be held responsible for this! It's just some sort of mix-up."

Candy considered that. "Maybe it wasn't

a mix-up at all. Maybe it was deliberate."

"Deliberate? What do you mean?"

"I mean, it's possible someone else switched those jars, on purpose."

"On purpose?" Sally Ann repeated, incredulous. "So you're saying I'm being framed?"

"It's one possible explanation, yes."

Sally Ann looked stunned. "Why would someone do that?"

"That's what we have to figure out," Candy said. "It all goes back to those jars. If what you just told me is true — that you left out a jar of your own pickles this morning — and Wanda found a different jar filled with poisoned pickles when she stopped by, then the most logical explanation is that someone switched them — a third party."

"Then we have to find this . . . this third party," Sally Ann said. "And fast, before they cook my goose!"

"Is there anyone who has a grudge against you," Candy asked, "someone who might do something like this to you?"

Sally Ann shrugged. "It's possible, I suppose. I've lived here for a long time. I've made plenty of friends over the years, and a few enemies. But I can't think of anybody in particular who might be behind this."

"Well, *something* strange happened with

those jars," Candy said. "If they *were* switched, we have to prove it some way. We have to make sure you left out your own jar of pickles, since that's a key point. Is there any way we can verify that?"

"I give you my word," Sally Ann said, holding a hand over her heart. "And my word has always been good around this town."

"I appreciate that, Sally Ann, but we need something more solid."

"You don't believe me?"

"It's not a matter of belief. It's simply a matter of fact."

"Well, if that's the case," Sally Ann said with a sniff, "then I know for a fact I left my own jar of pickles out on that stoop. And I *can* prove it!"

Twenty-One

Candy shut off the lights and locked both office doors behind them. Outside, the rain had picked up again. It fell from the sky at a steady pace, pattering against the sidewalks and glass storefronts, creating a steady rhythm. Beyond, she could hear the rumbling waves as they crescendoed against the nearby shoreline, then hissed and fell back.

Sally Ann had rezipped her black raincoat and plunked the broad-brimmed hat back down on her head, so low it almost touched her eyebrows, putting her face in shadow again. Candy buttoned up her own jacket and hunkered under her umbrella as she hurried up the avenue to Main Street, where she'd parked the Jeep. Sally Ann made off at a different angle, heading across Ocean Avenue to an old green Volvo station wagon.

Less than ten minutes later they both pulled into the long gravel-fringed driveway at Sally Ann's place. Candy half expected to find a police car waiting out front, on the lookout for Sally Ann. But they'd already been here and gone, and apparently they'd felt no need to hang around. Most likely they were out running down other leads, she thought. Still, she imagined they'd stop by again sooner or later.

Sally Ann's house was dark and looked deserted on this overcast night. No lights were on anywhere on the property or in the house. Here, a little further inland, the rain had given way to a fine mist and thick shrouds of fog, which lingered low over the treetops and were strewn across the gardens behind the house, creating an eerie landscape.

Sally Ann pulled up alongside the house ahead of Candy, jumped quickly out of her car, and headed back behind the house. By the time Candy brought her Jeep to a stop, Sally Ann had reached the goat pen. Located about twenty feet behind the house and sturdily built, it traditionally hadn't done a very good job of corralling her two animals. They had proved a clever and mischievous pair, and had caused plenty of trouble around town over the past few years.

But perhaps because she was the only one left, Guinevere had not attempted to break out of the pen. She waited impatiently inside, apparently put there by one of the police officers who had been out here this afternoon, Candy guessed. From where she sat inside the Jeep with the windows rolled up, she could hear the goat's unhappy bleats, a series of *meh-heh-heh-heh-hehs* in descending pitch, and watched through the still-flapping windshield wipers as Sally Ann reached the shed, flung open the door, and fussed with the nanny goat for a minute or two. Then, satisfied the animal was all right for the time being, she left it there where it was and locked up the pen again.

She started back toward the house but suddenly veered to her right, toward what looked like a small dark pile under a canvas tarp that had been staked down at the corners. Sally Ann approached the tarp cautiously and stopped several feet away. She knew what was underneath, but wasn't quite ready to have a look yet.

"I'll have to bury the poor thing, maybe out by the lilac bushes. She loved those bushes," Sally Ann told Candy once they were inside the house. She flicked on an overhead kitchen light and began to strip off her wet gear, throwing it over the back of a chair. "I always said she ate too much for her own good — that some day it would get her into trouble. I told her that over and over. But she never listened to me. She had a mind of her own."

Sally Ann paused, her face turning stormy. " 'Course, I never thought someone would poison her with a jar of pickles left on my doorstep."

"How's the other goat?" Candy asked as she leaned her umbrella against the wall by the door and unbuttoned her jacket.

Sally Ann shrugged. "As good as can be expected. She knows something's wrong and she's upset. They were like twins, you know — they've never really been apart. Cleopatra was the leader, of course, the alpha female, so to speak, while Guinevere was the follower. But she can be a troublemaker in her own right if she has a mind to it."

Sally Ann stuck her hands in her pockets as her shoulders sagged forward. "This is quite a blow. It's going to take a while for us both to cope with the loss. But somehow we'll manage. At least Guinevere was smart enough not to eat any of those pickles. She always was a bit of a fussy eater — for a goat."

"If there's anything I can do," Candy said sympathetically, "just let me know."

Sally Ann's gaze shifted toward her. "Now

that you mention it, there might be a way you can help out and give Cleopatra her due. You going to be in your office tomorrow?"

Candy thought about it a moment. "I'm not sure yet. It's Saturday. I have a lot scheduled. But I shouldn't be too far away. Just give me a call if you want to meet up."

Sally Ann nodded a single time. "Okay then. I might stop by." She crooked a finger. "So let me show you what we came to see — and put my own mind at rest."

Candy followed as Sally Ann headed out of the kitchen and into a dark hallway, which connected the kitchen with the living room and lower-floor bedrooms. Halfway along, under a steep staircase that led to the second floor, she stopped in front of a small wooden door, perhaps three-quarters of the normal height. "Basement," she said, indicating the door. "You'll have to duck a little."

She pulled open the door and tugged on a string along one inside wall. A single naked overhead bulb flicked on as a cool, musty draft drifted up from below.

Candy looked over Sally Ann's shoulder and saw a narrow rickety wooden staircase descending to their left, into inky blackness.

"Furnace is down there," Sally Ann said,

"and the wash machine. But here's what I wanted to show you."

Candy had already noticed. The open triangular-shaped area under the upper stairs was outfitted with shelves of various heights and depths. Narrower shelves also lined the side walls. The shelves, mostly full, held a variety of cans, jars, and bottles. Candy noticed homemade tomato sauce and applesauce, jars of honey and jams, some canned goods like chili and soups, as well as coffee, molasses, maple syrup, apple cider vinegar, and more.

This was Sally Ann's makeshift pantry and cold storage.

"I keep the pickles here, on this big middle shelf," she said, pointing to a deep shelf under the stairs. It held more than two dozen jars, by Candy's quick count. "I make up a full batch every year," Sally Ann continued. "They usually last me until late spring, and if it's a particularly good batch I'll save a few jars for a later time. That's what these are."

She indicated a smaller group of jars off to one side. "And these," she said, taking a step down and focusing in with her thick index finger, "are, as I suspected, my last two remaining jars from the Sweet Pickle Deli."

Candy spotted them now, toward the back of the smaller group, tucked into the wedge near the rear of the shelf. She tilted her head slightly. Something about them didn't look quite right.

"I bought those jars myself, right in the deli when it was still open, so I can vouch for their authenticity," Sally Ann went on. "I had three jars before last winter, like I said earlier. Still have two. So, you see," she concluded, turning back toward Candy, "I couldn't have put that jar from the Sweet Pickle Deli out on the stoop this morning for Wanda. Because if I had, there'd only be one jar left here on the shelf. Simple math."

Candy could see her logic, although she was taking Sally Ann's word about the number of jars she'd had last winter. But that wasn't what caught Candy's attention. Instead, she was focused on the jars themselves, rather than how many remained on the shelf.

"Could I see one of those?" Candy asked, pointing toward them.

Sally Ann gave her a skeptical look. "Why, something wrong?"

"They look . . . different," Candy said hesitantly. "I'd just like to get a closer look."

Sally Ann considered the request for a moment and then shrugged. "Okay, I'll bring them up to the kitchen." She reached out across the shelf and corralled the two jars, which she held close to her body as she retreated up the steps.

Under somewhat better light, she set the two jars down on the kitchen table.

"They look different than the jar I saw this afternoon," Candy observed, leaning over and getting in closer. "The labels are green but a different shade, and the lettering looks different, like it's another font, similar but not the right one. Or, I guess, *this* could be the right one and the others weren't. These jars are different in size and shape too. They're a little taller and narrower. The one I saw this afternoon was thicker and shorter."

She straightened and looked over at Sally Ann. "Did the Sweet Pickle Deli sell different types of pickles in different jars, with different labels? Or could these be from another batch, maybe made in a different year than the one I saw this afternoon?"

Sally Ann shook her head. "There were a few varieties of pickles, sure, but far as I know the jars and labels were all the same. He was cheap — he bought everything in bulk to save money." She waved at the jars. "The labels on these have faded over the years, and they're probably a little dusty from sitting on that shelf for so long. But the pickles are just fine. Here, I'll show you."

She stepped forward in a quick, unexpected movement, took one of the old jars from the Sweet Pickle Deli, and with a little effort unscrewed the lid.

"What are you doing?" Candy asked in surprise. "I thought you were saving those."

"No time like the present," Sally Ann replied with a wistful smile, and reaching into the jar with her fingertips, she withdrew a juicy spear and took a bite.

Candy was horrified. "Sally Ann! What if those are poisoned?"

The other woman simply shook her head. "Not a chance. Like I said, I bought these myself. They've never left my pantry." She took another bite of the pickle. "Trust me, they've never been tampered with. Unless they were poisoned back when they were made, of course. But I doubt that. They should be perfectly fine."

And she was right. As she finished one pickle and started in on another, the minutes ticked by and Candy watched nervously. But Sally Ann showed no negative reaction to the pickles. In fact, they seemed to lift her spirits a little.

"Here," she said, holding out the jar toward Candy. "Try one. They're delicious.

Unlike anything you've ever tasted."

"I don't think I should."

"You'll be sorry if you don't." She wiggled the jar at Candy. "Trust me," she said in a voice with a commanding edge to it. "I wouldn't put you in danger if I wasn't positive about what I'm doing."

Something in her tone convinced Candy, who finally relented. After all, she told herself, she had to see what all the fuss was about. At worst, if she took a small bite, she'd wind up in the hospital having her stomach pumped.

But there was no need for a trip to the hospital, as Sally Ann was true to her word.

The first pickle, unlike anything she had ever tasted, went down before Candy knew she'd finished it. The aroma was earthy and fragrant, the flavors still fresh and tangy, with an uncanny crispness, as if the pickle had been made the previous day, not five or more years ago. And certainly not like anything she'd ever bought in a supermarket — or a farmer's market, for that matter.

"What's in them that makes them taste so good?" Candy asked as Sally Ann, who was on her third pickle, held out the jar again. Candy couldn't refuse a second one.

Sally Ann shook her head. "No one knows. Many tried to pry the recipe from Old Man

Maurice, but he never gave up his secrets — not that anyone ever expected him to. He was not what you'd call a people person. He was a grouchy old cuss."

"You had some run-ins with him, didn't you?" Candy asked.

With her thumb Sally Ann pointed off behind the house. "Because of the goats. He lived on the next street over. They got into his gardens a few times. Practically came to fisticuffs, I don't mind telling you."

"Between you and him?"

"Between him and the goats," Sally Ann replied. "He got so angry he filed a complaint against them at Town Hall. And he threatened to take me to court. Said my goats had destroyed his property. He wasn't the first, of course. But he wanted me to get rid of them. Said they were a nuisance to the community. A hostile presence affecting his quality of life. But he cooled off after a while, and nothing much came of it."

Candy let that go for the moment and turned back to the jars. She was struck by something else about them. "The colors on the jar I saw this afternoon were brighter and more vivid than on yours. These are faded."

"Well, sure," Sally Ann said. "Makes sense. Labels will do that over the years."

"But if that's true," Candy said, "then the label on the jar I saw this afternoon should have been faded as well — if it was an actual jar from the Sweet Pickle Deli. But it wasn't. It looked . . . new."

"So what are you saying?" Sally Ann asked. "You think Maurice made up a new batch?"

"Maybe Maurice," Candy said thoughtfully, "or maybe someone else. After all, if that jar wasn't authentic like these are" — she waved a finger at Sally Ann's two jars — "then it could have been made by anyone, really, and left there on that table today. The same goes for the other two jars, including the one left here at your place. If you were duplicating the jars from the Sweet Pickle Deli, and wanted to poison them, you wouldn't even need to know Maurice's actual recipe, really. You'd just have to know what the label looked like. That's what everyone, including Wanda, Doc, and Ned, responded to. That's what attracted them. We have no idea, at least right now, what the pickles from those jars actually *tasted* like — though Wanda might be able to tell us when she's feeling better."

"So who do you think did it?" Sally Ann asked. "Who made those pickles?"

Candy gave it a lot of thought before she

shook her head. "I don't know yet, but I'm going to find out. I promise you that."

TWENTY-TWO

Candy's cell phone rang first thing the next morning.

She usually muted it overnight, so it wouldn't wake her too early, but because of all that had happened the previous day, she'd left it on. She thought she might get an early call from Wanda, or even Julia von Fleming, checking in about the upcoming book signing. But the caller identified on the touchscreen was someone completely unexpected, unconnected with the newspaper, the book signing, or even the blueberry farm.

It was a call from Tristan Pruitt.

Tristan was a scion of the wealthy Pruitt family, who lived in Boston most of the year but maintained a nearby summer home in the form of an English Tudor-style mansion on a prime piece of property just off the Coastal Loop overlooking the ocean. Candy had met him a few years earlier when she'd been working in a local pumpkin patch with Maggie. Tristan had appeared mysteriously one morning and hopped onto a Halloween-themed hay wagon ride Candy and Maggie were operating in the pumpkin patch as a way to make some extra money. As it turned out, Tristan sought Candy's help in solving a mystery involving a stolen book from his family's library, and in the process of searching for the book, Candy had uncovered a murderer.

At the time she'd thought, way in the back of her mind, that there might actually be a spark between her and Tristan, and possibly even a future. But they'd never had a chance to spend much time together to see what developed. He lived and worked primarily in Boston and New York, and only made it up to Cape Willington on occasion. They'd done their best to keep in touch, and he'd been out to the farm a couple of times over the past year or so. But they both led busy lives, and their communications had become less frequent. She realized they hadn't talked in months.

Why would he be calling her at this hour? she wondered.

She keyed open the call. "Hello, this is Candy."

"Candy, it's Tristan. Sorry to call so early.

Hope I didn't wake you." He sounded a little breathless, and distracted, as if he'd been awake for a while and had a lot on his mind.

"No, I was up. There's . . . well, there's been a lot going on."

"I heard about what happened yesterday. Damn shame about Ned and the others. Are you okay?"

When he spoke, she could hear the concern in his voice, but she assured him she was fine — or, at least, as fine as possible with a murderer on the loose.

"Any idea who's behind this?" he asked.

"Lots of speculation but nothing concrete so far."

"That's the reason I called," Tristan said. "I might have something concrete for you."

Candy's ears perked up. "Really? What?"

He hesitated. "I'm not sure it's something we should discuss over the phone. Can you meet me?"

"When?"

"Now? Or as soon as you can?"

Candy was surprised. "You're in town?"

"I'm out at the house. I arrived a few hours ago."

A few hours ago? Candy glanced at her bedside alarm clock. It was just after eight. She knew it was about a five-hour drive from Boston to Cape Willington. *He must have been driving all night,* she thought.

At this revelation, she settled onto the edge of her bed as she considered his request. "I was going to stop in to see Maggie this morning. In fact, I'm headed over there shortly," she said, "and I have to be at a book signing at eleven, plus a few other stops today." She paused, thinking back over what he had said. "But yes, of course I can come over, if you think it's important."

"It is," Tristan said. "When can you get here?"

There was an urgency in his tone that touched something inside her. She knew he wouldn't be making such a request for a frivolous matter. Something was up, she thought, and it sounded serious. "Give me half an hour."

Five minutes later she was downstairs, with Tristan still on her mind. What could have caused him to make a special trip to Cape Willington, driving through the night so he could meet with her first thing in the morning? Had something happened to someone? Perhaps to his aunt, Helen Ross Pruitt, matriarch of the Pruitt clan, whom Candy had met several times over the past few years? Or was it something else?

Something to do with the jars of poisoned pickles?

What kind of inside information could he have?

She found her father out on the porch in his favorite rocking chair with his coffee and newspaper, wrapped in a wool sweater against the chilly, dew-soaked morning. Usually on weekdays he headed off to the Main Street Diner for breakfast with Finn, Bumpy, and Artie, but they often took a break on weekends.

However, as Candy walked out onto the porch, Doc glanced up at her and checked his watch. "Sounds like the boys are assembling at the diner in a little while," he told her in a voice that cracked a bit, as it sometimes did early in the morning. "I guess they want to hash over all that happened yesterday. I thought I'd head over shortly. Want to come along? Finn might have some news from the police station."

Candy hesitated for only a moment. "I would, Dad, but I have a busy morning. Lots of meetings. But tell Finn to give me a call if he's heard anything interesting."

She was hesitant to say anything about Tristan Pruitt, since she wasn't sure how confidential she should be about meeting with him. Doc seemed to sense that

213

something was going on, but he was used to his daughter's sometimes enigmatic ways, especially when she was chasing down a mystery, so he kept any questions he had to himself.

Instead, he said, "I'll let him know. And if you get a chance, swing by the diner and say hello. I'll buy you a cup of coffee."

"Are you going to the book signing?"

"Possibly. I might wander over and check it out."

While her father finished his coffee and paper, Candy stepped off the porch and headed around the side of the house toward the chicken coop behind the barn. She'd started with a dozen chickens a few years ago, and while she'd lost a few since, they remained good producers, providing a steady supply of small brown eggs for her and Doc, as well as neighbors and co-workers.

As usual, she spread some chicken feed on the floor of the coop, checked their water supply, and collected half a dozen still-warm eggs in a wire basket. Then she wandered over to the vegetable garden. It occupied a flat plot of land between the barn and the upward-sloping blueberry fields, which were just about picked out. In a week or two they'd start mowing down the fields in preparation for next year's crop.

But it was the vegetable garden that concerned her. She'd been so busy lately that she hadn't had much time to devote to it. It needed weeding and watering, and some tender loving care. But where was she going to find the time, with all that was going on at the paper and in town?

There's so much that needs to be done around here, she thought with a touch of melancholy as she picked a few ripe tomatoes and cucumbers. She and Doc had talked about putting in a hoophouse, but they still hadn't had a chance to do that. They wanted to expand their blueberry fields. They'd talked about building a small farm stand and moving into retail operations, rather than staying a strictly wholesale business. But they'd been so busy lately they hadn't had a chance to do any of those things.

I miss working here at the farm, she thought with a sigh. *I may have to make some changes soon.*

At the paper, she'd held onto the title of interim managing editor for more than a year now, rather than accept an offer to become its actual editor, because she'd never been certain how long she wanted to remain in the position, since it took up so much of her time. Over the past few months, and even during harvest season, she felt she'd been spending more and more time in town, and less and less time at the farm. She was beginning to feel an imbalance in her life, but she hadn't yet decided on a definite course of action, since she enjoyed both jobs.

With a last look at the garden and a shake of her head, she headed back toward the house and gathered her things. Before she headed out the door, she sent a text to Maggie, saying she was headed over to Pruitt Manor, and she'd stop by the bakery as soon as she could. She left a short time later, following Doc out of the dirt driveway as he drove off to the diner in his pickup truck.

It was a short ten-minute trip to Pruitt Manor. Although the clouds of the previous night had moved on, the morning had a certain rawness to it, with a damp, penetrating feeling and lingering bands of fog and mist, mostly in the low spots. Like Doc, she'd thrown on a sweater and wore thin early-season gloves against the cold steering wheel.

She drove along the ocean on the Coastal Loop, headed into town past River Road and Main Street, and as she rounded a northwesterly curve, she could see the peaked roof of Pruitt Manor poking out above the treetops. Just beyond, on a rocky outcropping of land, stood Kimball Light, a privately owned lighthouse and one of two in Cape Willington, the other being English Point Lighthouse to the north.

A few minutes later, Candy turned onto a private driveway that led between two five-foot-tall stone pillars. The black iron gate stood open, as it usually did, so she drove on through, noticing the small, tasteful sign alongside the road, announcing PRUITT MANOR — PRIVATE PROPERTY.

She followed the winding gravel driveway before pulling into a wide, paved courtyard that fronted the house. A dark blue BMW was parked off to one side. It was the only car she could see, since the multiple bay doors in the detached garage were all closed.

In fact, the entire place looked like it was closed up for the season, which she imagined it was. As far as she knew, Mrs. Pruitt and her entourage had decamped for Boston right after Labor Day. Blinds were still drawn tight in all the windows, and the house looked dark and deserted.

She pulled up behind the BMW, shut off the engine, and climbed out of the Jeep. But before she could start toward the house,

Tristan emerged to greet her.

He was dressed casually, in expensive jeans, an untucked white shirt, and loafers without socks. He approached her with a weary smile and gave her a hug. "Thanks for coming so quickly," he said. "I know it was an unusual request, but it couldn't be helped."

He tried to keep his tone light, but she could hear an edge of concern in his voice. "It's no problem," she said, then added, "I'm happy to help any way I can."

Tristan nodded and pointed toward the house. "Then why don't you come on in and let's talk. I think we can definitely use your expertise."

TWENTY-THREE

He led her along a flagstone walkway, through a heavy wooden entry door, and into the manor's foyer, with its leaf-and-acorn-patterned oak floor, ornate wood paneling, heraldic designs, and family portraiture. On the left, a grand staircase ascended to the second floor.

It was both impressive and intimate at the same time, and Candy remembered that on previous visits, the place had had a warm, aristocratic feel. Today, however, it felt hollow and empty, unlived in. It was also a tad chilly inside, so she kept her sweater on, though she took off her gloves and stashed them in her pockets.

"Sorry about the climate in here," Tristan said as he continued through the foyer into the long hallway beyond. "They set it at fifty-nine degrees for the winter and I still haven't figured out how to override the system to raise the temperature. I have a text into Hobbins for the password." Hobbins was the butler for Helen Ross Pruitt, Tristan's aunt.

"Is Mrs. Pruitt here?" Candy asked, following Tristan along the unlit, shadowy hall. As she passed open doors to the left and right, which led to various rooms, she noticed they were all in shadows, though she caught sight of cloth-draped furniture and expensive rugs.

"No, she remains in Boston. There's some big social event this weekend to kick off the season, I think. She said she couldn't miss it. And Hobbins is with her, of course. So I'm on my own up here. Have you had breakfast?"

Candy said she had not.

"Good, I called the inn and asked them to send over some coffee and Danish. They delivered it right before you arrived. We're set up in the kitchen."

It was an impressive array of goodies, including a dozen different types of Danish, many maple- or toffee-glazed and enhanced with an assortment of almonds, raisins, pecans, and cheeses, as well as fruit-filled pastries and buttery croissants. Everything was still warm, as if it had just come out of the oven. Coffee, tea, and juice, along with fresh fruit, were also available. "And I think

I can scrounge up some cereal, though I'm not sure we have milk," Tristan said with a half frown. "The fridge and freezers were emptied when Aunt Helen relocated south, and I haven't had a chance to replenish anything."

"This is fine," Candy said, and she took a plate and moved to the pastry tray. "In fact, it's more than enough. I wasn't expecting breakfast."

"I thought it's the least I could do, asking you to come out here so early."

"Well, it was a very nice thought," Candy said as she surveyed the culinary offerings, then added innocently enough, as a way to get the questioning started, "So, I take it this is an impromptu visit to Cape Willington?"

Again, looking a bit weary, Tristan took a mug and filled it with coffee. "You could certainly say that. I didn't know I was coming here until almost midnight last night."

She turned to him. "What made you decide to make the trip? You said you could use my expertise. About what?"

"We had . . . a communication," he said, and taking a plate, joined Candy, selecting several items from the tray before moving to a small white table set off to one side of the kitchen. She finished filling her plate

221

and joined him.

Once they were settled, he continued, "A package arrived yesterday afternoon at Aunt Helen's place on Beacon Hill."

"A package?"

"An envelope with a letter inside," he clarified, and reached for a battered leather soft-sided briefcase sitting on the floor near his feet. He pulled it up into his lap, lifted the top flap, and took out a manila folder, which he laid on the table between them. The briefcase went back down on the floor with a soft slap.

"Aunt Helen contacted me as soon as she received it. At first we thought it was a joke — but given what happened here in town yesterday, we've decided to take it seriously. We contacted the police in Boston, of course, and pulled in our attorney to help us deal with the situation. But I came up personally to meet with the Cape Willington police later this morning. I've also asked for a private meeting with Mason Flint and the members of the town council."

Candy had yet to take a bite of her Danish as she focused on the manila folder on the table in front of her. She couldn't help shivering, not sure if it was caused by the house's chilly temperature or the thought of what might be inside that folder.

"Go ahead," Tristan urged, and he pointed at it with a finger as he lifted his cup of coffee. "Take a look."

Although her curiosity was strong, she hesitated just a moment. What could be inside the folder that was so important it had prompted Tristan to make an overnight trip to Cape Willington?

She reached out and pulled the folder toward her, flipping open the cover. Inside was a single sheet of paper with writing on it.

"That's not the original, of course," Tristan continued. "The Boston police have that, as well as the original envelope. It was postmarked in Cape Willington on Tuesday, by the way. No return address, of course. We're still trying to trace it, but it could have been sent by anyone."

Candy lifted the sheet of paper and began to read. There were only a few lines:

The poisoned jars are just the beginning. There are more where those came from. Don't let it get worse. Deposit two hundred thousand dollars into an account number to be provided. Consider the money a loan for the town, since you're its wealthiest resident. It's the least you can do. Details to follow.

That was all it said. But Candy knew what it meant.

By threatening more lives, someone was trying to extort a lot of money from the Pruitts, and from the village of Cape Willington.

TWENTY-FOUR

Candy's first reaction was one of disbelief. "Two hundred thousand dollars? That's insane."

Tristan nodded. "We thought so, too, of course. And it's not like we can lay our hands on that kind of cash in a day or two, no matter what anyone thinks."

"But why was this sent to you — or to your family?" Candy wondered. "Why not send it to Mason Flint, or even to us at the paper so we could pass it on to the proper authorities?"

Tristan shrugged. "Simple. Because the town itself would have a hard time coming up with that kind of money. But whoever sent it to us thought we'd have the assets to pay up. And, to be honest, we have people looking into that — just in case."

"You mean you're thinking of complying with his crazy request?" Candy wiggled the paper in her hand.

Tristan took a few moments to answer. "We don't know yet. That's why I drove up here. It's why I'm meeting with the police and the town council this morning. We're investigating our options — and keeping everything on the table for the moment."

"And you said the envelope was postmarked here in Cape Willington? On Tuesday?"

Tristan nodded.

Candy mulled this over. "That implies premeditation, of course. It's further proof those jars of poisoned pickles were not an accident. Someone's been planning this for a while."

"That's the way it appears, yes."

"So whoever's behind this has been in town for at least a few days."

"Maybe longer," Tristan said.

"Right, maybe longer." But even as she said this she knew what that meant. He was implying the pickle poisoner could be someone she knew, a villager, perhaps someone she ran into every day — the same implication she'd made to Sally Ann the night before.

Could one of the villagers — a local — have had a disagreement with the town itself, with the way it was being run, with a member of the town council or the municipal government? Could someone be seeking revenge for something she hadn't even considered? Some perceived slight or argument that had boiled over into murder?

She tried to think about all that had happened in town over the past few months, something that might have sent someone off on an act of revenge and murder. But nothing came immediately to mind.

What's more, she reasoned, if that was the purpose — to get back at the town — why use a jar of pickles bearing a label from the Sweet Pickle Deli? Why target Sally Ann, or Wanda, or the official judges, or the elderly woman up in Cherryfield?

The pieces just didn't seem to fit together.

She set the letter down on the table, folded her arms in front of her, leaned forward, and carefully read through it again, and then again. "If the person who wrote this note is to be believed," she said finally, looking up at Tristan, "then it sounds as if he or she could still be around — still be here in town." She pointed with her pinky at a line in the text. " *There are more where those came from.* ' That indicates more jars will be left around town, and apparently more people will die, unless you pay up."

"I agree. That's seems to be the implication."

Another thought came to Candy. "But why show this to me?" she asked, looking up at Tristan. "You're meeting with the police and members of the town council this morning. You've turned the original over to the Boston police. You've contacted the proper authorities and you're looking into legal implications, as well as the possibility of doing this financially. You and your family seem to have covered all the bases. So why bring it to my attention? And why make sure I saw it first, before you met with the other people in town?"

Tristan settled back into his chair as he considered how to respond. His face was cloudy for a moment as he thought, but finally he smiled. "Well, I guess it's because of all the people I've talked to, or I'm going to talk to, I believe you're the one person who can most benefit from this information. As I said earlier, we're interested in your expertise. You've solved these kinds of cases before. You helped out my family when we had a problem a few years ago. Aunt Helen personally suggested I contact you as soon as I got to town and show you the letter."

"Really?" Candy couldn't help but feel a bit of satisfaction at that.

Tristan nodded. "She thinks if anyone can

solve this mystery and save lives — and help us avoid paying out two hundred thousand dollars to some extortionist, I might add — it's you. She's even suggested we hire you again, secure your services as an investigator, pay you a per diem and that sort of thing, as she did before — on an unofficial basis, of course."

Candy waved a hand. "That's not necessary. I'm just as involved in this whole affair as you are. Dad and I were both there in the gym yesterday. I touched that jar of poisoned pickles myself, so my fingerprints are all over it. I have no doubt that, as least from the perspective of the local police, we're both suspects, just like everyone else in town."

She looked down at the letter again. "But this does change the situation. It's no longer just an alleged act of revenge. This escalates everything."

"It certainly does," Tristan agreed. "And makes the whole situation potentially more dangerous." He paused and ran a hand through his uncombed hair. "I have to admit, I had reservations about bringing this information to your attention. The last thing I want to do is put you in danger, or make you a target of any sort."

Now it was Candy's turn to smile. "I

wouldn't worry about that too much. Last night I thought I'd already become a target, but, well, it turned out to be a false alarm — at least, I think it was."

She didn't feel it was necessary to go into any more details about the shadowy figure in the baby blue pickup truck who appeared to be following her the previous night, and he didn't ask. Instead, he said, "Well, be that as it may, the truth is that you seem to have a knack for solving these sorts of mysteries. You have instincts the rest of us don't — and, to be honest, you're good at what you do."

"I know," Candy said, lifting an eyebrow. "Scary, isn't it? I don't really understand it myself. It's not something I plan to do. I just start, well, asking questions and poking around."

She looked down at the sheet in her hands again, read through the text a final time, then placed it back in the folder and slid it across to Tristan.

"Keep it," he said, pushing it back toward her. "As I mentioned, it's a copy. Maybe it can be of help in some way. I do have one request, though."

"And what's that?" Candy asked.

"I'd like you to keep all this confidential, just between us — at least for the next day or so. I don't know what the reaction from the local police and the town council will be, but my guess is they'll want to keep this hushed up for now, to avoid any sort of panic in town."

"Makes perfect sense," Candy said.

"And there's something else I need to talk to you about," he said. His tone still serious, he placed his folded arms on the table in front of him, leaned forward, and lowered his voice, even though they were alone in the house. "And again, I'm counting on your discretion. We've had . . . well, we think our family might be under attack on another front."

"Under attack?" Candy echoed. "That sounds ominous."

"It's not unintentional," Tristan admitted. "Frankly, we're worried — myself and Aunt Helen, especially. We have evidence that someone has been digging around for information about our family's financial assets, particularly our real estate holdings here in Cape Willington."

"With what purpose?" Candy asked, feeling the skin on her arms prickle just a bit. She pulled her sweater a little tighter around her.

"We don't know for sure, but we've had reports that someone has been researching the original deeds to our properties."

"Deeds?" Candy responded, trying to keep her voice even, though it came out strained.

"I know, it probably sounds crazy, but there have been rumors around town for years — decades, really — about a set of original deeds to properties in town that allegedly supersede all other existing deeds. As the story goes, a local Native American tribe was awarded the first deeds to the land that would one day become Cape Willington, in part for aid they provided to the colonies during and after the Revolutionary War. If that story is true, it could cause havoc around here. But those deeds are long lost, if they existed at all."

"And now you think someone is searching for them?"

Tristan shook his head. "I know. It sounds ridiculous, doesn't it?"

"Not at all," Candy said. "In fact, I might have some information for you." And she told him how, the previous summer, she and her father had come across an old treasure chest, which had been buried in the woods behind Crawford's Berry Farm, a nearby strawberry-picking operation now run by a friend of theirs, Neil Crawford. "We determined that it had once belonged to a

232

man named Silas Sykes, who buried it near a cabin he owned at the time," Candy explained. "He lived around here about a hundred and fifty years ago, and he was, among other things, a scoundrel and a thief."

"I think I've heard something about that," Tristan said, intrigued, "but I don't know the details."

"Well, apparently Neil's father, Miles, dug up the treasure chest. It was filled with bags of gold coins and some jewels . . . but we learned there might have been some old deeds in the chest as well."

Now she had Tristan's full attention. "I haven't heard this part of it," he said.

"Well, it's not common knowledge," Candy admitted. "Only a few of us know about the deeds."

"And what happened to them? Where are they now?"

"That's just it. No one knows. If Miles Crawford found them in that chest, he either hid them, gave them to someone else, or destroyed them."

"And you think these might be the original deeds to property here in Cape Willington?"

"That's the rumor," Candy said. "Neil, who took over the berry farm after his father's death, has spent the past year trying to find out what happened to those deeds, or if they exist at all. But so far he hasn't made much progress. He's in Vermont right now, selling off his old property so he can move to Cape Willington full-time."

"I'd like to talk to him at some point," Tristan said. "This could be what they're looking for — and yes, our sources indicate the Sykes family might be behind this search into our family's assets."

He went silent then for a few moments as he pondered their next move. "It's something we will have to look into — but not at the moment," he said finally, as if reaching a decision. "First, we have to solve this issue about the pickles and this extortion note. Once we've dealt with that, we can follow up on the property deeds — maybe work together with Neil to try to figure out what happened to them."

"Is it possible everything is connected somehow?" Candy asked.

Tristan let out a thoughtful sigh. "I don't know, but whatever's going on, we have to get to the bottom of it as quickly as possible." He indicated the manila folder still sitting on the table in front of Candy. "Because lives might be at stake."

"I'll do what I can," Candy said, taking up the folder. She checked her watch. "And now I have to get running."

Tristan downed the last bit of coffee in his mug and took a final bite of Danish. "I have to head out too. I'll be around for the next few days. Call me if you come across anything interesting, or if you need help. And whatever you do, be careful. It sounds like we both might have enemies out there we don't even know about."

TWENTY-FIVE

Enemies.

It wasn't a word she had considered until now, but she wondered if Tristan was right. Were their collective and individual enemies lining up against them, as well as against the village itself? Were they, in essence, under attack from some outside group or force? And if so, what could they expect to happen next? What would their enemies' next moves be? How serious were the threats?

Despite what she'd read in the letter, she had a hard time understanding why anyone would want to do harm to their sleepy coastal town or any of its residents, who were just average folks going about their daily business as best they could.

But then she thought about the shadowy figure from the night before — and the not-so-shadowy figures she'd run into over the past few years, those with murder on their minds. By solving a few mysteries around town and exposing a few murderers, often through harrowing encounters, she'd certainly made some enemies. But she'd never thought of it that way before.

And, as she hopped back into her Jeep and stuffed the file with the extortion letter into her tote bag, which she'd left on the passenger seat during her meeting with Tristan, she decided not to dwell on it right now.

Other more pressing matters called for her immediate attention.

So, for the moment, as she fired up the engine and started off toward Ocean Avenue, she tried to put thoughts of enemies, revenge, and murder out of her mind. She couldn't worry about the consequences of her past actions, even to her own safety. She simply had to do what she thought was best for the town — and for herself, her father, and her friends. That's what had always driven her before, and it remained her sole motivation now.

The early morning fog and mist were burning off, and the sun was starting to peek through a thin overcast sky, which lightened her mood a little. Off to her right, the calm, crisp blue ocean gave her some peace of mind, as it always did.

At the traffic light she made a left-hand

turn onto Ocean Avenue, which was naturally busy on this Saturday morning in early fall, and managed to snag a parking spot at the upper end of the avenue, where it met Main Street. Shutting off the engine and grabbing her tote bag, Candy jumped out, locked up the Jeep, crossed the street, and at a brisk pace headed south along the sidewalk to the Black Forest Bakery.

Inside, Maggie appeared to be under siege, but Candy wasn't really surprised. Even though it was now officially off-season, the town's small yet vibrant commercial area was still quite active on Saturdays, and many shoppers and strollers stopped in at the bakery for coffee or tea and a fresh-baked pastry or two. Plus, it was only a few doors from the Pine Cone Bookstore, where customers were beginning to gather for the book signing at eleven. Obviously some of them had stopped by the bakery first.

The place was humming, and the line at the counter nearly stretched out the door. Candy paused just inside the door and waved to Maggie, who was busy helping customers. She barely had time to wave back.

For a few moments Candy hesitated as she checked her watch. It was nearly nine fifteen. She had a couple of other stops to make that morning, and she wanted to drop by her office if she had time to get a little work done. She could come back when the bakery wasn't so busy.

Or, she thought, she could do something unexpected. . . .

On an impulse, she moved through the crowd and joined Maggie behind the counter. "It looks like you could use a little help," she said as she stashed her tote bag under the counter and reached for an apron hanging on a nearby hook.

Maggie turned to her with a look of surprise. "Well, hello stranger! Haven't seen you in a few days."

"I know, time flies, doesn't it?" Candy said. "You seem a little overwhelmed, so I thought I'd pitch in for a while behind the counter."

"Well, I could certainly use the help. We didn't expect to be this busy this late in the season. We've been mobbed all morning."

"I think I remember how all this works," Candy said, glancing over at the cash register and at the baked goods arrayed in a number of well-lit display cases around the shop. She'd worked for Herr Georg at the bakery for several years before taking the job at the paper. Maggie had replaced her behind the counter the previous year.

"Hey, this will be fun!" Maggie said, her face brightening. "It'll be like Martin and Lewis, back together again!"

"Like Laurel and Hardy!"

"Abbott and Costello!"

"Hope and Crosby!"

"Lucille Ball and Desi Arnaz! Oh Lucy, I'm home!" Maggie said in a fake Cuban accent, and they both laughed as they bumped hips and turned back to their customers.

As she worked, taking and filling orders, pouring tea, wrapping up all sorts of goodies, and filling the cash register with coins and bills, Candy could feel her spirits lifting. Maggie always seemed to be able to chase away her blues. They'd been best friends since Candy's first days in town, and never had a cross word passed between them. They'd leaned on each other in tough times, celebrated each other's successes, and even solved a few mysteries together.

As the morning progressed, they chatted and joked, and waited for a lull in the action before bringing up the latest mystery.

"Who are your suspects?" Maggie asked in a low tone once Candy had filled her in on all the latest details.

"All fingers seem to be pointing to Maurice Soufflé at the moment," Candy

240

said, "though I have my doubts. The motivations seem too weak."

"Don't underestimate that guy," Maggie warned, her light mood evaporating. "He was a tough cookie. I had a couple of run-ins with him over his insurance policies when I was working for Stone and Milbury. He would endlessly check every detail, and argue with us about every single charge and fee. He accused us numerous times of cheating him. I dreaded doing business with him."

"So you think he could have done this?" Candy asked.

"When you look at the facts, sure. Like you said, the name of his deli is on those jars of poisoned pickles. That's pretty tough evidence to ignore."

The sun brightened then, streaming in through the store-front's windows, and the conversation turned to more everyday topics. Between the occasional onrush of customers, they talked about Doc and the farm, and about Maggie's daughter Amanda, who had just entered her final year in college at the University of Maine.

Eventually they were joined by Herr Georg Wolfsburger, the bakery's proprietor, who took a break from the kitchen to greet customers and hobnob with Candy and

Maggie, whom he called "my two favorite ladies!" In a more energetic mood than he'd been the day before, he worked the crowd and talked about some of his latest creations, which entertained everyone in the shop. In the past he had been somewhat flirtatious at times like this, but he had toned that down quite a bit since he and Maggie had become engaged the previous summer.

After he had disappeared back into the kitchen, Candy sidled up next to Maggie. "So have you two set a wedding date?" she asked curiously, giving her friend a nudge.

"As a matter of fact," Maggie said, "we've been talking about it quite a bit lately."

"And?"

"Well, we're thinking about next spring," Maggie said. "Since we're both staying in town through the fall and into early winter, we're going to keep the shop open as late as we can this year, possibly until Thanksgiving. We might head south to Georg's place in Florida for the Christmas holiday and New Year's, but we want to be back early in the year to do some upgrading here in the shop. Georg wants to put in some new display cases and shelving, do some painting, and spruce up the place before we open next year. He's already lined up Ray

Hutchins to do the work." Ray was a local handyman who often helped out Candy and Doc at the blueberry farm.

"So have you thought of a specific date?" Candy asked, bringing the conversation back to the pertinent subject.

"Well," Maggie said cryptically, "when do the blueberry fields reach full bloom?"

"Around mid-May, if we're lucky and get some warm weather. A few weeks later if not. Why do you ask?"

"Because," Maggie said with some hesitation, as if she were uncertain how her friend would react, "we're thinking of getting married out at Blueberry Acres, when the fields are in bloom. If that's okay with you and Doc, that is?"

"Okay?" Candy could barely contain herself from squealing with delight. "I think that's the best idea I've heard in a long time!"

Maggie let out a breath of relief. "I'm so glad you think so," she said. "We've talked about it quite a bit, and we'd really like to have the ceremony outside, instead of in a stuffy old building. And since we both love your farm, and Georg especially loves baking with blueberries, we couldn't think of a better place to say our vows."

Feeling an onrush of joy, Candy gave her

friend a tight hug. "It's going to be the best wedding ever. Just wait and see. We're going to have so much fun!"

"I know," Maggie said, "and Georg has promised to bake us the biggest wedding cake he's ever made!"

"I can't wait!" Candy said. "We can start planning right away. We'll have you and Georg out to the farm as soon as possible, so we can walk the property and find the perfect place for the ceremony. It will be," she promised her friend, "the social event of the year!"

TWENTY-SIX

Given all they had to talk about, Candy didn't leave the bakery until quarter to eleven, when she had to abandon her position behind the counter to head over to the book signing at the Pine Cone Bookstore. "I wish I could stay longer," she said, "but duty calls."

"This has been so much fun," Maggie said as Candy hung up her apron. "I'm so glad you came by — although I didn't mean to put you to work! We were supposed to have tea together."

"Honestly, it was a nice change for me," Candy said. "And I'm always happy to help out, so if you get too busy again, just give me a call."

Maggie smiled warmly. "You're the best friend ever."

"You too."

They hugged each other again, and with that, Candy grabbed her tote bag, said her good-byes, and headed out to the street, walking the short distance along Main Street to the bookstore.

She had hoped to stop by the general store first, to talk to Trudy Watkins about her presence at the cook-off contest, but she'd cut the timing too close and would have to do that after the signing. She also wanted to stop by the pizza place to talk to Phil, the manager, but that could come later as well.

Like the bakery, the bookstore was abuzz. It was not a large store, deeper than it was wide, meandering back into the nether regions of an old brick building, although it was well lit and welcoming, with amply stocked shelves, clever displays, and comfy stuffed armchairs where patrons could sit and read at their leisure.

An open space had been cleared out near the center of the store, where the staff had set up a wooden table piled high with copies of Julia von Fleming's cookbook, *Home-style New England Cooking.* Candy spotted Julia herself, decked out in a mustard-colored print dress with a short beige jacket and coordinating tulip-patterned neck scarf flecked with red and green, at the center of a small group of ladies who were wide-eyed and smiling, obviously enchanted at meeting a published author.

Before she had a chance to join them, Candy fell into a conversation with Aurora Croft, the bookstore's sixtyish owner, who with her face-hugging bowl-shaped haircut, beaked nose, and big round glasses bore an uncanny resemblance to an owl. The illusion was only compounded by her frequent hooting, as well as the fact that today her head was constantly twisting in one direction or another.

"Ooo, this is all so exciting!" she said, placing a hand gently on Candy's forearm. "I'm so glad you helped us put this together. What a brilliant idea! Hosting a prestigious author like Julia is a dream come true, and we can certainly use the boost in sales!"

"It looks like you have a good turnout," Candy said as several more people came through the front door and began working their way back through the shop.

"We've had to bring in extra chairs," Aurora said. "We're expecting a full house!"

As the eleven o'clock hour approached, the place did indeed fill up, with latecomers finding standing room only. Candy herself hovered at the fringes of the crowd, tucked between two shelves of books, where she could observe the proceedings without drawing too much attention to herself. She had her digital recorder in hand, just in case she wanted to capture any of the remarks, and took a few photos of the assemblage with her smart phone, which she could use in the paper or on the website if she needed to fill space.

At the top of the hour, Aurora took center stage to welcome her guests and introduce the author, and the crowd erupted into applause as Julia swept forward to stand beside the wooden desk. She warmly thanked the crowd and then picked up one of her books, launching into a description of her work, the challenges of running down some of the recipes, and how honored she felt at locating and preserving some of the recipes in her book.

"Many are heirloom recipes, dating back several generations," she informed her listeners, "and some were almost lost to oblivion. I managed to locate a recipe for peach cobbler that dates back to the end of the eighteenth century! There's also a recipe for cranberry pie, which goes back to the nineteen forties, that's absolutely scrumptious! It's a wonderful recipe for Thanksgiving or just a summer picnic. You'll find it on page ninety-six of the book. And one of my favorites is a recipe for a Christmas goose from a family that emigrated from Frankfurt, Germany. It was a rare find!"

"How were you able to verify the authenticity of the recipes?" called a voice from the back of the crowd, on the opposite side from where Candy stood. Candy shifted her gaze to see who had spoken and was surprised to see Wanda Boyle, apparently out of the hospital, demurely dressed in a maroon sweater and black pants. She looked a little shaky, and her face was somewhat pale, but otherwise she appeared to be okay, though her overall demeanor seemed very serious.

Which wasn't a surprise, Candy thought, since she'd been poisoned the previous day.

"Well, of course I'm relying on the honesty of the people and sources from whom I gathered the recipes," Julia said, smiling as she responded to the question without missing a beat. "I was quite meticulous in my research, I can assure you. All the recipes are properly documented. Now, as I was saying . . ."

But Wanda cut in again, interrupting her. "In your research, did you come across any stories of stolen recipes?"

That got everyone's attention. Candy saw many faces in the crowd craning around to get a better look at the person who was asking these odd questions.

Julia looked confused. "Stolen recipes?"

"There was an incident here in town a few years ago," Wanda went on, undeterred by the sudden attention. "An award-winning lobster stew recipe was stolen from one of our villagers. Caused quite a ruckus."

Trying to keep an indignant look off her face, Julia forced a smile, which made her jaws quiver just a bit. "As I said, I can assure you all the recipes in my book are properly documented. None are stolen."

"Were any of the people who provided the recipes properly compensated?" Wanda pressed.

Again, confusion clouded Julia's face. "Compensated?"

"Are you aware of any other recipes that might have been stolen around town? Say, four or five years ago? Maybe you heard something about it as part of your research?"

Julia thought about that a moment. "No, not that I can recall. Why do you ask?"

At that point, Aurora Croft stepped into the conversation. "Perhaps this is a line of questioning we should save until later, after the signing," she said in a thoroughly pleasant manner. "Now, why don't we move forward?" Addressing the crowd, she continued, "Ms. von Fleming's book is currently available for purchase at the counter, and then you can start lining up to have your copy signed."

Wanda's interruptions forgotten, the crowd moved quickly, surging forward to talk personally with the author or snag a book for her to sign.

Candy continued to hover for a while, listening to the cash register ring and watching as the patrons began lining up at the wooden table, behind which Julia von Fleming had seated herself. She was chatting easily and smiling again, the strange line of questioning from Wanda seemingly dismissed.

But Candy hadn't forgotten it, and she was determined to find out the reasoning behind it. Stashing the digital recorder in her tote bag and slipping its strap up on her shoulder, she began to make her way through the crowd, across the room toward Wanda, who remained planted to the spot upon which she stood, stoically surveying the scene before her. As Candy approached, Wanda's eyes flicked toward her and followed her as she approached.

Candy stopped a few steps away. "Wanda, I'm so glad you're out of the hospital, though I'm a little surprised to see you here today. How are you feeling?"

"Terrible," Wanda admitted with a strange

twist of her mouth. "I don't mind telling you, that was one of the worst experiences I've ever been through in my life. My stomach and throat still hurt. I could have died, you know."

"Thank goodness you didn't," Candy said, "but what are you doing here? Why aren't you home in bed recovering from your . . . terrible experience?"

"Because," Wanda said, lowering her voice conspiratorially, "I want to find out who's behind this whole poisoned pickle thing. And I have some new information that might help us solve the case."

"Us?" Candy echoed.

Wanda gave her a dark look. "You're not the only one who can solve a mystery, you know. I'm just as involved in this as you are." Her voice had taken on a defensive edge. "More, really. I'm one of the victims, you know . . . one who lived, fortunately."

"Yes, fortunately. What's this new information?"

Wanda's hooded gaze shot around the room. "We can't talk about it here. Too many ears. Why don't we head over to the office, and I'll show you what I've got."

Twenty-Seven

"So, why all the questions about stolen recipes?"

A pause. "I just wanted to hear what she had to say. She's apparently done a lot of research on local and regional recipes. I thought she might have heard something."

"About what?"

Wanda harrumphed, as if the answer was obvious. "About stolen recipes, of course."

"So you think Julia stole some of her recipes?"

Wanda waved a hand dismissively. "No, nothing like that. At least, that wasn't what I was after."

"Then what *were* you after?" Candy asked curiously.

They were sitting in her office at the newspaper. Candy was in her usual spot at her desk, while Wanda was sitting uneasily in a folding chair across from her. They were alone in the place. No other employees, interns, or volunteers were around to overhear their conversation. Candy's office door was open, and the hall beyond was dark and quiet. They'd locked the front door behind them upon their arrival, to make sure they were undisturbed.

"Mostly just confirmation," Wanda said esoterically, "because I already know the answer."

Candy put a hand to her forehead. "Honestly, I'm still confused. Confirmation about what?"

In response, Wanda reached into a battered tan leather briefcase that she'd brought along with her. It served as her mobile office. She dug around for a moment and withdrew a fairly new manila folder, stuffed half an inch thick with papers and documents. She held it up. "This," she said.

Candy eyed it skeptically. It was the second manila folder someone had showed her that morning. She hoped it didn't contain another extortion letter. "And what's that?"

For the first time today, Wanda's fairly glum mood disappeared. It was replaced by a smug expression, making her look like the Cheshire cat. "Something that's going to blow your socks off."

Candy looked down at her feet. "I'm not

wearing socks."

"You know what I mean. Here, take a look. Just be prepared to be shocked." She held out the folder.

Candy hesitated a moment, squelching a look of disbelief. She knew Wanda had a flair for the dramatic, as well as for self-promotion and exaggeration. She couldn't imagine that the file's contents would surprise her *that* much, especially after what she'd learned earlier in the morning from Tristan.

But she couldn't resist. She reached over and took the folder from Wanda. Then, leaning back in her chair, she set it on her lap and opened it. Her gaze narrowed as she began to page through the documents inside, scrutinizing them.

A few minutes later, she had to admit — if she'd been wearing socks, they would have been blown right off.

TWENTY-EIGHT

"How — and where — did you get this?" Candy asked, unable to contain her amazement. "I thought I burned this last summer, along with the rest of Sapphire's files."

"I'm sure you did exactly what you thought you did," Wanda said evenly, betraying nothing.

"But if I burned all those files, then how . . . ?" Candy looked more closely at the documents inside the folder, and a moment later she knew. "They're photocopies, aren't they?"

"Of course they are. They'd have to be, wouldn't they, if you burned the originals?"

"But how?" Candy repeated. Suddenly anger flared inside her, and she knew. "You sneaked into my old office one day when I wasn't there and went through my filing cabinet, didn't you?"

Wanda shrugged. "It wasn't on purpose. I wasn't spying on you or anything like that.

It was a completely innocent act. I was working on a story and needed a file that I'd loaned to you. Of course, this was over a year ago, but if I remember correctly, it had something to do with the Cape Willington Heritage Protection League. I was on a tight deadline, you weren't in the office that day —"

"So you went searching for it," Candy said in an accusatory tone, filling in the blanks, "in my office."

Still calmly, Wanda continued, "Like I said, I was on a deadline. It was a perfectly legitimate excuse. When I didn't find the file on your desk, I went digging for it in your old filing cabinet, yes. That's when I saw the bottom drawer, labeled *S.V.* It wasn't hard to put two and two together."

She paused as her gaze narrowed, and her tone turned tighter as well. "You never told anyone you inherited those old files after Sapphire's death. You never told anyone you kept them. You could have destroyed them right away — you probably should have, given what was inside them — but you didn't, did you? So you're really no better than me. You were curious about what they contained."

"Yes, I kept them," Candy admitted, knowing in her heart Wanda was right, "but

I never went through them all. Only a few of them, when I needed to do some research to solve a murder."

"So that makes you better than me?"

Candy could feel her temper simmering, but she wasn't about to let Wanda get the best of her. She changed her angle of questioning. "So how many of Sapphire's old files did *you* go through?"

"All of them, of course."

"Then you probably know some things about this village and its people you shouldn't."

"That may be true," Wanda replied, "but I'm not a blabbermouth. I can be discreet. I've told you that before. It's obvious, when Sapphire Vine served as the newspaper's community columnist before you, that she was a royal snoop of the first order. She dug into people's lives where she shouldn't. And she used some of the information she uncovered to blackmail certain people." Wanda pointed to the folder sitting on Candy's lap. "Like him."

Candy looked down at the opened folder. She'd already seen the now-familiar name on a number of the photocopied documents: Maurice Soufflé.

Wanda had copied Sapphire Vine's personal, secret file on the Sweet Pickle

Deli's owner, obviously compiled before the paper's onetime community correspondent had been murdered several years ago.

"A lot of what I found in those files was outdated junk, worthless stuff," Wanda continued, "so I tossed it. But some of it was surprisingly informational. You haven't gotten to the photo and documents in the back yet, have you?"

"No." Candy's voice sounded a little hoarse. She cleared her throat and glanced up at Wanda. "Do I want to?"

"If you want to solve this current murder case, you do."

That brought Candy back to the moment. She flipped to the last few sheets in the folder, skimming through them. "And what will I find?"

"I'll summarize it for you, if you'd like. As we both now know, Sapphire Vine was a gossip, a spy, and a blackmailer. That's why she was murdered five years ago. She snooped around too much. She pushed things too far. But before she died she managed to get the goods on this guy named Maurice Soufflé."

Suddenly curious, her anger fading, Candy asked, "And what did she discover?"

Wanda shifted in her chair. "Well, his real name, for one thing."

"So Maurice Soufflé was an assumed name?"

"Of course it was. It was just a silly invention designed to hide his true identity."

It took Candy a few moments, but she finally came across a document that revealed the real name of the owner of the Sweet Pickle Deli.

"Marcus Spruell," she read. It was from a photocopy of an old Rhode Island driver's license issued during the nineties. The photo showed a man in his late forties or fifties, with a narrow face, thick and curly dark hair, a tight straight mouth, shadowed eyes, and a dark mole on his upper cheek just left of his nose.

Candy had to admit she was impressed by the level of Sapphire's research, but then again Sapphire had spent years and years compiling all this information. "How the heck did she find all this stuff?"

"You already know the answer to that. She was nosy, tenacious — and a little crazy."

Candy had to agree with that statement, for she knew Sapphire's background, and her own secret identity.

"And what else did she find?" Candy asked, skimming through the rest of the documents.

Wanda filled in the blanks. "That Maurice

260

— or Marcus — was a pretty good cook, but also a low-level con artist in his younger days, bilking wealthy widows, promoting shady investments, that sort of thing. My guess is at some point he got into some pretty hot water with the wrong people down around Providence, so he decided to skip town, head north, and lay low here in Cape Willington for a while. Maybe he was even trying to turn over a new leaf, make himself legitimate. Who knows? But his past eventually caught up to him, thanks to Sapphire. She did some research and found out he'd been accused of stealing a number of things, including family recipes."

"Recipes?" Candy said. "What kinds of recipes?"

"Well, the pickle recipe, for one, according to the documents in that folder. The original, which Sapphire somehow located, is attributed to a woman named Mabel Kaufman. Of course, it's possible Mabel was related to Maurice, maybe an aunt or a maternal grandmother. There's no way of knowing for sure. But there's evidence he stole the recipes for a number of other dishes he used to establish his reputation. He built his deli business with them — and although some of the information Sapphire gathered was sketchy, it appeared he was trying to make some extra cash, big cash, off the recipes he'd stolen. He apparently approached some big corporation about spinning off his own product line of pickles and other related items under the Sweet Pickle Deli label."

"Stolen recipes," Candy repeated. "So that's why you grilled Julia von Fleming this morning."

"Exactly. Like I said, I just wondered what she'd heard. I was trying to corroborate what was in Sapphire's files. Unfortunately, Julia didn't seem to know anything about Maurice and his recipes."

The next piece of the puzzle clicked into Candy's mind. "So Sapphire must have approached Maurice with what she'd learned and threatened to blackmail him, like she'd done to others in town. Maybe that's why he left so suddenly, closing down the deli in the middle of the night."

Wanda smirked and leveled a finger at her, an orange fingernail leading the way. "Bingo."

"What happened after that?" Candy asked.

Again, Wanda shrugged. "It appears that was the end of it. Sapphire lost track of him. End of the trail. No one to blackmail. You can't use your leverage against someone you can't find. A few months later she was dead."

Thoughtfully, Candy closed the folder and set it on top of her desk. She considered what she'd just learned for a long time before she finally spoke again. "Wanda, I can't condone what you did. Photocopying Sapphire's files without my knowledge was sneaky and underhanded. All this time, you knew what was in the bottom drawer in my filing cabinet, and yet you pretended you had no idea."

"What you didn't know didn't hurt you," Wanda said without a degree of remorse.

"That's not the point."

"So what *is* the point?"

Candy thought about that question as well. Part of her wanted to fire Wanda right then and there. What Wanda had done was a betrayal of trust — *that* was the point, Candy thought. But something deep inside told her it would be a mistake. *Better to keep your enemies close,* she told herself, although she hesitated to think of Wanda as an enemy. She was more of a nuisance than anything else, and occasionally an adversary. But she was good at what she did, and her columns in every issue of the paper certainly helped drive circulation, keeping the publication solvent. Without Wanda, the paper might no longer exist in its current printed form, and they wouldn't be celebrating its bicentennial anniversary.

And, Candy had to admit, Wanda's snooping and duplicity had uncovered a critical piece of information that just might help them solve a crime.

In the end, Candy decided to focus on the positive rather than the negative. "I'm going to try to forget what you've done by going behind my back and photocopying those files, at least for the moment, and focus on the problem at hand — although I think when this is over, you should burn all those files you've photocopied, just like I did."

Wanda shook her head, her mouth tight in defiance. "Not going to happen. I have a job to do. Those files are too valuable to get rid of now. And despite what you might think, they're not all as incriminating as they might seem."

She pointed at the folder on Candy's desk. "Take that one, for instance. If this whole pickle poisoning thing hadn't happened, the information in that folder would be totally irrelevant — useless. Who would've cared that Maurice Soufflé was being investigated and blackmailed by a community columnist who died years ago? Absolutely no one, that's who. And that's what I found in most of the files I copied — disjointed facts, scribbled notes, seemingly worthless tidbits of information jotted on slips of paper. Not worth much right now, but at some point they might prove useful."

Candy was somewhat dismayed to find herself agreeing with Wanda. "Like now," she said.

"Like now," Wanda emphasized. "So what's our next move?"

For a few moments they stared at each other, and neither spoke. Finally Candy picked up the folder and handed it back to Wanda. "I don't know yet. Let me think about it."

Wanda took that as her cue to leave. "Okay, you're the boss." She stuffed the folder into her briefcase, rose quickly, and headed for the door. "Just don't think too long, though," she cautioned on her way out. "We have a murderer on the loose again. It might even be this Marcus Spruell character himself. So the quicker we find out what's going on, and end this thing before someone else dies, the better."

TWENTY-NINE

She's right, Candy thought after Wanda had left, tromping back along the hallway and shutting the main office door behind her. Much as she hated to admit it, Wanda, through her subterfuge, had uncovered some important information. Now she had to figure out how to use that information to uncover a murderer, before anyone else in town was harmed.

And not just people in town. Whoever was behind the poisoned pickles had targeted people outside of Cape Willington as well.

That got Candy to thinking. Three jars of pickles. Three possible targets. All linked to Maurice Soufflé, whom she now knew was actually a con artist named Marcus Spruell.

What had happened to him? Where had he gone when chased out of town as a result of Sapphire Vine's alleged attempt at blackmail? Had he sought revenge on certain people, using jars of poisoned pickles? If so, why now?

As she'd done in the past to help organize her thoughts, she pulled a legal pad out of a drawer and started jotting down what she'd learned so far:

- Three jars of pickles had been found — one at Sally Ann Longfellow's house, one on the pickled food table at the community cook-off, and one in a mailbox of a woman named Georgia McFee, who lived in Cherryfield, about thirty-five minutes away.

- All three jars appeared to be targeted at specific people. Julia von Fleming was convinced the jar of poisoned pickles left on the table at the cook-off had been meant specifically for her, since she'd written a negative column about the Sweet Pickle Deli a few years back, though she'd published the column under a pen name. Georgia McFee had beaten Maurice Soufflé, alias Marcus Spruell, in a private cook-off challenge held around the same time. And Maurice had been so annoyed at Sally Ann's goats that he'd filed a complaint with the local officials. Despite her doubts, Candy had to admit that Maurice was still the prime suspect.

- However, Candy was certain she and her father, along with everyone else who had attended the cook-off contest the previous day, were still considered suspects by the police. There was even evidence against Candy and Doc, since Doc had initially spotted the jar on the table and Candy's fingerprints were all over it. In addition, she had tried to give the tainted pickles to the three official judges for a taste test. Not good. However, she doubted Chief Durr seriously considered her or Doc a suspect, despite the evidence.

- Whoever had left the pickles on Sally Ann's doorstep would not have known that Wanda Boyle was stopping by to pick up that jar, and Sally Ann had said she'd left out a jar of her own pickles, which had not yet been found. Candy suspected the jars had been switched, but when and by whom?

- Sally Ann still had two jars from the old Sweet Pickle Deli, kept in the back of her pantry for special occasions, but the labels on them, as well as the shape of the jars themselves, differed from the one Candy had seen yesterday in the gym. And the pickles in Sally Ann's jars weren't poisoned, as Candy found out when she sampled them herself. Still, Candy wasn't quite ready to completely rule out Sally Ann as a suspect. She said she'd been out of town when the jars of poisoned pickles were found, but Candy was taking her word for it — just like she was taking Sally Ann's word that there were still two jars from the deli left in her pantry, allegedly proving she'd left out her own jar of pickles on the stoop for Wanda, and not one from the deli, suggesting the two had been switched.

- While he'd been living in town and running the deli, Maurice Soufflé had developed a reputation as a top-level cook but also as someone who was hard to get along with, throwing customers out of his store for what everyone else considered were minor infractions. It wasn't hard to imagine that his negative attitude could have eventually developed into a murderous one.

- From Sapphire Vine's old file on Maurice, photocopied by Wanda, they had learned the true identity of the owner of the Sweet Pickle Deli, and that Maurice/Marcus had a previous life, one as a con artist, among other things. Again, could something that had happened in the past have driven him to target several people around the area with jars of poisoned pickles?

- Finally, the Pruitts had received a letter attempting to extort two hundred thousand dollars from them, by threatening to harm more people in town, allegedly with more jars of poisoned pickles. The letter had been mailed from Cape Willington earlier in the week, indicating that the sender had been in town at that time. Sally Ann, for instance, had surely been in town then, but what about Maurice Soufflé? Could he have mailed it? Or was someone else behind the extortion letter?

There were other issues, she knew, though she wasn't sure how they related to the current crime. Maurice had been a thorn in the side of Mason Flint and the village's selectmen, she'd learned, badgering them about a permit for an outdoor dining area, for which he'd refused to pay. And he'd left behind unpaid financial obligations, including back taxes. Could that have been a motivation for murder, driven by revenge? Even Maggie had a run-in with him over his insurance policies. It seemed he didn't have a single friend in town.

Despite all the evidence against Maurice Soufflé, there was a possibility the jars had been left out by someone more familiar to them, someone around town, someone who had been at the cook-off contest yesterday and had an opportunity to place the jars in the locations in which they'd been found. Someone who had been in town to mail that extortion letter. But again, who? It could be just about anyone, including many of the town's most prominent citizens.

Then there was Marjorie Coffin's story about the box of late entries, including possibly a jar of poisoned pickles, left on the hood of her car. She'd carried the box into the gym herself, although it had become lost in the shuffle and never found. And Candy had spotted Trudy Watkins leaving the gym yesterday at a particularly opportune time.

Candy also jotted down a note about a

woman named Gloria, who had apparently worked at the Sweet Pickle Deli when it was still open, according to the teenaged girl who worked at the pizza parlor. She'd have to talk to the manager Phil about that.

She added another note at the bottom of the page, with a star beside it: *Shadowy figure? Baby blue pickup truck? Was I being followed, or did I imagine it?* She still didn't know for sure.

Candy read back over the list. It included everything she could remember. It was a good list, and several points jumped out at her. She'd already talked to a number of the people involved in the cook-off contest, but there were several more she needed to visit — people who might have some insight into what had happened in the gym yesterday, or who might know the whereabouts of Maurice Soufflé.

She knew, rightfully, she'd have to share some, or all, of this information with the local police, especially the details about Maurice's true identity. To do otherwise would be withholding evidence. But she'd been repeatedly warned to stay out of official investigations, which made her hesitate. After thinking it through, she decided she'd have to talk to Chief Durr and tell him what she'd learned. The sooner, the better. She also might be able to get a little information from him about the status of the official investigation. But first she had a few more leads to run down. Then she'd contact the chief and give him a full report.

She turned back to her computer and searched for a phone number for Georgia McFee but came up empty. However, she was able to locate a street address. She decided she'd just have to make a quick trip up there, since it wasn't that far, and she preferred to talk to Georgia face to face, anyway. She was in the process of checking out the quickest route to Cherryfield when the office's front door squeaked open and slammed shut again, making her jump in her chair, and she heard the strangest of sounds in the hallway, coming straight toward her.

THIRTY

It was a clattering of footsteps, unlike anything Candy had heard before, a combination of heavy steps stomping toward her, accompanied by uncoordinated higher-pitched clomps that seemed to reverberate through the building. Candy thought Wanda might have returned, but this didn't sound anything like Wanda. It was, in some way, otherworldly.

Then she heard the forlorn bleat of an unhappy goat, and knew who it was.

A few moments later, Sally Ann Longfellow peered in through Candy's open office door. She was dressed in faded dungarees that hung loosely on her, a threadbare blue flannel shirt, and a wide-brimmed straw hat. In her left hand she held a rope attached to the collar of Guinevere, her sole remaining goat, who seemed to want to be anywhere but here.

"I saw your Jeep parked up the street.

Hoped I might find you here," Sally Ann said gruffly, without preamble. "Like I said last night, I got something I need to talk to you about." She stepped into Candy's office, tugging in the goat, which seemed to want to go in a different direction.

Involuntarily Candy rose from her seat. "Sally Ann! And Guinevere! What a surprise!"

"Told you we might stop by," Sally Ann said, "and here we are."

"Yes, here you are — a little unexpected, but that's fine. But . . . I didn't think you'd bring the goat along."

Sally Ann glanced at the animal. "Didn't want to leave her alone, after what happened yesterday. She's been pretty depressed since you-know-who passed away."

"You mean Cleopatra?" Candy ventured.

The goat bleated sadly, and Sally Ann put a shushing finger to her lips. "We don't mention that name," she told Candy.

"Oh, sorry, I didn't mean to . . ." Candy paused, her brow wrinkling. "But a depressed goat?"

"Animals have feelings, too, you know," Sally Ann said in the critter's defense.

"Yes, I'm sure they do." Candy tried to regroup and motioned to a chair as she ran a hand through her hair. "Well, why don't you sit down?" she said, settling uneasily back into her own seat, hesitant to put herself down at the goat's height.

Sally Ann waved away the offer. "Don't need to. Not staying long. This won't take long."

"Okay, so what did you want to see me about?"

"Got something for you." Sally Ann reached into a back pocket of her dungarees, which looked decades old, and withdrew a twice-folded, misshapen piece of paper, soiled with bent corners. She unfolded it with thick fingers, smoothed it out against her stomach, and handed it to Candy, who took it hesitantly. She turned it in one direction. Then another. A long paragraph was written on it in an unsteady hand with heavy black ink. Candy tried to decipher the handwriting.

"What's this?" she asked.

"It's Cleopatra's obituary."

Candy looked up at Sally Ann with uncertainty. "Obituary?"

"I thought you could run it in the next issue of the paper."

Candy scanned the first few lines. "An obituary . . . for a goat?"

"She was a good citizen of this village, just like everyone else. Sure, she had her run-ins with a few folks, but she was murdered just like Ned Winetrop. I thought she deserved an appropriate send-off. The funeral's tomorrow morning."

Candy couldn't keep the skepticism out of her voice. "A funeral . . . for a goat?"

"Eleven o'clock, out at my place. I'm expecting quite a turnout. Despite what you might have heard, Cleopatra had a lot of fans in this town. I'm hoping you can make it. Wanda too. Maybe you can take a few photos, do a little write-up."

Candy turned her attention back to the obituary and read it more carefully. It was roughly worded, with a number of spelling and grammatical errors, and would need some editing, but she could probably salvage it, maybe publish a short paragraph to appease Sally Ann.

She heard a crackling sound behind her and swiveled around. While she'd been reading, the goat had made its way across her office and was sampling some papers she'd left out on the credenza under the window. "Hey, not those!" Candy shouted.

Sally Ann yanked on the goat's cord. "Guinevere, behave!"

The goat bleated again and changed tack, angling toward a potted English Ivy sitting in the far corner of the credenza in front of the window. "No, leave that alone!" Candy said, reaching toward it, but she was too late. The goat had flicked out its tongue and lassoed a tender shoot, yanking it toward her. The pot tipped over, spilling out clumps of moist dirt. Candy managed to catch it just in time, before it went over the edge and onto the floor.

Sally Ann finally corralled her animal as Candy set the pot upright, scooped some of the spilled dirt back into it, and then placed it on a high shelf, out of the goat's reach. "Guinevere, that's not meant for you," she said, trying not to sound too scolding.

"She's just upset," Sally Ann said in the goat's defense.

Candy eyed the goat warily. "Yes, I'm sure she is."

"So you'll make sure this obituary gets into the next issue?"

Candy placed the paper on her desktop next to her computer. "I'll do my best."

Sally Ann nodded once, emphatically. "That's all I can ask. I'll keep an eye out for it. And I'll look for you in the morning."

Candy sighed. "I'll try to be there, but I have another event at two."

"It shouldn't take long. Half an hour or so. You'll mention it to Wanda?"

"Yes, of course," Candy said.

She thought they were about done, and expected the other woman to leave before her goat caused more damage. But a strange look came over Sally Ann, and her expression changed. Her lower lip protruded, and her eyes began to water. After a few moments, Candy realized the other woman was becoming emotional.

"She was a good goat," Sally Ann said. "We'll all miss her a lot."

"Yes, we will," Candy said supportively. "Everyone in town knows how important those goats are to you."

"You're going to find out who did this to her, right?"

On an impulse, Candy rose, stepped forward, and gave Sally Ann a big hug. "I promise you, I'll do my very best. We'll find out who's behind those poisoned pickles. And you can rest assured that if I have anything to say about it, justice for Cleopatra — and for Ned — will definitely be served."

THIRTY-ONE

After Sally Ann and Guinevere left, heading back down the hallway and out the door with a clattering and stomping of footsteps, accompanied by one or two bleats, Candy resettled herself at her desk and went back over the notes she'd made earlier.

Her next steps seemed clear — two stops in town and one out of town. But before she left, she fished out her cell phone and made several quick calls — to her father, to Finn Woodbury, to Maggie at the bakery, and even to Mason Flint, inquiring whether any of them had heard of someone named Marcus Spruell. But, perhaps not surprisingly, she came up blank. The name rang a bell with no one.

Next she conducted a quick computer search of the newspaper's digital archives of previously published stories, again finding nothing about Marcus Spruell. Lastly, she conducted a quick Internet search, but again, she found no references to anyone of that name.

She checked her watch. It was close to one, still early afternoon. Plenty of time to make a few house calls, including a thirty-five minute drive to Georgia McFee's place in Cherryfield, and talk to a few people. She took a few minutes to locate Georgia's place using an online map. It looked easy to find, on a side road off of the village's Main Street. Candy figured she could be there and back well before dinnertime. She wasn't sure the woman would be home. Georgia might still be in the hospital. But Candy decided to drive up anyway.

Five minutes later she was out the door and headed up Ocean Avenue. When she reached her Jeep she kept going, crossing the street at the light.

Before she left town, she wanted to talk to Trudy Watkins at the general store.

Zeke's was a busy place just about any time of the day. Like many New England general stores, it offered a wide range of goods, from fresh produce, everyday groceries, dry goods, and an extensive array of gourmet foods and wines to clothing, plants, toys, gifts and souvenirs, office supplies, books and magazines, DVD rentals, live bait, and even homemade sandwiches, soups, fudge, and cookies. In the winter the store was also stocked with sweaters, hats and gloves, and an assortment of sleds and toboggans, which were replaced in the summer by sunglasses, suntan oil, flip-flops, and beach towels. An old-fashioned candy counter was a big attraction for kids and families, and a space by the front window had been set up with chairs and a table, so customers could sit and play checkers, or just watch as pedestrians and traffic went past.

Trudy had run the place with her husband, Richard, for more than twenty years, and they were constantly changing and adding to the store's offerings. Candy stopped by often, sometimes at lunch for a quick sandwich, sometimes after work for milk, cheese, and a loaf of fresh-baked bread, and many times just to look around to see what she could find. She was often pleasantly surprised, whether she picked up the latest paperback mystery novel, a greeting card designed by a local artist, a new pair of flannel pajamas, or a jar of spicy gourmet mustard or apple-cinnamon butter.

As she pushed through the front door, she was greeted by the warm smells of coffee, chocolate, and fresh-baked goods, along with the more subtle fragrances of beeswax candles and milled bar soaps, mixing with the ever-present scent of old wood and natural oils. She headed back past the shelves and aisles, trying not to let herself get distracted by all the items she passed, and made her way toward the checkout counter along the left wall, which stood in front of a floor-to-ceiling shelving and display unit packed with all sorts of canned items, cake mixes, condiments, salsas, and boxes of cereal.

She spotted Trudy talking to a customer while bagging another woman's purchases. Other customers stood in line, so Candy patiently hovered nearby until Trudy had a few free moments.

As she waited, she noticed a young man stocking some of the shelves to her left, on the far side of the counter. He seemed to be watching her out of the corner of his eye as he worked, which made Candy feel a little self-conscious. She hadn't seen him in here before. He was in his late teens or early twenties, a lean young man with shaggy blond hair and a wispy moustache, which he probably felt made him look older. His blue-eyed gaze, Candy thought, was a little intense for someone his age.

As Candy moved among the shelves, biding her time, he continued to glance in her direction. She finally nodded a greeting at him but got no reaction, although he did avert his eyes and seemed to rededicate himself to his work. But his gaze still flicked in her direction from time to time.

Maybe I just remind him of someone, Candy thought. She toyed with the idea of approaching him to say hello, but the line at the counter finally cleared out, so she headed toward the cash register instead.

"Candy, I thought that was you," Trudy said with a pleasant smile. She was a tall, slender, gracious woman, with horn-rimmed glasses and long graying hair pulled back into a neat bun. Today she wore a colorful tulip-patterned apron over a blue-and-white gingham dress. Candy recalled that Trudy liked to collect vintage aprons, which she often wore around the store. "It's always so good to see you. How are things over at the newspaper?"

"Just fine, Trudy, thanks. We did have some trouble over at the cook-off contest, though."

"Oh, yes, I was so sorry to hear about that," Trudy said, her smile fading. "Ned was such a good man. I've known him for years. I still can't believe he's gone! We'll miss him around here."

"We sure will," Candy agreed, "and to be honest, that's sort of the reason I stopped by today — to talk to you about the cook-off contest."

She hesitated as Trudy gave her a questioning look, then plunged on. "I couldn't help but notice you were there yesterday, in the gym during the contest." Candy was careful to keep any negative tones out of her voice. She didn't want to sound threatening or accusatory, only curious.

Trudy looked a little surprised. "Oh, I didn't know you'd seen me. I had hoped to keep a low profile," she admitted, "since I wasn't sure I was supposed to be there. But I just wanted to see what was going on. It all seemed so exciting, so I snuck in for a quick peek. I hope that's all right."

"It's fine," Candy assured her.

"Of course," Trudy continued, "being the owner of a commercial establishment, I wasn't able to enter any of my own recipes in the contest."

"Yes, that's unfortunate," Candy agreed, "though we wanted to keep the event geared toward amateur cooks. I'm sure you understand."

Trudy nodded. "It was a wonderful idea regardless. We have so many talented people around here! I can't wait to see who the winners were. You'll announce them in the paper, right?"

"In the bicentennial issue, in early October. So how long were you at the event yesterday?"

"Oh, well, let's see." Trudy glanced down at the counter as she bit her lip. "Not for very long, I'm afraid. Richard's been homebound with leg problems, as you might have heard, and I didn't want to leave the store for too long. My nephew, Brian Jr., kept an eye on the place while I was gone." She pointed with a thin finger toward the blond-haired teenaged boy, who was still stocking shelves nearby.

"Oh, yes, I saw him earlier," Candy said, turning. She waved at him. "Hello, Brian Jr." To Trudy she added, "I thought I noticed a family resemblance."

"He's named after his father, Brian, who is Richard's youngest brother. We call them Brian Sr. and Brian Jr., to distinguish between the two. They live in Ellsworth now but Brian Jr. is staying with us for a while. He was looking for work, and we needed the help around here. It's a blessing to have him around." Trudy motioned to the teenaged boy. "Brian Jr., come and say hello to Candy."

Somewhat reluctantly, and with some additional coaxing, the young man walked to the counter, shook hands with Candy, and muttered a few words before disappearing into the back room.

"He's a little shy until he gets to know you better," Trudy said, "but he's a good worker, and he helps us out a lot. We couldn't do it without him. I hope he stays around for a while."

"He seems like a nice young man." Candy steered the conversation back onto the proper track. "So, about the cook-off contest — I was wondering if you noticed anything unusual while you were there yesterday?"

"Unusual? At the cook-off contest?" Trudy echoed, her brow furrowing. "In what way?"

"Anything that seemed strange or out of the ordinary. Maybe someone engaged in a suspicious activity, or something you might have heard that didn't sound quite right. I'm trying to find out how that jar of pickles got onto that table, and where it came from."

Trudy looked alarmed. "And you think I might know?"

"I'm talking to a lot of people," Candy said, "just trying to gather information. I don't suppose the police have talked to you?"

Trudy's hand went to her chest. "The police? Good gracious, no! Why would they want to talk to me?"

"They're interviewing everyone who was there yesterday. It's just standard procedure in any investigation of this sort. We're all hoping someone might have seen something or have some information that might help find the person behind Ned's death."

"Well, I can certainly understand that," Trudy said, "and I'd love to help any way I can. But I just didn't see anything that struck me as unusual. If I had, I would surely let you know."

Candy gave Trudy her card. "Well, if you do think of anything, let me know. Or just give the police a call. We're hoping to solve this as quickly as possible."

"Yes, I should hope so." Trudy took the card and glanced at it before she pushed it into the front pocket of her apron. "It's always hard to believe when something like this happens around here. This is a good community, you know, filled with good people. I remember when you could trust everyone in town, leave your doors unlocked, and never have to worry about your safety. But times have changed. I hate to say this, but you can't trust anyone anymore."

THIRTY-TWO

Once back outside and headed down the street, Candy decided to postpone her trip to the pizza parlor until later. The sky appeared to be lowering again, and she wanted to make sure she talked to Georgia McFee before it got too late in the day or turned stormy. If all went well, she figured she'd be back in time to talk to the manager at the pizza place before he went home for the day.

The drive northward out of Cape Willington was a colorful one. Most of the trees lining the road were just beginning to turn, but some, like red maples and white ashes, were already well into their seasonal change, displaying brilliant reds and yellows.

Like everyone else in New England, Candy kept track of peak foliage season. She knew that areas in the north of Maine, places like Aroostook County and Presque Isle, usually reached peak color during the last week in September, while it took until the second week in October for peak to reach Cape Willington. Still, there were low pockets of landscape she passed where colder air had settled at night, causing the foliage to change ahead of schedule. These areas in particular always fascinated her with their unexpected beauty.

The road north took her out of Cape Willington to Gouldsboro, then east on Route 1 until it turned north again at Milbridge, following a river that flowed into Narraguagus Bay. Traffic was light and she made good time, entering Cherryfield at a little past two. It was a quaint village, though more spread out than Cape Willington. She passed a stately bed-and-breakfast with a white picket fence and, a little further on, the small settlement with a town hall and a general store, before heading on northward and back out of town.

She found Georgia McFee's place with little trouble. She spotted the mailbox where the third jar had been left. A dirt lane beside it led back to a ramshackle house half-hidden behind a rise in the driveway, sitting in a hollow a hundred feet back from the road.

Pulled up beside the mailbox with the Jeep's engine idling, Candy surveyed the house and the surrounding property from the road, but she could see no one from her vantage point. In fact, the place showed no signs of life, with darkened windows and a general stillness about it. She wondered for a moment if anyone was home, although she spotted an old sedan parked to the side of the building.

Only one way to find out.

She backed up a few yards, shifted gears, and turned the Jeep into the dirt lane, progressing slowly toward the house. If Georgia was here, Candy didn't want to alarm the woman. She stopped in front of the house, shut off the engine, and climbed out. Walking around the front of the Jeep, she shaded her eyes against the brightening sun and saw a curtain flutter at one of the front windows. She'd been spotted.

A few moments later the front door opened and an elderly woman in a green cardigan sweater stepped out onto the porch. "Can I help you?" she asked in a tone that was neither friendly nor hostile.

"Hi, I'm Candy Holliday. I'm the managing editor of the *Cape Crier* down in Cape Willington."

"I know who you are," the other woman said. "I don't get the *Crier* anymore but I visit your website." She paused. "I love Wanda Boyle's columns. She seems like

291

such a wonderful person."

Candy took a few steps forward and folded her hands in front of her to project a casual presence. "Yes, well, that's good to hear. Wanda's columns are very popular. People seem to like them."

"Yes, we do," the elderly woman said. Then she added, sounding concerned, "I heard she had some trouble yesterday."

Candy nodded. "Yes, that's true. She's bounced back, but she had a rough day. I heard you did as well."

The woman raised her shoulders dramatically and made a face. "Yes, I suppose I did. But it was my own fault. I should never have opened that jar of pickles, knowing the man behind them."

"Hmm, yes, I wonder if I could ask you a few questions about him?"

Georgia McFee made a face. "I've already talked to the police. They asked me questions for two hours. I told them everything I know."

"What about the jar itself?" Candy asked.

"The jar?"

"Did you notice anything odd about it? Anything about the label, maybe, or the shape of the jar?"

Georgia took a few moments to think about that. "Not really," she said finally.

"Did it look different in any way from the jars sold at the Sweet Pickle Deli years ago?"

Again, the other woman thought a moment before saying, "Not that I noticed."

Candy had hoped Georgia might be able to corroborate what she'd discovered at Sally Ann's house, that the jar she saw had a newer label and a different shape than the original jars from years ago. But it seemed she wasn't going to get that, so she tried a different line of questioning. "When was the last time you saw Maurice Soufflé?"

Georgia shivered at the mention of his name, and her face darkened. "The last time? When he threw me out of his shop, I guess."

"And when was that?"

"Five or six years ago. I don't remember exactly."

"Have you heard from him since? Do you have any idea what happened to him?"

Georgia sighed deeply. "As I said, I answered all these questions for the police. If I knew, I would have told them. But no, I have no idea. He just disappeared one day, and that's the last I heard of him."

Candy decided to tip her hand a little. "Are you aware that Maurice Soufflé was a fake name, something he made up?"

That caught Georgia's attention. "I

suspected as much, but no, I didn't know that for sure. He insisted over and over again it was his real name."

"Well, I don't believe it was," Candy said. "In fact, with Wanda's help, I believe we've discovered his real name."

At this piece of information, Georgia studied Candy carefully, to determine if she was kidding or telling the truth. "And what might that be?" she finally asked.

"We believe his real name was Marcus Spruell." She paused to let this bit of information sink in. "Does that ring a bell?"

Georgia's brow wrinkled and she tilted her head. "Spruell? Hmm, yes, it might."

"Really?" Candy felt a quiver of hope. "What can you tell me about it?"

"Well, I heard that name up in Bangor, when I was living there with my first husband. This was many years ago, of course, before I moved to Cape Willington and then came here after my second husband passed away. It seems to me there was a Spruell family living in Old Town, up past Orono. I worked with one of the daughters. Don't remember her name, though."

"Old Town? That's north of Bangor, right? That would be, what . . . ?" Candy had to think about it a minute. "An hour and a half from here?"

"Something like that, maybe a little less," Georgia confirmed. "I don't know much about the family, but I think the mother was a sickly woman. Needed lots of care. They lived on an old estate that had been fairly glamorous at one time — for Old Town, of course — but the impression I got was that it had begun to fall into disrepair. Something about a wayward son who drained away all the family's money."

"How would I find this estate?"

Georgia shrugged. "I don't know really, since I've never been there myself. If you head north from here and catch Route 9, that will take you to the outskirts of Bangor. That's a little over an hour. Head north another twenty minutes or so and cross the river. You'll have to ask around once you get there. For all I know, the place is gone."

She paused, her mouth tightening again. "But if it isn't, and you find Maurice — or Marcus, or whatever his name is — and he's the one who's behind this poisoned pickle thing, would you do me a big favor?"

"And what's that?" Candy asked.

"Tell him Georgia McFee sends her regards. And then make sure he spends the rest of his life in jail."

THIRTY-THREE

She hadn't expected to make a side trip to Old Town, but she also wasn't going to pass up a chance to track down Maurice Soufflé, aka Marcus Spruell. Besides, she thought as she left Georgia's place and headed north again, she'd learned another valuable piece of information that could easily fit into the overall puzzle. If Marcus's mother had been sickly and needed attention, it could explain his frequent disappearances for a day or two at a time, closing down his deli on short notice, so he could head back to his family's estate to take care of her.

Was she still alive? Candy wondered. Was she still living at the estate? Would she know anything about her son's whereabouts? Did the Spruells even still own property in Old Town? It was probably a long shot, Candy knew, and it could be a wild-goose chase, but she felt she had to run down every lead, no matter where it led.

As was typical for many New England rural roads, Main Street turned into Beddington Road once it left Cherryfield's borders. It was a simple two-lane road, framed for the most part by tall trees and vegetation that pressed in close from either side, though occasionally she passed solitary white-clapboard frame houses and weathered barns that stood on cleared pieces of land, surrounded by miles of nothing. There were few cars on the road and she made good time, pushing the speedometer as far above the posted speed limits as she dared.

As she neared Route 9 the landscape opened up a little, and she passed a few rolling patches of blueberry fields. Up ahead, low dusky hills rose above the relatively flat land. She turned west at the junction of Route 9 and goosed the gas pedal. She managed to find a classic rock station with minimal static on the radio and settled in for the ride.

In a little over an hour she reached the outskirts of Bangor. At the village of Eddington she turned north again, along the east bank of the Penobscot River. Bangor, Orono, and Old Town were all located west of the river, in a line from south to north, and there were only a few places to cross, one to the south at Bangor and one to the north at Old Town. As Georgia had suggested, Candy opted for the north crossing, but it took her another half an hour to get there. She stopped to gas up and then continued across the bridge, over the Penobscot River and into Old Town.

It was a typical small New England city, with a mixture of churches, storefronts, red-brick buildings, and residences, many of them two-story white-clapboard structures with black shutters but some of Victorian design. Main Street ran north and south along the river, while Center Street continued west through town

It wasn't a large city, with fewer than eight thousand residents, but Candy didn't want to drive every street checking the names on mailboxes. So she considered the other possibilities.

She knew there was a museum on Main Street — she'd visited it a few years back with her father. She could inquire there about the Spruells, but she suspected the place was probably shut down for the day. She seemed to recall it closed at four P.M., and it was approaching four thirty in the afternoon. A barbershop or beauty salon might be a good idea, but she didn't spot either of those as she drove through town.

She could stop at a drugstore but doubted a cashier would know the information she sought. Or she could always stop at the police station to make inquiries, but she thought that would cause more complications than she was ready to deal with right now.

So, in the end, she decided to just stop in at a bar or tavern and ask a bartender. They usually knew what was going on around town. It seemed her best bet.

She found a bar and grill that looked promising, on south Main Street in a plain-looking structure, so she parked the Jeep in an open spot right in front of the building, locked it up, and pushed through the establishment's front door. Inside, she found a typical tavern atmosphere, with low lighting, dark woods, and multiple flat-screen TVs tuned to Saturday afternoon baseball and college football games. Along the left wall was a long bar with a highly polished countertop. She found an empty stool at one end, sat down, and ordered a glass of white wine from a distracted bartender who came and went quickly.

Then she waited, glancing frequently at her watch and turning often to survey the place.

It didn't take long for the bartender, a

thirtyish man in a black T-shirt, with a thin pale face and a long brown ponytail that stretched halfway down his back, to return, his curiosity piqued. "Looking for someone?" he asked, trying to sound as helpful as possible.

Candy gave him a warm smile, crossed her legs, and leaned forward, placing one elbow on the countertop. "Waiting for someone, actually. I'm afraid I'm a bit late." She glanced at her watch again to emphasize the point. "We were supposed to meet up about an hour ago but I got delayed. He's an old friend of mine. Perhaps you know him? His name is Marcus Spruell?"

"Spruell?" the bartender repeated. He looked a little disappointed, as if he'd hoped Candy might be single and available — which, of course, she was, though she wasn't about to tell him that. "Don't know of anyone named Marcus," he said after a few moments, "but the old Spruell place is located on Old Town Road, out past the trading post and the freeway. Don't know if anyone still lives out there, though. Last I heard the place was all boarded up."

Candy brightened. "Really? Well, maybe I'll look for him there. I might have mixed up the meeting time. I appreciate the information. So how much do I owe you?"

She left him a relatively generous tip, as well as a nearly full glass of wine, and headed back out to the Jeep.

She had trouble finding Old Town Road, until she stopped and asked someone for directions. In town, she was told, it was known as Gilman Falls Avenue, but changed to Old Town Road out past the Stillwater River on the west side of town. "Why is nothing simple anymore?" she muttered to herself as the gunned the Jeep again and headed northwest.

A short time later she passed by the Old Town Trading Post — just a gas station and convenience store, really — and then drove onward, over Interstate 95 and, a little further on, past a golf course on the left. After that were occasional single-family homes on the left and right, a mixture of ranch-style properties and farmhouses. The vegetation on either side of the road became dense again, with tall grasses and lots of pines in among the deciduous trees in various stages of color.

She began to watch the mailboxes closely, slowing so she could read the names on the sides. It was another ten minutes before she came upon one that read SPRUELL. Beside it a dirt lane, showing only two parallel ruts with unkempt grasses between, led back among the trees. From the road, no house was visible.

Candy sat for a moment alongside the road, debating whether to drive or walk down the dirt lane. She finally decided she'd feel more secure if she stayed inside the Jeep, so she nosed it past the mailbox and headed back through the trees.

The lane wove around a little before emerging into an open area. Up ahead to the left, on a slight rise, stood a meandering white-clapboard farmhouse. It had been added on to several times over the years, with a large rectangular two-story main structure and a series of smaller attached lower sections butted onto one side of it, all with similar designs and rooflines. The final add-on looked as if it served as a breezeway, connecting the main residence to a towering three-story barn, which stood taller than anything else on the property. Several single-story buildings were attached to the far side of the barn, making for a long and impressive-looking residence. Off to one side was an additional building that could be a garage or storage unit, and she spotted another outbuilding back among the trees.

The house and barn were still in decent shape, though they both needed painting, and the surrounding grass was uncut, giving it a shabby appearance. Hardly an estate in the traditional sense, but at one time it certainly must have been a property of note.

Some old farm equipment was parked off to one side, but Candy saw no vehicles — cars, trucks, or tractors — in the driveway, which looped around in front of the house, the barn, and other outbuildings.

Still moving slowly, she followed the loop around and pulled the Jeep to a stop in front of the long house. With a final glance around, she shut off the engine and climbed out.

Standing in the dirt driveway beside the Jeep, she studied the property, turning a full circle. Except for the faint rustling of leaves and tall grasses, it was deathly quiet. The sky had darkened on her way up here but the rain had held off and the wind had lightened. She could hear the sounds of no man or animal. Not even a car passed by.

She turned back to the main building. At first glance, it seemed no one was home. The farmhouse wasn't boarded up, as the bartender had said, but the windows were dark and lifeless. The place looked abandoned.

She suddenly felt uneasy, like an intruder. She also had a distinct sense that someone was watching her, though who or from where, she could not tell.

Perhaps it was just her imagination getting the better of her.

Perhaps not.

Still, she was determined to check out the place, as long as she was here, so she crossed the driveway and walked up onto the small covered porch that fronted the main building. She pulled open a rusted screen door, which creaked ominously on old hinges, and knocked on the wooden door.

She waited.

Nothing.

She knocked again.

A wind freshened from the northwest, and the house creaked a little on its foundations. Somewhere a loose shutter flapped with muted thuds. She stepped back and studied the facade of the house from left to right and back again. No faces in the windows. No fluttering curtains. No interior lights snapping on to indicate someone might be inside.

She knocked on the door a final time, then stepped back again. There would be no response, she knew. If someone was here, he or she wasn't about to open up the door, let alone talk to her.

It appeared her first instinct was the correct one — the place was empty. The sickly woman who had once lived here was gone, and no other family members seemed to have laid claim to the place. She had a vague disturbing feeling that it was just being left to rot.

She stepped down off the porch and angled to her left, walking the dirt driveway along the length of the building, studying the main structure and add-on sections, glancing from window to window and door to door, until she reached the three-story barn.

There she stopped. The barn doors were shut tight, as were two tall, narrow windows in the second story. Candy glanced back and forth, just to make sure a final time she was alone, and then stepped forward to the dual doors, which appeared to slide in either direction on metal tracks. She reached out a hand and tentatively tested them, pushing on either side to see if it gave, and then on an impulse she grabbed a metal handle and attempted to slide open the right-side door.

It refused to budge.

She tried the other side. It gave just slightly, moving an inch or two, giving her a small space so she could peer inside. She stepped closer and put her left eye close to the gap, but mostly she saw only dusty darkness inside. The barn had a wooden floor and several open levels, with stout beams and numerous areas for storage. On the ground floor, bales of hay were stacked to one side, and an older red tractor was parked further back. There were workbenches with tools and scattered farm equipment. None of it looked like it had been touched in ages.

She slid the door shut again and stepped back. Nothing to see here.

She continued walking past the barn, following the curve of the looping driveway toward the garagelike building on the right. It had two bay doors that appeared to open upward, though both were closed. Each door had a series of small windows in it, so she headed toward the doors and, when closer, peered inside. An old riding lawn mower was parked in one bay, and in the other was an aged sedan that looked as if it hadn't moved in decades.

But then she noticed tire tracks left by the sedan, leading into and out of the garage.

So it *was* being driven by someone — and from the freshness of the tracks, it appeared it had been moved recently.

She stepped back from the garage, turning toward the house again, and the barn.

And finally to the outbuilding back among

the trees. It was separate from the rest of the buildings, set off by itself, a small single-story place, perhaps even a single room inside, with a wooden front door set to the right, two dark windows, and a stone chimney.

A cottage, she realized.

She saw the dirt path then, winding from the back of the garage to the cottage.

Her eyes strained.

Were those footprints on the path?

Was someone living there?

Should she go knock on the door?

For several moments she didn't move, rooted to the spot upon which she stood, uncertain.

Then she remembered why she'd come here. One person and a goat were dead. Two others had been seriously poisoned. The Pruitts were being extorted for two hundred thousand dollars. More people could potentially be harmed.

She took a deep breath, steeled herself, and started through the tall grasses alongside the garage toward the path and the cottage. But she'd taken only a few steps when she saw the front door of the cottage open and a thin, ragged man emerge.

He carried a shotgun, with the muzzle aimed down toward the ground. But from the look of him, he'd have no problem pointing it in her direction if he had to. He was heavily bearded, his hair long and gray and uncombed, with a lined face, weathered cheekbones, shadowed eyes — and the dark circle of a mole on his upper cheek just left of his nose.

With a jolt, Candy realized who he was.

The man previously known as Maurice Soufflé, owner of the Sweet Pickle Deli.

"Marcus Spruell," she said under her breath.

THIRTY-FOUR

"Don't come any closer," he said in a low, threatening tone, his voice sounding gravelly, as if he'd just eaten a bowl of pebbles. He brandished the shotgun a little to emphasize his point.

Candy stopped dead in her tracks and held up both hands in a gesture of surrender. "Don't worry, I won't," she said.

"Who are you and what are you doing here?"

"My name is Candy Holliday, and I just want to ask you some questions."

His lips ground together, as if he were thinking, possibly trying to remember if he'd met her before. "You're trespassing on my property," he said finally. "I could shoot you right where you stand and no one would find fault with me." His dark gaze focused hard on her. "They might not even find your body."

Candy stood frozen, unmoving, with her

hands still held up. "Please don't do that. I don't mean any harm." She paused, and decided to push her luck a little. "You're Marcus Spruell, aren't you? You used to own the Sweet Pickle Deli in Cape Willington?"

If her words meant anything to him, he didn't show it. His face remained impassive. "What of it?" he muttered after a few moments.

"Have you heard what's going on down there?"

He nodded, almost imperceptibly. "I've heard."

"Someone has died, eating pickles from jars with the Sweet Pickle Deli label on them, and two other people were poisoned."

He took a few moments to respond. "I don't know anything about that."

"So you didn't poison those pickles and put those jars out where people could find them?"

"Bah!" He spat out the word. Candy almost expected him to add *humbug*! "Now why would I do a stupid thing like that," he asked angrily, "especially with the name of my old deli on those jars?"

Good question, Candy thought. But she had a response. "You had a lot of enemies in town when you left. Some people think you wanted to get revenge."

"Revenge?" He said the word uneasily and made a face. "Fools. Jealous fools. Glad I left when I did."

Needing a moment to think, to try to figure out her next question, Candy turned to survey the house and barn before returning her gaze to the cottage. "How long have you lived out here?" she asked.

He brandished the shotgun again. "None of your damn business."

She pressed on. "You're out here alone, aren't you?" When she received no response, she asked, "When did your mother die?"

That seemed to visibly affect him. The muzzle of the shotgun aimed back down toward the ground at his feet. "Two years ago," he said softly.

"And you were taking care of her, weren't you?" Candy asked. "That's why you used to close down the deli and disappear for a day or two. She needed you."

He seemed to shrug, though she couldn't be sure. "I did what I could."

"Is that where you got your recipes? For the pickles and your other dishes? From your mother?"

Again, no response, other than a tight glare.

Candy finally lowered her hands, though

she didn't move otherwise. "Some people say you stole those recipes," she said, trying to make it sound as nonthreatening as possible.

Now he bristled and sneered at her. "Where'd you hear that? From *her*?"

"*Her?* You mean Wanda?"

"Who's Wanda?" he growled.

"I don't . . . who were you just referring to?"

"*Her!* That woman! Gloria!"

"Gloria?"

It was the same name the teenaged girl had said to her last night at the pizza parlor: *"There was one person who might have worked here back then, when the place was a deli,"* the girl had told her. *"I think her name was Gloria. . . ."*

Candy forged ahead. "So, this Gloria . . . she worked for you at the deli, didn't she?"

"Of course she did. And she was always a problem, from the very beginning," the ragged man said with obvious contempt. "Told me she wanted a cut of the profits. Wanted me to make her a co-owner. Imagine that! *I'm* the one who put up the money for that place, not her! I'm the one who built that business and made it a success, not her! She was just a hired hand, a contributor of sorts, yes, but . . ." His voice trailed off and his glare returned. "Like I said, it's none of your business, is it?"

"Someone has died," Candy said, "and others still might. Our town is being threatened. If you know something that could help us get to the bottom of this, you should tell us — tell the police, someone. . . ."

"No!" he said emphatically.

She chanced a step forward. "Mr. Spruell — Marcus — if you . . ."

"No," he said again, in a lower, more threatening tone. "I have nothing more to say to you, or to the police, or to anyone." He raised the muzzle of the shotgun. "Now get off my property before I stop being a nice guy."

Candy knew she had already pushed her luck as far as she dared. She nodded and turned, heading back to the Jeep, but then she paused and turned back toward him. "I'll leave my card," she said. "If you want to talk later, or think of something else you'd like to . . ."

But he cut her off. "Don't bother. Just get out."

The whole way back to her Jeep she could feel his eyes boring into her back — and perhaps the muzzle of that shotgun as well. It seemed to take a long time for her to walk across the dirt driveway, along the length of the house. She heard thunder somewhere far off to the west, and the crunch of the ground under her shoes as she took each step.

At the Jeep she went to the passenger-side door and opened it, chancing a look back as she did so. He was still standing there in front of the cottage, the shotgun still in his hand, though the muzzle was lowered toward the ground again.

She reached into her tote bag, dug around, and pulled out one of her business cards. She thought of walking it back to him, but immediately dismissed that idea.

Instead, she walked up onto the porch of the main house and pulled open the screen door just a tad. She slipped her card into the gap between the door and the frame, and then closed the screen door tightly, so it held the card securely.

It was the best she could do.

She took a final look back at Marcus Spruell — dark, angry, ragged, without a hint of civility on his bearded face — then returned to the Jeep, climbed inside, started the engine, and drove off.

THIRTY-FIVE

It looked like a mirage — a ghost that came out of nowhere.

At first it didn't register in her mind, which was preoccupied with other thoughts — of Marcus Spruell and jars of poisoned pickles, of labels old and new, of shadowy figures and dead goats, and even of Maggie, Herr Georg, and impending weddings.

So when she saw it, she had to blink several times, clearing her vision and her mind so both could focus on the baby blue pickup truck turning off the main drag onto a side road, glimpsed from the corner of her eye.

By that time she'd been driving all afternoon and into the evening — five hours on the road already — and the weather had worsened again. After clearing up earlier in the day, the low clouds had returned, and as she turned off Route 1, heading south on the Coastal Loop toward Cape Willington, a light rain began to fall, making visibility hazy. Feeling tired and hungry, she drove through the dusky twilight and gathering shadows in a bit of a daze, following a line of cars that stretched six vehicles ahead of her.

She was only a mile or two down the road when she spotted the baby blue pickup truck, which had been some distance in front of her. It slowed, red taillights flaring, and made a right turn onto a narrow side road. Initially, it didn't quite click in her mind, but when she drew near the side road and saw the truck's taillights receding into the distance, she realized what it was: the vehicle she'd encountered the night before, driven by the shadowy figure who had appeared to be following her.

She couldn't pass up the opportunity to follow it, so she checked her rearview mirror and pulled off to the side of the road, where she waited patiently for the traffic behind her to pass. She then made a quick U-turn and headed back the way she'd come.

She drove slowly until she spotted the side road the baby blue pickup truck had taken. She'd passed it numerous times before but never paid it much attention. A small, almost unreadable sign at the intersection identified it as West Shore Road.

In this section of Maine, numerous small, craggy-coast peninsulas jutted south into the cold waters of the North Atlantic. Cape Willington sat at the southern tip of one such peninsula. None were very long or very wide, maybe five to fifteen miles in length and about the same in width. Candy figured this small road cut across the northern end of the peninsula, probably skirting a large body of water known as Dandelion Pond before it reached the opposite coastline a few miles to the west. From there, the driver of the baby blue pickup truck could turn either north, following the western leg of the Coastal Loop back up to Route 1, or south along the coastline-hugging road before reaching the peninsula's southern tip, curving around, and coming into Cape Willington from the west.

There was a small harbor along that northwestern shore, Candy knew, and most of the homeowners in that area were lobstermen or fishermen or those who made a living off the sea in some way. A little further down was an old mill, and near that was a small nine-hole public golf course, called the Old Mill Course, which featured several holes along the ocean. But other than that, there wasn't much in this part of the peninsula.

As she followed the distant taillights of the baby blue pickup truck, staying a respectable distance behind, she passed small, isolated wood-frame houses, nothing fancy, usually with dirt or gravel driveways. Some had garages but many did not. She also spotted a few mobile homes here and there. Like many backwoods roads in Maine, this one was lightly traveled, carrying only local traffic. Tourists and visitors to the cape tended to stay on the eastern road into and out of Cape Willington.

It took only about ten minutes to drive straight across the northern section of the peninsula. Up ahead, Candy saw the baby blue pickup truck brake briefly at the intersection with the western coastal road before turning south and heading further down into an unpopulated area. As the road shadowed the coastline and the houses thinned out, the truck picked up speed, and Candy was tempted to goose the gas pedal to keep up. But the low rolling clouds coming from the west had squeezed out the last of the day's light, and an inky blackness settled over the wet road, lit only by the Jeep's weak headlight beams. Candy was patient and kept the distant taillights in view as much as possible, but at times they disappeared around curves in the road, only to reappear on the straightaways.

She passed what looked like the old mill and the golf course, both dark. With the limited visibility on such a curvy road, Candy eased off the gas pedal even more, which put her further behind the baby blue pickup truck, until eventually she lost sight of it completely.

She wasn't too worried, though, since she knew there weren't many places the pickup truck could go. In a few places side roads, or often just dirt lanes, led off the main western road, and she eyed those carefully as she passed by, in case the pickup truck had turned off onto one of them. But she saw no signs of that, so she continued straight ahead. She could always circle back later and search those roads more thoroughly, if needed. She also kept an eye on driveways and mailboxes, just to see if anything jumped out at her.

They were only a few miles outside of Cape Willington when the red taillights popped back into view, brighter than before. The truck was braking and making a turn to the right, toward the ocean. It was still some distance ahead but Candy realized she was familiar with this area and, for the first time, thought she might know where the pickup was headed — though she hoped she was wrong.

The road led to a few houses on a ridge of land overlooking the ocean. The first one in line, which Candy could almost see from the main road as she approached the turn-off, was a tan and stone single-level house with an attached garage, illuminated now by the pickup truck's headlights. There were several vehicles parked in the driveway, and the baby blue pickup truck pulled in beside them. A cord of wood was piled on one side of the driveway, and an American flag on a tall flagpole occupied a prominent spot in the front yard.

Candy slowed as she neared the turnoff and finally pulled off to the side of the road. She left the Jeep running but killed the headlights, just in time to see the lights of the pickup truck go out also. A moment later the driver emerged.

Candy could make out nothing specific about the person, due to the distance and the shadows. But whoever it was moved quickly, heading into the house.

She turned on the Jeep's headlights again and inched forward, toward a row of mailboxes just ahead. She angled the headlights so she could read the name on the side of the first box: WATKINS.

Candy's guess had been right, as much as she hated to admit it. The baby blue pickup truck, driven by the person who apparently had followed her the previous night — the shadowy figure, as she thought of it in her mind — had stopped at the oceanfront home of Trudy and Richard Watkins.

THIRTY-SIX

She killed the headlights again, turned off the engine, and sat for a while in the Jeep by the side of the road, waiting and watching, arms folded in front of her against the oncoming chill. Was this a quick stop by the driver of the pickup truck, just to say hello to Trudy and Richard? Was some sort of meeting taking place? Were they friends? Or did the driver actually live there?

As time stretched on, Candy began to sense it was the latter. The house looked buttoned up for the night. Exterior lights were extinguished, though a warm interior glow continued to show through the curtained windows. The pickup truck in the driveway didn't move, nor did any of the other vehicles. It appeared no one was going anywhere.

Candy waited a reasonable amount of time, then started the engine again and edged away before flicking the headlights back on and increasing speed. She continued south, following the narrow, winding coastal road, which would soon loop around the southern tip of the peninsula and take her eastward to Blueberry Acres and Cape Willington.

So what did it all mean?

She had a hard time believing that either Trudy or her husband had been the person who had followed her the previous night, and as far as she could recall, neither of them drove a baby blue pickup truck, since she'd never seen it around town before yesterday.

Trudy's nephew Brian Jr., who was helping them out in the store, *was* new in town, and Trudy said he was staying with them — here, in this house by the ocean, where the Watkinses had moved half a dozen years ago after selling a large farm property they'd owned inland. It was, Trudy had told Candy a few years ago, their dream retirement home, though neither of them planned to retire for a while.

The baby blue pickup, then, must belong to Brian Jr. But did that make him her alleged follower — the shadowy figure? The lean, blond-haired young man certainly fit the description of the person who had appeared to stalk her on the village's rainy streets the night before. She could imagine him in a baseball cap and black rain jacket, walking down the street in front of the pizza parlor.

But why would Brian Jr. have any interest in her?

For a few moments she was tempted to turn around, drive back to the Watkins place, knock on their front door, and start asking questions. But while she was still contemplating her next move, her cell phone buzzed. She slowed as she fished it out of her tote bag.

"Candy, it's Tristan," the voice at the other end said.

Her mood brightened immediately. "Tristan, hello! This is an unexpected call — and a pleasant surprise."

"Hope I'm not interrupting anything."

"No, not at all — just out for a . . . drive."

"Have you had dinner tonight?" he asked.

She had to think about that. "Honestly, I don't think I had *lunch*. In fact, I think the last time I had anything to eat was at breakfast with you at Pruitt Manor."

"You must be starving then. Interested in meeting me at the Lightkeeper's Inn in, say, twenty minutes?"

"I'm on my way. Hey, how'd everything go today?"

"I'll tell you over dinner."

As she keyed off the call and slid the phone into a pocket of her cardigan, she realized just how hungry she was, and stepped a little harder on the gas pedal. She toyed with the idea of stopping in at Blueberry Acres to change, since she'd pass close by it on the way into town. She'd been in her current clothes all day, though she'd dressed nicely enough that morning, in fairly new jeans and a pale green mock turtleneck top with her long tan sweater.

Although a little wrinkled and shapeless, given her travels that afternoon, her outfit would still be appropriate for the Lightkeeper's Inn, which wasn't an overly fancy place, so she decided to skip Blueberry Acres for now. She had another stop she wanted to make first.

She drove into town about ten minutes later and found a parking spot halfway along Ocean Avenue. It was close enough to the Lightkeeper's Inn, but upon climbing out of the Jeep, Candy headed in the other direction first, up the broad avenue to Main Street, then left at the corner and down to the end of the street, to the pizza parlor.

The place was still open, so she pushed through the door and approached the counter, hoping she wasn't too late. But it was a long shot, she knew, since it was nearly seven thirty.

"Hi, is Phil the manager around?" she inquired.

A minute later she was back outside. Phil had already gone home for the evening. She'd have to come back in the morning to talk to him.

Huddled under her umbrella, she followed the route she'd taken the night before, walking the short distance along the Coastal Loop toward the inn. Though the weather wasn't quite as rough as it had been the previous evening, she still felt a certain rawness in the air, and pulled her sweater tighter around her.

She found Tristan at a table near the dining room's stone fireplace, checking his phone, with a bottle of wine and two filled glasses waiting for the both of them.

"Hope you don't mind that I already ordered us something to drink," he said, looking up as she sat down across from him.

"I'm glad you did. It's been a long day," she said, and they clinked glasses before sipping the wine.

After exchanging pleasantries, Tristan told her of his meetings with the police and the town council. "They listened," he said, "but I'm not sure there's much they can do about it at this point. As you pointed out, that letter is evidence of a premeditated situation, but that's about all we can conclude from it right now — until something else turns up in the investigation."

"Now that you mention it," Candy said, "there have been a few new developments." And she told him of her discovery of Maurice Soufflé's real name, of her trip to see Georgia McFee in Cherryfield, and how Georgia had pointed her to the Spruell estate in Old Town.

When she'd finished, Tristan whistled softly. "Wow, you've had a busy day. Have you told the police about all this?"

"No, not yet, I haven't had a chance," Candy said, pulling out her phone, "but I guess there's no time like the present, right?"

She called the station and talked to the duty officer in charge, repeated everything she'd just told Tristan, and promised to stop by first thing in the morning to make an official statement and perhaps talk to Chief Durr.

"The chief's not going to be happy with me when he hears all this," Candy told Tristan as she keyed off the phone and laid it on the tabletop. "He's warned me repeatedly to stay out of these investigations. But I can't help myself. For some reason, I keep getting pulled into them."

"I'm sure he appreciates your help," Tristan said, "even though he'll never admit it to you."

They ordered, and talked about the events around town, including the paper's bicentennial issue. As their food arrived, they also discussed the current activities of the members of the Pruitt clan, and the situation out at Blueberry Acres.

"Because I'm so busy at the newspaper, I just don't have enough time to devote to the farm anymore," Candy lamented, "and it's becoming a problem. Dad's getting too old to do it all by himself. He needs my help, now more than ever."

"Could you hire someone to help out? A farm worker?" Tristan asked, genuinely interested.

"We could . . . if we had the money. We run on a very tight budget."

"So what are you going to do?"

Candy thought about the question for a moment as she savored a spoonful of lobster bisque. "I've been thinking about it a lot lately," she admitted, "and I'm toying with the idea of leaving the paper."

"Quitting?" Tristan asked, surprised.

"Moving on to something else," Candy clarified. "Freeing up some time. Getting back to the farm. Getting my hands dirty again."

"It's a big step."

"It sure is, especially when we really need the money I bring in from the paper. But if we can generate more revenue out at the farm, that will make up for it."

She told him then of some of the improvements she and her father had talked about making at the farm — expanding the blueberry fields, putting in a hoophouse, perhaps setting up a farm stand and starting a retail operation during the picking and harvest season. Later, they shared a tiramisu for dessert, and after a final few sips of wine, headed out to lobby.

"You're welcome to come by the house for a nightcap, if you'd like," Tristan offered.

But Candy demurred. "I think I'll just head home. It's been a long day, and I have a lot going on tomorrow. But I'll take a rain check, okay?"

"I'll hold you to that. This was fun. We should do it again real soon."

Saying their good-byes, she headed in one direction, out the long side hallway to the porch, while Tristan went out another door to the back parking lot.

Candy exited the building and had just stepped down from the porch onto the sidewalk when she sensed someone coming her way from the shadows up ahead. Momentarily spooked, thinking her follower from the previous night might have returned, she halted and backed up quickly onto the porch, stepping off to one side, hiding herself in the shadows there, hand clasped tightly to the wooden railing.

She waited as footsteps approached, and then a figure emerged from the gloom, walking hurriedly along the sidewalk toward the inn and quickly climbing the steps to the porch. The figure headed straight toward the side door from which Candy had just emerged.

Had the figure glanced over, she would have seen Candy standing off to the side. She didn't, obviously preoccupied with something, but Candy could see her well enough. She was dressed in dark colors, with a slick black raincoat over dark pants and black boots. She'd tucked her hair up under a black knit cap and wore black gloves. The only splash of color was an umbrella tucked under her arm. It displayed a tulip pattern in colors of pink, yellow, and purple.

Candy almost said something to the

woman — a brief greeting, a simple hello. But it all happened so fast she never had a chance.

Julia von Fleming crossed the porch in seconds and was gone, inside the building, before Candy had a chance to speak to her.

Thirty-Seven

Finn Woodbury called her just after nine o'clock the following morning. "You coming into the diner today?" he asked after a quick greeting.

Candy was up but not dressed. She could hear her father rattling around downstairs, and could smell coffee brewing. The rain had ended, and the weather outside her window looked promising, brighter and a little warmer than the past few days. But she hadn't been out to enjoy it yet, as she'd lounged a little longer in bed than usual, her mind working over everything she'd learned the previous day, and thinking about her dinner with Tristan Pruitt the previous evening.

"Don't think we have any plans to, Finn. Why?"

"Heard some surprising news out of the police department this morning. You might want to make a trip into town."

"What have you heard?"

"I'd prefer to tell you in person."

Candy hesitated. It was a Sunday morning, and she'd hoped to get a few things done around the house first before heading out for the day's events. But if Finn said he'd heard something, and he'd taken the time to give her a call, she knew it must be important. "We'll be there in twenty minutes."

"I'll hold a spot in the booth for you," he said, and ended the call.

She dressed quickly and headed downstairs to tell her father to put a hold on breakfast. "Finn's got something for us," she told him.

Doc didn't need too much convincing. "Sounds good. I was feeling like blueberry pancakes anyway, and it'll save me from cleaning up the dishes."

Ten minutes later, they were headed toward town in Candy's Jeep, saying little between them, each caught in their own thoughts.

Finn, Bumpy, and Artie were waiting for them in the corner booth at the diner. Whenever possible, they'd all contributed to her efforts to solve the murders that had plagued their small coastal village, especially Finn, given his background in police matters. Numerous times, Candy had attempted to get him to reveal his secret source inside the Cape Willington Police Department, but he'd remained as tight-lipped as ever. "It's not a secret source if everyone knows who it is," he'd told her more than once.

That morning he looked like he had an especially good tidbit for her, but when she found out what it was, she was more surprised than she ever expected to be.

A former big-city cop, now retired, Finn ran the annual local theater production and managed the village's Memorial Day festivities, among other tasks. Today his beard was neatly trimmed and he wore his trademark tweed jacket, patched at the elbows and fraying at the ends of the sleeves, over a white collared shirt. Sitting next to him, Bumpy was bighearted and big-chested, although he'd lost a few pounds over the past few years. He had a wide, ruddy face and an easy grin. Today he was dressed in a green polo shirt with a *Hemmings Motor News* logo on it, a sign of his passion for classic cars. The third member of the group, Artie, was a distinguished-looking gentleman with thin steel gray hair combed straight back and wire-rimmed glasses set on his bladelike nose. He sometimes grew out a well-groomed goatee but today he was clean shaven.

The three of them were talking to each other in low voices as Candy and Doc arrived and slid into open spots in the booth. Coffee arrived almost before they were seated, and they ordered quickly, knowing the menu by heart.

After Juanita the waitress had gone, Finn leaned forward, elbows on the tabletop, a strained expression on his face. "You're not going to believe this," he began in a voice so low Candy could barely hear him, "but there's been another death — apparently a murder."

"Another one?" Candy said, trying to process this information. "Here in Cape Willington?"

"But how can that be?" Doc added. "I didn't hear anything about it on the news this morning."

"That's because they're keeping it hushed up for now," Finn said, and to Candy he added, "No, not here in Cape. Out of town."

"A jar of poisoned pickles again?" she asked.

But Finn surprised her when he said, "No, not pickles this time. Something more common — a fatal gunshot wound. A shotgun, actually."

Candy felt a chill, and was going to ask

where the body was found, but it was her father who spoke up. "Finn, enough with the dramatics. Just tell us what's going on."

Finn nodded and sighed. "Okay, here's what we know: Sometime late last night, an anonymous call came into the CWPD. The caller, who apparently used a disguised voice and an untraceable number, told the police there had been a fatal shooting at a farmhouse up near Old Town."

"Old Town?" Candy's breath caught in her throat, making it hard for her to get the words out.

"That's right," Finn confirmed, not noticing her reaction. "So, after some hemming and hawing, the police down here contacted the police up there, who finally checked out the lead sometime around midnight. They indeed found a dead body at this property on the outskirts of town — a pretty nice place in its time, from what I've heard. It was reportedly abandoned a while ago but apparently some hermit-type guy was still living in one of the outbuildings. They called in the crime scene boys from Augusta, who arrived just before dawn, and they're conducting a full investigation."

"So what does this have to do with us?" Doc asked, his face screwed up in confusion.

"Because of who the victim was — this hermit who was living there," Finn said.

"And who exactly was he?"

The volume of Finn's voice fell a shade lower as he continued, and his words were harshly spoken. "Someone we all knew. Someone who used to live and work here in town. Apparently his real last name was Spool or Spruell or something like that, but all of us knew him by another name." He paused, then said, "It was Maurice Soufflé. And he's dead as a doornail."

THIRTY-EIGHT

"It seems this guy Maurice — though now we know that was not his real name, as most of us suspected — has been hiding out in Old Town," Finn continued. "It's his family's place, from what I've heard. They're still piecing together the details, but apparently Maurice's mother was in poor health, and when she passed away a few years back the place started going downhill."

"You mean Maurice Soufflé has been living that close to us this whole time?" Doc asked, still finding the story hard to believe.

"Yup, that's the skinny," Finn said. "But I'm not sure any of us would have recognized him even if we'd run into him while up there on a day trip. Initial reports said he had a beard and apparently looked pretty ragged, like a hermit — a completely different appearance. Not even the people who lived around him knew who he was, or that he was there at all. The police have been conducting some interviews with local people, but they haven't turned up much. No one really knew much about him. They're all as surprised by this as we are."

That caused quite a stir around the table, and Doc and the others quickly launched into a general buzzing, all of them speaking at once, trying to make sense of what they'd just learned, speculating on the reason for Maurice's death and who might be behind it.

Except for Candy, who said not a word. She sat with her hands folded in her lap, gazing out the window at Main Street, her mouth a thin line, lost in her own musings.

Marcus Spruell is dead, she thought. *Someone killed him just hours after I visited him.*

That could mean nothing, and it could mean *everything.*

Most importantly: Was there a connection between her visit and his death? Had someone followed her to his place and murdered him after she'd left?

Could it have been the person in the baby blue pickup truck — Brian Jr., the nephew of Trudy and Richard Watkins? Or someone else — someone she didn't know about yet?

The questions gave her shivers. And the implications were too serious for her even to consider, starting with her personal safety.

Could her own life be in danger now?

Another sobering thought came to her: She'd left her business card lodged in the screen door of the Spruell house. The police would know she'd been there. They'd probably consider her a prime suspect. And what would they think of her phone call to them last night, when she'd informed them of Maurice Soufflé's real name and his current location at the Spruell estate in Old Town?

She got the answer to that last question much sooner than she expected.

As she sat staring out the window, watching passersby with a thousand thoughts going through her head, a sudden silence fell across the corner booth. The buzzing of Doc and the boys ceased abruptly. She sensed their general uneasiness, and shifted her gaze back toward the table.

All their eyes were on a newcomer who was approaching the booth.

Candy turned to see who it was, and felt her stomach lurch.

It was Chief Darryl Durr of the Cape Willington Police Department — and he was looking right at her.

From the expression on his face, he didn't appear to be too happy.

"Well, this is an unexpected development," Doc said softly, so only those in the booth could hear. "Wonder what he's doing here."

"Somehow I don't think it's a social visit," Artie muttered ominously.

But Candy didn't pay attention to either of them. In fact, she barely heard what they'd said.

Her eyes were fixed on the chief's.

He came toward them, walking past the other booths and counter seats, and stopped right in front of her. His gaze went to the men sitting around the booth, turning his attention away from Candy for the moment as he tipped his hat. "Doc. Finn." He nodded to the others. "How's everyone doing today?"

"We're doing okay, Chief," Doc said, as amiably as possible. "How's everything going with you?"

"Good as can be expected, I suppose, given what's going on around town," Chief Durr said.

"Any developments in the poisoned pickle murder case?" Finn asked, fishing for information.

The chief nodded, almost imperceptibly. "Possibly. But nothing I can reveal at the moment."

"Well, if there's any way we can help out,

let us know," Bumpy said lightly, in an effort to ease the tension they all felt.

"As a matter of fact," the chief said, "that's why I'm here. One of you can help me out a lot." Now his gaze shifted back to Candy and locked on her. "Thought I might find you here this morning, Ms. Holliday. I wonder if you and I can have a word?"

Candy gulped. "A word? With me?"

"What's this all about?" Doc piped in.

"Well, for the moment, that's between me and your daughter, Doc." The chief took a step back and made a waving motion with his hand. "Shall we?" he said to Candy.

"Where are you taking her?" Doc asked a little defensively.

Chief Durr turned toward Doc with a tight smile. "We're just going to step outside for a few minutes so we can have a private chat." His gaze shifted back to Candy. "Aren't we, Ms. Holliday?"

"Umm, yes, Chief." She turned and laid a hand on top of her father's. "It's okay, Dad. Just a little business we have to discuss. I'll be right back. Keep the coffee warm for me."

"Holler if you need anything, pumpkin," he said, not totally convinced by her words.

"I will, but I'm sure the chief will take good care of me."

The chief's smile broadened. "You have my word."

He turned then, heading out of the diner. She followed, feeling like she was walking in a dream.

She knew, in her heart, what this was all about. But once they were outside, on the pavement off by themselves, where they could talk in relative privacy, the chief made the reason for his sudden appearance at the diner quite clear.

"I heard you called the station last night," he said without preamble.

"Yes, I did."

"And you were supposed to come by the station this morning and file a statement," he continued.

"I'm still planning on doing that."

"Good, the sooner the better." His smile looked incredibly strained. "Because I'm trying to figure out exactly what the hell's going on here."

For the moment, Candy decided to play innocent. "What do you mean?"

He looked perturbed by the question. "You know exactly what I mean. I'm talking about your whereabouts yesterday afternoon. You made a trip up to Old Town, didn't you, and stopped in to see this person —" he paused long enough to pull a small notebook out of a shirt pocket, which he referred to briefly before continuing, "— this Marcus Spruell fellow?"

Candy nodded, remaining calm. *At least one of us has to,* she thought. "Well, yes, I did stop by to talk to him, but I called the station last night to let you know —"

The chief cut her off. "We know you called, Ms. Holliday, but what we didn't know was that you visited his place yourself. Of course, we know that *now,* because you left your business card right there, at the scene of the crime, where it was found this morning. And according to this bartender fellow who contacted the local police up there, a woman matching your description stopped in at his bar yesterday afternoon and inquired about this Spruell character — said you were his friend and you were meeting him there."

Candy didn't say anything.

The chief took her silence for confirmation. "I suppose that was a fabrication of some sort, and I assume you were digging around for some information about the Spruell place, which the bartender said he provided to you." The chief's gaze focused in on her, hawklike. "Perhaps you'd care to elaborate."

Again, Candy remained silent for now,

344

uncertain of what to say. She didn't want to dig herself in any deeper.

So the chief took a different approach. "Why don't we start with something simple? We know you were at the Spruell place yesterday afternoon, but we don't know the specifics. So why don't we start there? What time did you arrive, and when did you leave?"

Candy decided there was no point in trying to hide anything. The best course was to be completely honest. So she cleared her throat and said, "I got there a little before five, and I wasn't there very long. Maybe ten or fifteen minutes. Just time for a quick conversation."

"So he was alive at that point?"

"Yes, and he was still alive when I left."

The chief accepted that bit of information before he continued, seeming a little less frustrated now that she was starting to answer his questions. "And what did you two talk about?"

"About the deli. About the poisoned pickles." She explained that Marcus Spruell and Maurice Soufflé were the same person.

"Yes, I got that. And what did he say about the pickle jars?"

"He seemed to indicate that he wasn't involved with them or with the murder of

Ned Winetrop."

"Did he give specifics?"

"No."

"What else?" the chief asked, prompting her.

"Well, we talked about his mother."

"And . . ."

"She died a few years back. He was taking care of her before she passed away, and I guess he just stayed on, living in that little cottage back among the trees."

"And what else?"

Candy hesitated a moment, but again, decided to hold nothing back. "He seemed to indicate he was being framed by someone named Gloria, who used to work for him at the deli years ago. She apparently stayed on for a while when the place became a pizza parlor, but I don't know much more than that." She paused. "I told him he should go to the police and tell them what he told me."

"But you waited until now, this morning, to tell *me* all this?"

Again, Candy didn't answer.

The chief gave her a stern look. "Ms. Holliday, let me be perfectly blunt. You could be in a heap of trouble here. Why, I could arrest you right now on suspicion of murder."

"Murder? Of Marcus Spruell? But I didn't

have anything to do with that, Chief," Candy said emphatically.

"That may or may not be true. But there's obviously evidence you were there at his place, possibly just an hour or two before the actual murder." He paused, tipped back his cap, and rubbed his forehead. "I've got people pressuring me on this one, Ms. Holliday — Candy. People higher up than me. I'm trying to run interference for you, but you've got to give me something to go on."

"Like what?"

"How did you find this Spruell character in the first place?"

She repeated and elaborated on the story she'd given to the duty officer the previous evening, telling the chief about the old files of Sapphire Vine's that she'd burned the previous year, and how Wanda Boyle had photocopied them before they'd been destroyed, and how Wanda had produced the file Sapphire had kept on Maurice Soufflé. She told him that, years ago, Sapphire had uncovered Maurice's true identity and details about his previous life as a small-time con artist. And she speculated that Sapphire had been blackmailing Maurice, which caused him to skip town and disappear.

The chief listened carefully, and when she was finished, he said, "I need to see that file."

She had expected that. "I don't have it. I'll have to get it from Wanda."

"Today," he said. "Bring it by the station as soon as you have it, and you can make a formal statement then. I need to know everything you've been up to."

"Okay, Chief, I'll be sure and do that."

"Good." He nodded. "I'll look for you. And let me be perfectly clear about one more thing: We have a murderer on the loose. This is a dangerous business. The last thing we need is another dead body, especially if it's the body of the local newspaper editor and blueberry farm owner. So no more amateur sleuthing. Whatever you do, try to stay out of trouble. And if you uncover anything else, you call me first. Got it?"

Candy was tempted to salute him but fought the urge. Instead, she said, quite contritely, "Got it, Chief."

THIRTY-NINE

All in all, she thought she'd gotten off fairly easily during her encounter with Chief Durr. It could have gone much worse, she reasoned. And he was probably right: He could have arrested her, given all the evidence that pointed to her involvement not only in the murder of Marcus Spruell, but of Ned Winetrop as well. She'd been at the scenes of both crimes. Her fingerprints were on the jar of pickles Ned had dipped into. She'd left her card at the Spruell place, right where it could easily be found, and she'd made inquiries about him in Old Town.

I'm definitely in a sweet pickle, she thought with morbid humor as she wandered back into the diner, *and I've got to find some way to get myself out of this.*

There was, of course, one simple way to resolve it: find out who was behind the murders — despite the chief's warning to stay out of it — and clear her own name.

But how to do that, without getting herself killed or thrown in jail?

As she reentered the diner, she was surprised to find all eyes on her. It made her feel self-conscious but there was nothing she could do about it, so she forced a smile and ignored the stares as she made her way back to the corner booth.

"So what was that all about?" her father asked as she resumed her seat.

"Just a friendly little chat with the chief of police," Candy said as lightly as possible.

"You in any trouble?"

"Not that I know of."

Her father gave her an inquisitive look. "Would you tell me if you were?"

"Believe me, Dad, if I really *was* in trouble with the police, you'd know about it."

"Did he say anything about the murder up in Old Town?" Finn asked.

"He mentioned it," Candy admitted, "but he didn't tell me anything new."

"Does he have a suspect?"

"If he does, he didn't tell me."

"He's not coming after *you,* is he?" Finn pressed.

Candy sighed and swept a few strands of hair away from her face before she answered. "Well, to be honest, I am sort of involved in this whole thing right up to my eyeballs."

Doc harrumphed at that, as if it was ridiculous to assume his daughter could be involved in murdering someone, and Artie said what they all were thinking. "Remember, no matter what happens, you always have our support," he told her. "Just say the word, and we'll mobilize this whole town on your behalf."

"Here, here!" Bumpy chimed in.

Candy was touched. "Thanks, you guys. That means a lot to me, and I just might take you up on it. But now, if you'll excuse me," she said, glancing at her watch, "I have a funeral to attend." To her father, she added, "Dad, if you need a ride back to the farm, just give me a call and I'll swing by and pick you up."

"Don't worry about me, pumpkin. I'll be fine."

She asked the waitress to pack up her food to go — just a buttered croissant and an assortment of fruit slices — and after saying her good-byes, made her way out of the diner before she had to dodge any more questions.

She knew they all meant well. She knew they all had her best interest at heart. And she hated holding back information from them. But she also knew that if she told them everything that was going on, she'd just cause them needless worry, especially her father.

She also knew she'd been in tight spots before, especially when she was trying to solve a local murder, and she'd always managed to figure a way out. She had every reason to believe she'd find a way out of this one as well. At the moment, she just didn't know how she was going to do it. But she had faith in herself and in her instincts. And she had at least the semblance of a plan of attack in mind.

As she walked along the sidewalk toward her Jeep, she realized she'd never contacted Wanda about the funeral, as she'd promised Sally Ann the day before, so she paused to send out a quick text message. In a second text, she added, *I told the chief about Sapphire's file on Maurice Souffle. He wants to see it. Could you drop it off at the station?* She then continued on, climbing into the Jeep and driving out on Gleason Street to Edgewood Drive.

Sally Ann had said to expect a big turnout, and she was right. Her front yard was like a grocery store parking lot on a Saturday morning, jammed with vehicles, as was the street leading out to her place. As Candy approached the end of Gleason Street, she also saw many neighbors walking in the direction of Sally Ann's.

"That goat must have had a pretty big fan club," Candy said with a shake of her head. "Who knew?" But it was a close-knit community, she thought, and they all supported each other in tough times, so perhaps it wasn't such an odd thing after all.

Sally Ann had put out quite a spread. She'd set up tables near the house with lemonade, fruit punch, and cookies available for those who were feeling a few hunger pangs. Out in the backyard, she'd set up an easel with an enlarged photo, draped in black, of Cleopatra herself in happier times. Groups of chairs had been arranged in various places around the yard, and Sally Ann had managed to find herself a small PA system with a microphone, which she'd set up back near the goat pen. A small group had already gathered around the microphone stand in anticipation of the event.

As for Guinevere, she was on a long tether, apparently to prevent her from wandering away or disrupting the proceedings, but she was surrounded by a number of well-wishers who kept her fed and contented.

Wanda Boyle must have known about the ceremony before Candy's text, because she had already arrived with her camera and notebook. Candy spotted a number of other people she recognized as well, including Melody Barnes from Melody's Cafe, Gus Gumm of Gumm's Hardware Store, Elvira Tremble and Cotton Colby of the Cape Willington Heritage Protection League, cabinetmaker Payne Webster and his fellow snowplow driver Pete Barkeley, local historian Julius Seabury, and shop owners Ralph Henry and Malcolm Stevens Randolph. Also hovering nearby were handyman Ray Hutchins, standing restlessly near some lilac bushes, and the reclusive Judicious F. P. Bosworth, rooted to a spot near the back of the crowd, clearly visible today as he curiously eyed the proceedings.

It's an impressive turnout, Candy thought as she surveyed the gathering. *Cleopatra would be pleased.*

Her gaze swept out toward the fringe of the crowd on the far side of the yard, scanning the faces, looking to see who else she might know. And there, standing all alone in the shadows of a small group of trees, wearing a baggy sweatshirt and a faded baseball cap, was a lean young man with shaggy blond hair. He appeared to be surveying the crowd himself, and looked noticeably surprised when his gaze shifted across the yard and he spotted Candy looking right back at him.

Realizing he'd been spotted, he took a few steps back under the trees, half hiding himself behind a thick trunk, hands jammed into the front pockets of his jeans.

Candy watched him for a few moments, debating her options. She quickly decided she should take advantage of this opportunity to finally confront her pursuer, in a relatively safe environment, to find out what was going on.

So without further hesitation, she made a beeline toward Brian Jr., nephew of Trudy and Richard Watkins, presumed shadowy figure and owner of a particularly suspicious baby blue pickup truck.

FORTY

Before Candy could reach him, however, a motor kicked into sputtering life somewhere nearby, and a puffy cloud of black smoke erupted into the air. The buzzing from those gathered in the yard rose an increment in pitch, and in its collective excitement, the crowd pressed forward and closed up around her, shifting her in a different direction and blocking the way, so Candy lost sight of her target.

Moments later, a small red farm tractor jerked forward from behind the lilac bushes. Heads craned and shorter observers stood on tiptoes to see that Ray Hutchins was driving it, and he was pulling a low flatbed cart upon which sat a large rectangular box. The box was made of good, new pine and looked as if it had been assembled just recently. It was slightly shorter than a typical casket but much wider, approaching four feet. Atop it sat a bushy green wreath.

Hand-painted on one side in pink letters were the words: *Our Beloved Cleopatra.*

As the tractor and its cargo inched across the yard, traveling a gentle arc along the outside rim of the crowd, the buzzing died away and a hush fell over those who had gathered to pay their last respects. Looking around, Candy noticed a few ladies dabbing at their eyes with handkerchiefs, and a few men as well.

Gentle music started playing then in the background — not much of a melody, but it was something a goat might have liked, Candy supposed.

"Sounds like a funeral dirge from the Middle Ages, doesn't it?" came a whisper from behind her.

Candy turned around. It was Maggie, appropriately attired in dark clothing, wearing sunglasses and a black ball cap.

"You made it!" Candy said happily, as she gave Maggie a quick hug.

"It was almost impossible to find a parking spot but I wouldn't have missed this for the world. Other than your cook-off on Friday, it's the highlight of the week."

"It's been a pretty eventful week," Candy pointed out.

"You're right," Maggie said, and quickly corrected herself. "Then it's the biggest event of the day, or maybe the hour, depending on what happens in the next twenty minutes. Because if there's an explosion or a car chase, all bets are off!"

Candy chuckled softly and was promptly shushed by several of those around her, who looked askance at her and Maggie. Holding a finger to her lips, Candy turned first toward her friend, who had sidled up beside her looking slightly abashed, and then back toward the proceedings at the front of the crowd.

Sally Ann Longfellow had finally made an appearance, emerging from a side door of her house. She was dressed basically the same way she dressed most days — nothing fancy, just faded loose-fitting dungarees and work boots, a flannel shirt with a fleece vest, and in the sole nod to the occasion, a wide-brimmed straw hat with a black band wrapped around the crown.

She came alone, with no one to accompany her. Apparently she'd decided to do the whole thing herself. She held in one hand a single sheet of paper.

"Cleopatra didn't have no specific religious denomination, nor any real religious affiliation that I know of," Sally Ann began once she'd reached the microphone, switched it on, and consulted her notes, "but she certainly deserves to go to goat heaven, if there is such a place. Now, I know she had her run-ins with a few of you. She did have a knack for slipping her bonds, that's for sure. I certainly admit she was a high-strung girl, and a hungry one at that. But she simply loved her freedom, she never meant to harm anyone, and she had a good heart."

Here Sally Ann tilted her head down and sniffled several times. She finally took a handkerchief from her back pocket and wiped her nose and eyes before continuing.

"She was born, of course, at the Mc-Quarry farm up by Dover-Foxcroft, where I got family, and she and Guinevere came to me in a trade when they were just kids. Cleopatra lived here in Cape Willington ever since, and I've always considered her a true member of this community."

Some supportive applause rippled through the crowd, and Candy even heard a few chime in, "Here, here!"

Sally Ann nodded appreciatively, sniffled again, and went on. "Thing is, she was here for only about nine years, just about half her life span. We'll never know why she was taken from us in the prime of her life, but she left her mark, and she'll always have a place in our hearts and memories."

She then proceeded into a litany of all the things Cleopatra loved, which included peanut butter, artichokes, chocolate-covered raisins, and wild berries. "She loved to play in snowdrifts and munch on icicles. Her favorite performer was Jim Carrey, and her favorite song was "Dancing Queen" by ABBA. She also loved Willie Nelson. Something about his voice appealed to her."

Sally Ann paused, took a moment to glance at her notes again, and then looked up to survey the crowd. "I'd like to thank the ladies of the Cape Willington Heritage Protection League for helping to set up today's event and bringing the refreshments, and to Ray Hutchins for helping me make the casket. The backhoe gets here in about ten minutes, at which time Cleopatra Long-fellow will be interred over by the lilac bushes she so dearly loved."

Sally Ann took one more glance down at her notes, then nodded and folded the paper in half. "So, anyway, that's all I have. I want to thank all of you for coming out today. Cleopatra would have been thrilled to see every one of you, I know that for a fact. What a wonderful turnout. It's very gratifying to see neighbors supporting neighbors."

That was it. She switched off the microphone as the crowd applauded again, the general buzzing of low conversation returned, and people began to step away, some heading toward the casket, while others made a beeline for the refreshments. Several women stepped forward to console Sally Ann in her moment of grief, including Elvira Tremble and Cotton Colby. Wanda Boyle was there, too, snapping a few photos with her digital camera and pulling a few quotes from those who had just witnessed the event.

"It was such a wonderful ceremony," Candy heard one woman tell Maggie, and others around them concurred.

"Very fitting for a goat," Maggie agreed, sounding a little caught up in the moment. "Very earthy. Unfortunately, no explosions, though."

"This thing's not over yet," Candy observed.

"True. I think I'm going to hang around for the backhoe. That sounds pretty exciting."

Candy laid a hand on her friend's arm. "You do that — and maybe grab us both a lemonade before they're gone."

"You read my mind. Where are you headed?" Maggie asked.

Candy pointed toward the stand of shade trees to the right of the lilac bushes on the far side of the yard. "I just spotted a young friend I need to talk to."

Maggie turned to look, squinting into the distance. "Anyone I know?"

"I don't think so, but stick around — we still might get that explosion."

They headed off in different directions then, Maggie toward the refreshments and Candy forward through the crowd. She walked at a measured pace, not hurrying but with a certain deliberateness, picking her way through the constantly shifting crowd, her gaze focused on her destination. Brian Jr. watched her approach and, when she was still some distance away, seemed to finally realize she was zeroing in on him. He retreated fully behind the trunk of the tree, and moments later she caught a glimpse of him retreating, heading back through the narrow stand of trees toward the road on the far side.

He had probably parked his truck over in that direction, she surmised; he was getting away.

She picked up the pace but the dispersing, meandering crowd still blocked her way. Finally she broke free into an open space and jogged toward the spot where she'd last seen Brian Jr., her eyes scanning the area ahead of her.

She soon reached the stand of trees and passed through, searching among the shadows for the young man in the sweatshirt and ball cap. She emerged on the far side, where a long line of cars was parked along Edgewood Road. Turning to her left, she followed the line of cars, still moving at a quick pace, searching for Brian Jr. and his baby blue pickup truck.

She finally spotted him up ahead. He'd just reached the truck and was climbing into the cab, although he stopped for a moment to glance back at her. She waved an arm. "Brian! Brian Jr.!" she called out to him. "Wait up! I need to talk to you."

He paused and seemed to consider that briefly before turning and sliding into the driver's seat. He pulled the door shut and started up the engine.

However, traffic was busy on the road as many of the cars, filled with mourners, were beginning to pull out of their parking spaces and drive away. Brian Jr. had to sit and wait for an opening, which gave Candy a chance to nearly catch up to him. But when she was just ten feet away, he found a break in the line of traffic and gunned the engine.

But he never managed to make his escape, for just then a man approached from the shrubbery on the left side of the road and stepped right in front of the truck, as if he were about to cross the road, causing Brian Jr. to quickly jam on the brakes. It took a moment but Candy recognized the man. It was Judicious F. P. Bosworth, who appeared to have purposely stepped out in front of the truck in order to delay him. Judicious raised both hands in an expression of surprise, doffed his black fedora at the driver, and mouthed a silent apology as he stood in front of the truck for several seconds, as if he couldn't decide which direction to go. He finally headed back the way he'd come, but his delaying tactic gave Candy a chance to catch up with the truck.

The driver's side window was rolled down, so she placed a hand on the lower window frame, as if she could physically restrain the truck from driving away. "Hi, Brian Jr. I wonder if I might talk to you a minute?"

He turned toward her, his face a little pale, looking embarrassed and somewhat nervous. His hands, with short chewed fingernails, tightly clutched the steering wheel. "I have to get going," he said.

Candy didn't budge, but she did flash him a reassuring smile. "This will take just a minute. You remember me, right? I'm Candy Holliday. We met at the general store yesterday? I know your aunt and uncle."

"Sure, I remember," he said with a slight nod of his head.

"Well, that's good." Her gaze swept across the truck's interior. "I couldn't help notice you drive a fairly unique vehicle. What year is it?"

It took him a moment to respond. "It's a sixty-seven Chevy," he said.

"It's a very distinctive color," she continued. "Tends to stand out in a crowd, you know what I mean?"

He nodded.

"I thought I saw a pickup truck just like this one Friday night on the Coastal Loop, over by the pizza parlor and the inn. This would have been around seven or so. You weren't out driving around at that time of night, were you? Just out of curiosity."

He shrugged. "I might have been."

"Because," Candy said, deciding to cut to the chase, "I had this strange feeling that someone who drives a baby blue pickup truck just like yours was following me around that night. I wonder why someone might want to do that, if someone was, you know, actually doing something like that."

"I don't know." His face was scrunched up, as if he hadn't fully understood her comment.

"Brian Jr., have you been following me?" she asked bluntly.

He looked contrite. "Maybe. But I was only doing what I was asked to do."

That caught Candy off guard. "Asked to? By whom?"

He ignored the question. Instead, he said, "There's something you should know. I'm not the only one. Someone else has been following you around."

That caught her off guard too. "Someone else?"

He nodded. "Someone who drives a white Volkswagen hatchback. I saw it around Cape Willington this weekend, and I saw it up in Old Town yesterday, before I lost it in traffic."

"You were in Old Town?"

Brian Jr. nodded. "Both of us were. I think the VW was shadowing you. That's why I followed it. Where it was headed after that, I don't know, because the driver must have spotted me in the rearview mirror, realized what was going on, and managed to give me the slip. Couldn't tell much about the driver, though. Kinda bulky. Wearing a dark knit cap. But there was something else I noticed, something important," he said earnestly.

"And what was that?"

"The car that was following you, the white VW hatchback? It had New Hampshire plates. Like I said, I just thought you should know."

And finally spotting an opening in the traffic, he gave her a quick nod, gunned the engine, and drove off.

FORTY-ONE

By the time Maggie caught up with Candy again, the backhoe had arrived. They wandered after it and, as they drank their lemonade, Candy brought Maggie up to speed on all the latest developments, including her encounter with Brian Jr., his admission that he'd been following her, and his revelation about a white Volvo with New Hampshire plates, which also apparently had been following her. As they talked, they watched the backhoe dig a deep, wide hole in a flat, open space just beyond the lilac bushes. Then they spotted the six or eight pallbearers who had gathered around the tractor and cart, and when the hole was ready, the pallbearers hoisted the pine casket up on their shoulders and laid Cleopatra Longfellow to a final rest with all the efficiency of a well-done farm operation.

"Oh, Cleopatra, we hardly knew ye!" Maggie memorialized, but Candy was a little less moved.

"We knew her just fine, and she died the way she lived — on the edge."

"She was just a carefree girl who loved her pickles. You really can't hold that against her."

"No, I suppose not. At least she had good taste. And, yes, we will miss her."

Before they left, they swung over to pay their respects to Sally Ann. Earlier there'd been a larger group surrounding her, but some had already stepped away. The two ladies from the Cape Willington Heritage Protection League remained, however, managing to look both smug and grief stricken at the same time. Cotton Colby was a little more businesslike in appearance, with a dark jacket over a dark blue blouse, while Elvira Tremble had opted for a black-and-white-patterned dress with a wide black belt, making an odd fashion statement.

First Candy, and then Maggie, stepped over to Sally Ann, gave the woman a hug, and said a few encouraging words. Sally Ann smiled appreciatively and thanked them both for coming. "What about the obituary?" she asked Candy, getting straight to the point that was on her mind.

"I'll make sure it gets into the next issue."

"Thank you," Sally Ann said sincerely, with a weak smile. "Cleopatra would like that. Her last hurrah, so to speak."

"She's had a good send-off, that's for sure."

For the most part Sally Ann seemed to be holding up fairly well, so Candy and Maggie said their good-byes and together walked back toward their cars. "Where are you headed this afternoon?" Candy asked her friend.

"I'll have lunch with Georg and then maybe stop by the library to hear Julia von Fleming give her talk this afternoon. You?"

"I'll meet you there," Candy said as she angled off in a different direction.

Hopping back into the Jeep, she turned toward town, and in a little more than five minutes she was back on Main Street. She parked at the lower end, down past the hardware store and bakery shop, and taking her tote bag with her, headed around to the pizza parlor on the corner, hoping to finally talk to the manager, Phil.

Since it was nearly noon, many of the tables were occupied, as customers munched on slices of pizza, salad, calzones, and Italian sandwiches. The smells brought a few quick hunger pangs, though Candy had just downed a glass of lemonade, but she pushed those aside as she made her way to the counter at the back of the restaurant.

"Hi, what can I get you today?" asked a bright-eyed teenaged girl, a different one than she'd encountered two days earlier.

"Actually, I'm looking for someone," Candy said. "I wonder if your manager is around? I think his name is Phil?"

Instinctively the girl turned and looked back over her shoulder, toward the kitchen. "I don't know if he's in yet," she said. "He sometimes comes in a little later on Sunday mornings." She turned back toward Candy. "But I'll go check for you."

A few minutes later she was back. "He's not here yet, but I texted him and he's on his way. He should be here in a few minutes if you want to wait around."

"Thanks," Candy said. "Can you let him know it's fairly urgent? You could say it's a matter of life and death."

"Sure. Would you like to order something while you wait?"

Although technically it was still morning, and although she still had the remnants of breakfast sitting on the Jeep's passenger seat, Candy opted for a small salad and a diet soda, then took a seat at a table by the front window to wait. People walked past on the sidewalk and cars zipped along the

Loop road. The weather was continuing to improve, and the sun was peeking out in places; with luck they'd hit the low seventies today, she thought. Beyond the road, she could see the great expanse of the ocean to the south, dark blue and relatively calm. She spotted the silhouette of a sailboat out on the horizon, and watched for a few minutes as it seemed to drift along slowly. She sipped at her drink, nibbled on the salad, and checked her watch.

The sailboat out on the horizon was making some progress, moving right to left, headed down east toward Jones-port and the Maritimes.

She drank and ate a little more.

It took nearly fifteen minutes, but finally the manager named Phil arrived. He'd apparently come in the back door, because she heard him talking to the staff in the kitchen, before he eventually made his way out to the dining floor.

After glancing at all the occupied tables, he walked over and stopped in front of hers. She'd seen him in here before, though she hadn't talked much with him, other than placing her orders at the counter and chitchatting a little. He was maybe in his mid-forties, with dark curly hair, a pale face, and heavy eyebrows. He was dressed casually in khaki pants and a yellow button-down shirt, and had tied a white apron around his waist.

"Hi, I'm Phil, the manager of this place," he said by way of greeting. "Someone said you were asking for me?"

Candy looked up at him. "Yes, hi, Phil. Thanks for stopping by to talk to me. I'm Candy Holliday, from the paper? I think we've met before. I'm actually looking for someone who might have worked here back when this place was the Sweet Pickle Deli. I believe she stayed on with you for a while as well? Her name was Gloria. Does that ring a bell?"

"It does, actually," Phil said, squinting his eyes just a bit and nodding. "Gloria was something of a legend around here, given the fact that she'd worked at that deli. We kept her on for a bit but, well, to be honest, I think she grew bored of this job. She'd been doing it for several years, going back to the deli days, and I think she wanted to branch out — maybe work at someplace a little fancier, or open her own restaurant, or something like that. She gave her notice one day and left shortly after. Haven't heard from her since."

"So you don't have any idea if she still lives around here?"

"If she does, I haven't heard, and I haven't run into her," Phil said.

"What did she look like?"

Phil put his hands on his hips and shook his head. "Shoot, I don't know. Average I guess. Brown hair, regular height, regular weight, maybe a few extra pounds. That sort of thing. Nice enough woman, though."

"Did she have any distinguishing characteristics? Anything that might make her stick out if I saw her?"

"Like what?"

"Well," Candy said, "like a birthmark? Or a tattoo?"

"I never noticed any of those things."

Candy thought a minute. "Did she have any unique speech patterns — maybe an accent or a phrase she liked to repeat over and over?"

Phil shook his head. "She was just a regular person. She was good at what she did, which was why we asked her to stay on. In fact, I wish she'd stayed around longer. She got along well with the customers. She helped out in the kitchen sometimes and seemed to know her stuff. She was good at coming up with recipes for dishes the customers liked. That's about all I can remember. It's been a few years, you know. Hard to remember back that far."

"Yes, I know, and I appreciate your time. Just one or two more questions, if you don't mind."

He waved a hand. "Shoot, I don't mind. Go ahead."

"Do you happen to remember her last name?"

Phil smiled, a little painfully. "You know, I was afraid you'd ask me that, but honestly I don't remember off the top of my head. I suppose I could check for you, though. I'm sure we have her record somewhere in the files." He seemed to indicate that it would take some time to dig it out, though.

"That would be helpful if you could do that, when you get a chance," Candy said. "And I have one final question. About how old would Gloria be now," Candy asked, "if you had to take a guess?"

"Oh, I don't know. Around my age? Forties, maybe?"

"Can you be more exact?"

"Forties or fifties?"

Hmm, nothing very specific, Candy thought. *It's just been too long. I guess this is a dead end.*

Out loud, she said, "Well, you've been very helpful, Phil. Thanks for speaking with me."

He paused. "Is this for an article or

something?" he asked.

"Something like that," Candy said as she rose. She dipped into her tote bag and pulled out a card, which she handed to him. Then she held out her hand, and they shook. "If you happen to think of anything else specific about Gloria, please let me know."

"Okay, will do, Candy," he said, and started toward the kitchen.

But after he'd taken a few steps he stopped and turned back. "You know, there is one thing I remember about her, now that I think of it," he said.

Candy had been in the process of hoisting her tote bag, and stopped mid-move. "And what would that be, Phil?"

A distant look came into his face, as if he was remembering something pleasant he hadn't thought about in a long time. "Well, she used to love tulips."

"Tulips? Like the plants? The flowers?"

"That's right," said Phil. "She sort of had a thing for them. Bought like earrings and key chains with tulip designs and notebooks with tulips on them — that sort of thing. She even had clothing with tulips on them. And she used to bring the plants into the store all the time and set them at the end of the counter. It was a real nice touch. The customers seemed to like it. Red was her favorite color but she liked the yellow and pink ones as well. So there you go. That's all I remember."

FORTY-TWO

Tulips, Candy thought as she left the pizza parlor, walking quickly with her eyes cast downward. Gloria liked tulips.

And, Candy realized as she turned the corner and headed back up Main Street, she'd seen tulips several times around Cape Willington over the past few days. She just had to remember when and where.

So where had she seen those tulips?

On Trudy Watkins, for one. When Candy stopped by the general store yesterday, Trudy had been wearing an apron with tulips on it.

But Trudy couldn't possibly be Gloria, could she? She didn't fit the profile. Their ages didn't match, for one thing. And Trudy had been in town for decades, so she couldn't have worked at the deli, since she'd been running the general store during that time.

So who else?

Candy could think of only one other person. Just last night, she'd spotted Julia von Fleming, dressed all in dark colors, except for an umbrella she'd been carrying tucked under her arm, with a colorful tulip pattern on it.

Now that Candy thought about it, she remembered that Julia had been wearing silver earrings with a tulip design at the cook-off contest on Friday. And a tulip-patterned neck scarf at the book signing yesterday.

Plus, Candy recalled, Julia was from New Hampshire, so her car would have New Hampshire plates. What kind of car did she drive? Candy wondered. She was sure she could find out easily enough.

According to Brian Jr., a white Volkswagen hatchback with New Hampshire plates had followed her to Old Town yesterday. But could she trust his account? Maybe he was trying to mislead her. After all, he admitted that he'd been following her over the past few days. Something strange he'd said stuck in her mind:

I was only doing what I was asked to do, he'd told her.

So someone had instructed him to follow her. But who? And why?

If he was *right,* however, that brought up

another question: Why would Julia have followed her?

Candy mulled that over. Could Julia have been trying to locate Maurice Soufflé, and followed Candy in the hopes of finding him?

Her mind was trying to connect all the dots, all the information she'd heard this weekend, and another thought struck her: Could Julia von Fleming actually have been the person who worked for Maurice Soufflé at the Sweet Pickle Deli years ago? In other words, could Gloria and Julia be the same person? They'd be about the same age, Candy thought. Their physical descriptions differed but Gloria could have altered her appearance to disguise herself as she morphed from Gloria to Julia von Fleming.

Finally, was there a link between Gloria and the person behind the poisoned pickles? In other words, could Julia have left out those jars herself?

Some of it made sense, Candy thought as her mind buzzed with the possibilities. But there was one prominent and mitigating fact that argued strongly for her innocence: Julia had almost eaten that poisoned pickle at the cook-off contest on Friday. If Candy hadn't intervened at the last moment, Julia would have wound up in the hospital, just like the others — or dead, like Ned. Why put herself in danger like that if she'd left the jar there in the first place?

Was it possible that Julia was responsible for Ned's death? Could she truly have followed Candy to Old Town yesterday and murdered Maurice Soufflé, aka Marcus Spruell?

Candy still had a hard time accepting it but, all in all, she thought, the evidence she'd just discovered pointed strongly in Julia's direction.

So . . . what to do about it?

Which direction to go first?

What was the proper way to handle this?

Candy was already halfway up Main Street and approaching Zeke's General Store, which was across the street on her left. Her gaze was drawn to it. Perhaps that would be a good place to start.

She didn't see the baby blue pickup truck parked out front, though it could be around back somewhere, if Brian Jr. had come here right after the funeral.

But when she pushed through the front door and scanned the place as she headed back past the shelves and aisles, she didn't see him anywhere in the store. She saw Trudy Watkins, though, behind the counter, in her usual spot. She was wearing a different apron today, one with teapots on it.

Fortunately, she wasn't dealing with any customers at the moment. She stood easily with her hands on the counter, so she was free to talk.

"Hello, Candy," Trudy said with a pleasant smile and an amiable nod. "It's so good to see you back so soon."

"Hello, Trudy," Candy replied as she approached the counter.

"We have some wonderful food samples out today." Trudy pointed to her left. "We're featuring our pickled zucchini. There are several slices on a tray right over there with some crackers, if you'd like to sample them."

"I might do that later. Actually, I just popped in briefly. I'm here on fairly important business, if you have time to answer a few quick questions."

Trudy's pleasant expression faltered. "About what?"

"Well, frankly, about the apron you were wearing yesterday."

"My apron?" Trudy had to think a moment. "Oh, you mean the one with the tulips on it? Yes, isn't that an attractive piece? I've had it for a few years. It's one of my favorites. I do tend to wear it a lot."

"Just out of curiosity," Candy said evenly, "can I ask where you got it?"

"Of course. Actually, it was a gift."

"From whom, if I may ask?"

At this question, Trudy hesitated, and a guarded look came to her eyes. "Well, it was from someone who used to live here in town. This was many years ago, of course. She used to come in here all the time, and we'd chat about various things. We discovered we had a lot in common, including a mutual love for tulips, so one day she brought me the apron as a gift. I've had it ever since."

"Do you happen to remember her name? The woman who gave it to you?" Candy asked.

Again, Trudy hesitated. For a moment Candy thought she was going to draw a blank, or simply refuse to answer, but finally, in a soft whisper, she said, "Her name was Gloria."

FORTY-THREE

"She was a very nice young woman," Trudy continued, her voice rising in volume. "Very smart, I could tell, and she had a wonderful sense of humor. We got along fairly well — until she left town a few years back."

"So you two were pretty good friends?" Candy prompted.

Trudy's mouth had formed a tight line, and she appeared to have grown more cautious in her answers. "We were acquaintances, yes, though I don't know if I would have called us friends."

"Would you recognize her if you saw her today?" Candy asked.

In response, Trudy turned away and walked along the counter toward the tray of food samples. "You really should try one of these pickled zucchinis," she said, changing the subject, and ate one herself, a small sliced sample. Beside the tray, a small placard, printed in neat block letters, described the dish. "I made them myself, using an old recipe from my grandmother. They're really quite good. I would have entered them in the contest — if I wasn't excluded from it, of course."

Candy followed her along the counter. Sensing that Trudy was holding something back, she pressed on with her line of questioning. "Gloria would probably be in her forties now, I think. Back when you knew her, she had brown hair and apparently carried a few extra pounds, but she could have changed her appearance. She might have slimmed down, dyed her hair a different color, changed her makeup, adopted a new accent, that sort of thing."

Trudy's eyes darted from side to side. "Well, I don't know."

"Her eye color would be the same, though," Candy continued, "and she'd have the same height and basic figure. Maybe she had some other distinguishing characteristics that you might recognize, since it sounds like the two of you spent some time together."

Trudy shook her head but said nothing.

"If there's anything you might know — anything you could tell me about her — it could be very important." Candy paused. "It could save someone's life."

"Well, it's just . . ." Trudy rapped nervously on the counter several times with her open palms. "The truth is, I really just don't know for sure."

"Know what?" Candy prompted.

Trudy took a long time to answer. "Well, it's possible I might have seen someone who looks like Gloria, and I might have thought it was her at first. But I'm sure I was mistaken. It was probably because of that apron with the tulips I'd been wearing. For some reason it got me to thinking about her, because she liked tulips too. My memory isn't what it used to be, you know. I mix people up all the time." She waved a hand in the air dismissively, as if that settled it.

"Where do you think you saw her? Has she been here in the store?"

Again, several moments of silence passed as Trudy's eyes shifted back and forth. Finally she shook her head. "I'd rather not say anything else right now. I don't want to make myself look like a fool."

"Was it Julia von Fleming?" Candy asked, hazarding a guess. "Since she apparently likes tulips too. Maybe that's why you thought she looked like Gloria?"

Trudy's face scrunched up, as if she was giving this some serious thought. "Yes, you know, that might be possible. In fact, I think that's exactly what happened. I must have seen Julia wearing something with tulips on it, and I just got confused."

"When was this?" Candy asked. "When did you see her?"

"Well, she was in here on Thursday night, during the canning demonstrations." Trudy's expression lightened. "You remember. Wanda mentioned it in her column, in the last issue. That was a wonderful event, you know. We should do that more often. We had a great turnout, and it was very educational. Wanda was here the whole time, taking photos and conducting interviews for a longer story. It should make an informative article for your paper."

"How long was Julia here?" Candy asked, steering the conversation back on course. "When did she arrive and leave?"

"Oh, she didn't stay long, as far as I remember. She was here for only a little while. Apparently she'd driven over from New Hampshire that afternoon and she was a little tired. I hadn't seen her around here before, but then someone told me who she was. It was very exciting to have a published author in the store! As I remember it now, she was wearing a sweater with tulips on it, and it must have triggered something in my brain. I guess I just came to the wrong conclusion."

"So you initially thought Julia looked like Gloria?"

"Well, yes, that might be what I thought at first," Trudy admitted, "but as I said, I'm certain I was wrong. And just to make sure, I went to the cook-off contest on Friday to double-check. I wanted to get a second look at her. I was going to talk to her then but she seemed very busy and, well, as I said, I just wasn't sure. And I didn't want to make a fool of myself."

She continued on, sounding almost breathless, as if everything she'd been holding inside over the past few days was tumbling out of her. "And then, after what happened at the cook-off contest — well, I was shocked! I got very worried. I began to think something strange was going on again. That's why I asked Brian Jr. to keep an eye on you. I knew you'd try to solve Ned's murder, and I knew you might get yourself into trouble, so I wanted to make sure you had a bodyguard nearby in case something happened to you."

"A bodyguard?" Candy said, surprised. "So *you're* the one who told him to follow me?"

"It was the least I could do," Trudy admitted. "He's such a good young man. He was only trying to help. And he knows karate. I was afraid . . . well, I guess I really don't know what I thought might happen to you. But I wanted to be ready in case something did."

"And this was prompted by the arrival of Julia? The fact that you thought Gloria and Julia might be the same person?" Candy clarified.

Trudy nodded, rubbing her hands together nervously.

"Did she give any indication that she recognized you?" Candy asked.

Trudy shook her head. "Oh no, nothing like that. I'm sure she doesn't know who I am."

Candy was silent for a few moments as she processed this information. Finally, she said, "Well, this is very helpful, Trudy. At least now I know who's been following me for the past few days."

"We just wanted to be there to help if you ran into trouble," Trudy said in Brian Jr.'s defense.

"I wish I'd known that. I have to tell you, I thought it was the poisoned pickle murderer coming after me."

"Oh, I'm so sorry!" Trudy said, genuinely contrite. "I told him to stay out of your way and not to bother you unless you needed his help, but I guess he took that part a little too seriously. I apologize if he disturbed you."

"I was just a little worried, that's all, since I didn't know what he was up to."

Trudy frowned. "Well, that wasn't our intention at all. As I told you yesterday, we villagers have to look out for each other, especially with all that's been happening over the past few years. I've talked about this with some of the other folks in town, and we all agreed you should have someone close by if trouble breaks out. That's why I asked Brian Jr. to keep an eye on you — because if something really *did* happen, and you really *did* need help at some point, I wanted to make sure at least one of us is there. And right now, Brian Jr. is that designated person — except when he's working, of course, like yesterday evening. He worked the late shift, since we stay open late on Saturdays."

So that's why he was absent when I ran into Marcus Spruell up in Old Town, she thought. He had to head back to the store to relieve his aunt, and left Old Town before the confrontation out at the Spruell estate developed. "Well, I appreciate your concern, and at least now I know what he was up to. But do me a favor. The next time he follows me, tell him to stay out of the shadows and show himself. That way, at least I'll know who's coming after me."

FORTY-FOUR

As she left the general store, Candy checked her watch. It was a little past twelve thirty. Julia von Fleming's talk at the Pruitt Public Library was scheduled for two o'clock. Still a little early to head over there, Candy thought.

And what would she do when she encountered Julia again? Ask her point-blank if she was actually a woman named Gloria? Accuse her of leaving out jars of tainted pickles and murdering people?

She could go to the police with this latest information, but there wasn't much she could prove — at least, not yet. Everything she'd learned so far was more or less hearsay. Brian Jr. had spotted a white VW hatchback with New Hampshire plates, sup-posedly following Candy up to Old Town. Julia was from New Hampshire. A woman who used to work at the Sweet Pickle Deli allegedly liked tulips. Julia liked tulips. Did that make her a murderer?

Candy decided she needed more information — hard evidence.

And the best way to get that was to go right to the source.

Waiting for a break in the traffic, she crossed Main Street and headed down Ocean Avenue. Her office was nearby, just down the block, but at the moment she paid it no attention. As she moved along the sidewalk she was facing the other direction, away from the buildings and toward the angled parking spaces that lined the avenue for its entire length. On certain days and at certain times of the year, all these spaces would be filled, but there were some empty spots today, since it was a Sunday, and many of the downtown businesses were closed. She scanned both sides of the street as she walked. Once she was about halfway down, she spotted the white VW hatchback, parked in a space on the right-hand side at the lower end of the avenue, near the inn.

Candy approached the vehicle cautiously, watching it out of the corner of her eye, until she determined there was no one inside. She slowed even more, studying it. New Hampshire plates. Brian Jr. had been right about that, at least. She left the sidewalk and walked around the vehicle quickly. An unfinished drink in one of the front cup holders. Maps and CD cases on the passenger seat. An old blazer, some boxes and brochures, an umbrella, and a long ice scraper in the backseat. The cover was pulled over the hatchback section in the rear, so she couldn't see what might be hidden in there.

Nothing to indicate the car belonged to Julia von Fleming. Lots of folks from New Hampshire, and all the New England states, visited Cape Willington often, sometimes for just a weekend jaunt. This car could belong to someone from Concord or Manchester or Nashua, over for a few days before the leaf peepers arrived and clogged up the hotels and restaurants. It didn't necessarily have to be Julia's vehicle.

Candy stepped back onto the sidewalk, her mind a jumble of thoughts.

Could Gloria and Julia von Fleming really be the same person? It certainly seemed possible. Gloria had disappeared several years ago, and the rise of Julia von Fleming had taken place at roughly the same time, maybe even a year or two later. Both were involved with the food industry in some way. Phil the manager had said Gloria was aiming for something higher in her career. Could she have written a popular regional cookbook and re-created herself as someone more glamorous?

It wouldn't be the first time something like that had happened, Candy thought.

But what about motivation? Again, Candy saw some possibilities that might make sense. On Friday night, she recalled, she'd run into Julia at the inn, and learned that Julia considered herself the primary target of the poisoned pickles — presumably left for her by Marcus Spruell, aka Maurice Soufflé, as retribution for a negative column she'd written about his place when it was still open, under the anonymous pen name Yankee Food Girl.

That at least established a basis for animosity between the two. Could it have escalated from there? Marcus Spruell, when she'd encountered him at the business end of a shotgun up in Old Town yesterday, said Gloria had wanted a cut of the deli's profits. He'd called her "a contributor of sorts" to the business, but what had he meant by that? A financial contributor? Or had she lent something else to the operation? Her recipes, for instance? In her file on Maurice Soufflé, Sapphire Vine had found evidence that, in his prior life as a low-level con artist, Maurice had been accused of stealing a number of things, including family recipes.

Sapphire had also discovered that the original pickle recipe Maurice used — the one that had made the deli so famous locally — was actually attributed to someone named Mabel Kaufman. Could that be a relative of Gloria's? Could Maurice have stolen her family's recipes and used them to enrich himself, cheating her out of a financial reward in the process?

It could certainly be motivation for murder.

But then there was the matter of Julia and the poisoned pickle — the one fact Candy couldn't ignore, since she'd been there and seen it happen with her own eyes.

At the cook-off, Julia had been aware of the existence of a jar from the Sweet Pickle Deli. She'd brought it up in conversation, in fact, anxious to try one of the pickles. When Candy had quizzed her about it later, Julia said she'd "heard whispers" and "people talking" about its existence. But she'd been overly vague about it, Candy thought. Could she have known about the pickle jar because she'd put it there herself? If so, why almost eat one? She'd almost had it in her mouth, and was about to bite down on it. If Candy hadn't batted it away at the last moment, Julia probably would have wound up in the hospital like the others —

or worse.

If she'd placed that jar there herself, why eat a pickle from it, if she knew it was poisoned? Why put herself in danger like that? She easily could have avoided eating it. But instead, she'd actually seemed *excited* about eating it.

That fact alone, Candy thought, could disqualify Julia as a suspect. Who would be so foolish to do such a thing? Surely it proved that Julia couldn't be the poisoner — or the murderer.

Could she?

Candy thought back over everything she knew about Julia, and realized she couldn't remember much. Julia lived in New Hampshire and was the author of a popular regional cookbook. Other than that, she knew little of Julia's background. Candy had contacted her first a few months ago, true, but Julia had offered to serve as a judge at the cook-off — although Candy had planned to discuss it with her anyway. Now that she thought of it, it was Julia who suggested they set up multiple events this weekend, though Candy had agreed readily with that idea as well. And it was Julia who had arranged and negotiated with the ladies of the Cape Willington Heritage Protection League for her appearance fees and travel expenses.

She had artfully maneuvered her way into town for the weekend. Had she done that on purpose — as a way to put herself on the scene so she could disrupt the weekend's events with jars of poisoned pickles? But again, Candy asked herself, why would she do such a thing? What could she hope to gain?

Then she remembered the extortion letter sent to the Pruitts.

Money, she thought. In the end, it must be about the money. Put out some jars of poisoned pickles. Make some threats in an anonymous letter. Collect the financial windfall.

Candy stood for the longest time on the sidewalk near the white VW hatchback, thinking.

Julia had a two o'clock event at the library to prepare for. Where might she be right now?

If the VW really *did* belong to Julia, and it was parked here in the street, then she must still be nearby, probably in her room at the Lightkeeper's Inn, getting ready for the library event.

Candy stood looking in the direction of the inn for the longest time, trying to figure out what she might say to Julia, and how she might handle this appropriately. She'd have to be extremely delicate in her questioning, and strive to make any accusations not sound like accusations. But the exact words she might use eluded her at the moment.

Still without much of a plan, and acting more on an impulse than anything else, she continued on down the avenue, vaguely hoping that Brian Jr. was somewhere behind her, lurking in the shadows and keeping an eye on her — just in case she needed backup.

FORTY-FIVE

As she reached the inn, climbed the steps to the wraparound porch, and entered through the side door, she still had no idea what she was going to say. She'd just have to make it up on the spot — not a very smart approach, but it was the only plan she had.

She walked down the long hallway and came to the lobby, where she paused, half-hidden behind a door frame at the end of the hall. She spotted Alby Alcott, the bearded assistant innkeeper, behind the front desk, dealing with some new arrivals. She thought of approaching him, but hesitated. She didn't know which room Julia was in, and wasn't sure if Alby would tell her, despite the fact that they'd known each other for years. He was a stickler when it came to the privacy of his guests, she recalled, and wouldn't release the information easily.

She could ask him to buzz Julia to let her

know she had a guest, but that would tip Candy's hand, and she didn't want Julia to know she was coming just yet. Some part of her told her it would be better to catch the other woman off guard. The first step, however, was simply to find out what room she was staying in.

Candy turned around and walked back the way she'd come, pulling out her phone as she went. At the other end of the hall, right before the door that exited to the porch, was a carpeted stairway leading up to the rooms on the second floor. Candy turned into the stairway, took a couple steps up, and paused there while she made a quick call to Elvira Tremble, who as a member of the Cape Willington Heritage Protection League had helped with the arrangements for Julia's stay.

"I need to talk to her about this afternoon's event, and I just wanted to stop in and see her real quick," Candy said. "Do you happen to remember what room she's in?"

"Room two fourteen," Elvira said without hesitation.

Candy thanked her, ended the call, and continued on up the stairs.

Two fourteen was about midway along a hallway that paralleled the one below. Once

Candy located the room, she walked past it several times, double-checking the number, running over in her head what she was going to say for a final time.

She checked her watch. Julia would probably be leaving for the event at the library fairly soon. If Candy was going to make her move, she had to do it now.

She stepped forward and knocked on the door.

She heard a rustling inside, and had to wait a few moments before Julia opened up. The cookbook author was dressed in a black bathrobe and her hair was fluffed up, as if she'd been in the process of combing it out when she heard the knock.

She seemed naturally surprised to see Candy. "Oh, why, hello!" She smiled weakly, and her wary eyes indicated she wasn't prepared to entertain a guest at the moment. "I thought you were one of the hotel staff. What an unexpected . . . visit."

Candy launched right into it. "Hi, Julia. I'm sorry to intrude," she said quickly, "especially since I know you're getting ready for your talk at the library this afternoon. But I wonder if I could come in for a minute? I just have something real quick I need to talk to you about."

"Does it concern the event at the library?"

Julia asked.

"Actually, it's . . . something else," Candy admitted. When Julia looked hesitant, she added, "I promise I won't take up too much of your time. It's very important."

Julia finally relented, stepping aside and opening the door wider. "Well, I think I can spare a few minutes. But I'm on a tight schedule, as you know. I'm loading up the car before I head to the library, and heading home right after the presentation, so I have to finish packing as well."

"I understand that," Candy said, moving quickly into the room. "I won't keep you long."

Julia motioned toward a chair. "Why don't you have a seat while I finish getting ready? I'll be right back." And with that she disappeared into the bathroom, shutting the door behind her.

Rather than sitting, Candy hovered, her gaze sweeping around the room. It was cozy yet plush, with a rose and cream color scheme, maroon carpeting, dark colonial furniture, a queen-sized four-poster bed, and a small sitting area with a love seat and easy chair. A window at the opposite end overlooked the back of the property, so Julia hadn't managed to snag an ocean-view room. But the accommodations looked comfortable enough, and certainly a pleasant place to spend the weekend while in town.

Candy had a fleeting thought to search the room while she had a chance. If Julia really was the person behind the poisoned pickles, she might have stashed a few jars here somewhere, maybe in the closet or in her luggage, where they'd be close at hand if she wanted to put any others out. That would certainly be the evidence Candy needed.

She took a few steps toward the bed. Julia had brought two suitcases with her. One suitcase, its lid closed, sat on a low folding stand nearby. Another was lying open on the bed.

Candy inched toward the one on the bed first, her heart beating a little too loudly for her own comfort. A quick scan told her there were no pickle jars inside. She moved next to the one on the folding stand, glancing around as she went to make sure Julia was still in the bathroom. In a quick movement, she lurched forward, raised the suitcase lid with a couple of fingers, and again scanned the contents. Typical clothes, blouses, scarves, underwear, and so forth.

No jars of poisoned pickles.

She lowered the lid and backed quickly

away, returning to her original spot near the door. The bathroom door was still shut. So far, so good.

Where else could Julia have hidden the jars if she had them? Under the bed? The mattress sat high, due to its colonial frame with a high headboard. Looking underneath wasn't much of a problem if she bent over a little. Nothing there.

Nearby, just inside the entry door, was a small closet for coats and wardrobe items. She took a few steps toward it, opened the closet door, and peeked inside. A few clothes hanging from a rack, some still in dry cleaning wrappers. An ironing board tucked into one corner, and an iron on a high wooden shelf. Three or four pairs of shoes, but nothing else on the floor. Nothing on the shelf.

Candy closed the door and stepped back just as the bathroom door swung open and Julia emerged. She'd tamed her hair and finished her makeup, and had changed into a black skirt and lavender-colored blouse, though she was still in her stocking feet. She padded over to the dresser, flipped open the lid of a black felt jewelry box, and started digging around inside. "So, what did you want to talk to me about?" she asked with her back toward Candy.

A scattering of thoughts ran through Candy's mind. What to say? *I think you're Gloria, the woman who used to work at the Sweet Pickle Deli, and . . .*

And then what?

Are you the person behind the poisoned pickle jars? Are you the extortionist who sent a letter to the Pruitts demanding two hundred thousand dollars . . . or else?

Did you murder two people and a goat?

Of course, none of those responses would work, so instead she said, "I just wanted to stop by and thank you again for coming this weekend, for serving as a judge at the cook-off contest, and for taking part in these other events this weekend."

Julia still had her back to Candy as she plucked several different earrings out of the jewelry box and, turning toward the mirror, held them up to her right ear one after another to see which one she liked the best.

Several of them, Candy noticed, had tulip designs.

"Oh, well, dear, it's been my pleasure. I've told you that, haven't I? You have such a wonderful little town here. I know I've been around for only a few days, but I already feel as if I've lived here for years. The villagers are such wonderful people, and have been so helpful during my stay."

"Hmm, yes, that's good to hear," Candy said, distracted by the earrings. "You know, that last pair you tried looked very nice."

Julia stopped and turned toward her. She indicated the earrings she was currently holding up alongside her cheek. "Which ones? These?"

"No." Candy pointed toward Julia's hand. "The other ones, the purple and silver ones, with the tulip design."

"Oh, those. Yes, they're among my favorites. And they go well with my outfit today, don't you think?"

"Yes, I do. I take it you like tulips?"

Julia waved a hand as she turned back to the mirror and started putting on the earrings Candy had chosen. "I guess you can tell, can't you? I have ever since I was a little girl, when my grandmother used to buy them for me every birthday. I was born in March, you know, which is when the daffodils and tulips arrive in New England. I have all kinds of items and accessories with tulips on them."

"Yes, I noticed the umbrella you've been carrying around, and that scarf you had on at the book signing yesterday."

"My, my, you have quite a memory." Julia's gaze flicked to her through their reflections in the mirror. "I do tend to favor them, that's true."

Candy went on, as if just talking blithely. "I noticed Trudy Watkins likes them too. I was over at the general store yesterday and she was wearing an apron with a tulip pattern on it. She says it's one of her favorites. It was given to her as a gift, years ago, by a woman she used to know, named Gloria. She liked tulips too. You don't happen to know a woman named Gloria, do you?"

The silence that followed was noticeable. Julia had not frozen — she calmly finished putting on the second earring, studying herself in the mirror over the dresser as she brushed a hand over her clothes, smoothing out any wrinkles. But her expression had visibly changed.

"Why would you think I know this Gloria person?" she said finally, her voice low but steady.

"Because you seem to have a lot in common. You both like tulips, for instance."

"You've been paying an awful lot of attention to tulips this weekend, haven't you?"

Candy shrugged innocently. "Strangely enough, I've seen them quite a lot over the past few days. I thought it was kind of interesting, really."

"Yes, it is. Perhaps we should start a local tulip-lovers' club."

"Perhaps. That's not a bad idea, you know. This other woman — Gloria — she would be about your age," Candy continued, "and just about your height. Someone said the two of you could have been mistaken for each other."

"Is that right?" Julia said.

"It's just what I've heard."

"It isn't that unusual, you know. I've been mistaken for other people before. It happens."

"That's true," Candy said. "It's probably just a coincidence."

"Well, I hope I get to meet this Gloria person someday. She sounds . . . intriguing. Now, if you'll excuse me, I really must . . ."

"Can I ask you what kind of car you drive?" Candy cut in, knowing her time was running out.

"My car? But — ?"

"Because a friend of mine saw a white Volkswagen hatchback yesterday up in Old Town. It had New Hampshire plates, so I thought it might have been you."

Another stretch of silence. Finally, somewhat huffily, Julia said, "Have you been *spying* on me?"

Candy took that as a positive response to her question. "So it *was* your car then?"

"I went to see a friend who lives around

there but —" Julia stopped again. With dark eyes flashing and arms crossed, she finally let down her guard. "I'm not quite sure what you're getting at, or what you think I might have done," she said, her mouth twisting a little as she tried to muster a smile, "but whatever it is, I assure you I wasn't involved. And even if I was, there's not much you can do about it. Let's say, for the moment, that I did go to Old Town yesterday, to see an old friend. Let's say I do resemble this person you mentioned — Gloria — with the suggestion, I suppose, that we're the same person, as ludicrous as that sounds. Let's say I'm the one who gave Trudy Watkins that apron, and let's say I used to work at the deli and somehow miraculously reinvented my life, wrote a cookbook, and conspired to come here to Cape Willington so I could poison a number of your villagers with tainted pickles. Let's say I'm even responsible for the death of that goat they buried this morning. Let's say that's all true."

Her gaze tightened. "Do you know what I'd say to that?"

Candy hesitated, but finally asked, "What?"

"I'd say, *'Prove it.'*"

FORTY-SIX

"You can stand here all day and ask questions and make accusations," Julia continued, her voice taking on a harder edge. "But you'd better have a darn good reason for doing so. I came here at *your* request, I don't mind reminding you. I'm doing this as a *favor* to you and the townspeople. I don't need to have *wild* and *unfounded* rumors about me spreading around town and ruining my reputation, which I've worked very hard to establish over the past few years. So unless you have something solid — something you can take to the bank, or to the police — you'd better not waste any more of my time. In fact, I think you should leave."

To emphasize her point, Julia shifted and started toward the door. But she stopped halfway and turned back to Candy. "By the way, if you recall, I almost ate one of those poisoned pickles. I could have died, you know. I didn't say this at the time, but something like that should have never happened. Obviously it speaks to the way your event was run. If I wasn't such a kindhearted person, I would sue you and the paper over what happened."

Her gaze narrowed. "Oh, and there's one more thing. If you talk to the police, I'll tell them I saw *you* put that jar out on the table Friday, but I held the information back because I wanted to protect you. *You* were the one who handed *me* that pickle to eat and almost poisoned me. *You* were up at Maurice's place in Old Town yesterday. *You* could easily have killed him. You're more of a suspect right now than I am, so who do you think they're going to believe if we start telling stories about each other?"

She took a few more steps toward the door and turned back once more. This time her smile was almost genuine. "But I'll tell you what: I'm not going to do any of those things — unless, of course, I'm forced to. Instead, as a favor to you, I'll pretend none of this happened. We'll just put this conversation behind us, so we can get through this afternoon's event peacefully, and then I'll be on my merry way."

She walked the rest of the way to the door and pulled it open.

There wasn't much more Candy could say. Julia was right. Candy admitted it.

She had nothing concrete — no solid evidence. There was no way to tie Julia directly to some of the incidents that had occurred around town that weekend, nothing she could prove, no accusations she could make that would withstand scrutiny by the police or the courts.

At least, not yet.

"Sorry to disturb you," Candy said. "I'll see you at the library."

She barely remembered the next few minutes. She assumed that she'd left the inn and walked down off the porch and up along the sidewalk to her office, but she didn't remember anything about the journey. Her mind was too occupied with other thoughts, running over and over in her head the conversation with Julia.

She finally looked up and didn't remember where she was for a moment. Then she saw the opera house across the street, and Town Park down toward the ocean, and familiar shops and restaurants, and remembered she was on Ocean Avenue in Cape Willington.

She stopped and looked back down the street, toward the inn.

"I think I just uncovered a murderer," she said with a shake of her head, "and I have no idea what to do about it."

Her office was nearby. She needed a few minutes to settle and think this through. It seemed as good a place as any.

It also would give her a chance to verify at least one fact.

Once up in her office, she walked to the window and looked out at Ocean Avenue. From her vantage point on the second floor, she could see both sides of the street, and for a good distance in either direction, left and right. She could also just barely see, far down to her right, the hood of the white Volkswagen hatchback. She could wait. She had some time. If Julia was going to the library to give her talk, she'd have to leave soon, and she'd have to drive.

Candy could at least verify the owner of the VW. She'd just wait here until she could visually do that.

But ten minutes later she was interrupted. She heard someone opening and closing the front office door, and footsteps coming down the hallway toward her office. Moments later, Wanda Boyle poked her head in through Candy's open door. "Hey, what the heck are you doing here?" she asked.

"I'm working," Candy said, never taking her eyes off the white Volkswagen. "And what are *you* doing here?"

Wanda held up a familiar manila folder. "Making a copy so I can drop it off at the station, just like you asked. So, are you working on the paper or on the case?"

Candy admitted it was the latter.

Wanda took a few steps into the office. "You uncover any more clues?"

Candy said that she had.

"You close to solving it?"

"I might have already — that's what I'm trying to figure out."

"So what are you looking at?"

"I'm waiting for someone."

"Who?"

When Candy didn't answer, Wanda said, "It wouldn't be Julia von Fleming, would it?"

Candy's head snapped away from the window. "Why would you say that?"

"Because," Wanda said with a fiendish little grin, "I talked to Brian Watkins Jr. just a little while ago. I saw you chasing after him at the funeral and wondered what that was all about. So I did a little digging of my own, asked him a few questions. He told me everything."

"He doesn't know everything," Candy said, sounding a little defensive.

"He might not, but it's enough for me to guess what's going on. Let me see if I got this straight: Brian Jr. was shadowing you because his aunt asked him to keep an eye on you, in case you needed his help in some way. So yesterday he notices you're being followed by another car, this one with New Hampshire plates. Of course, Julia von Fleming is from New Hampshire. So put two and two together, and what does that mean?" She paused before she offered the answer herself. "*I* think *you* think Julia followed you yesterday up to Old Town and murdered this Spruell character — same guy who used to own the deli, right?"

Candy had to admit she was impressed with Wanda's grasp of the situation. "Something like that, yes. But there's nothing I can prove. I haven't found any evidence yet to tie her directly to any of the crimes. I need hard evidence, and I don't know how to get that."

Wanda considered that for a moment before she said, "Have you thought of setting a trap?"

"A what?"

"A trap. You know, like in the movies. You create a situation in which you fool your mark — in this case, that would be Julia — into thinking that something's happened that hasn't really happened. That way you confuse her and get her to reveal whatever it is she doesn't want you to know about." Wanda grinned. "See? Simple."

Candy thought about it a minute as she turned her gaze back to the street — just in time to see Julia von Fleming come up the sidewalk with her bags and stop when she reached the white Volkswagen hatchback. She pulled out a key fob and pressed it, unlocking the doors and hatchback. She first walked behind the car, lifted the hatchback, and moved a few boxes around inside, opening them and checking them, as if she was looking for something.

Unfortunately, from where Candy stood, she couldn't see what was inside the boxes. "That's where it must be," she said to herself as Julia closed the hatchback, put her bags in the backseat, and climbed into the driver's seat. She started the engine, and Candy watched in silence as Julia backed out of the parking spot and did a hard U-turn right in the middle of the avenue. She gunned the engine and headed up the street, toward the library.

Just then Candy's phone buzzed in her back pocket. She pulled it out and read the display. It was a local number. She slid her finger along the display, answering the call. "Hello?"

"Candy Holliday?"

"Yes?"

"Hi, this is Phil over at the pizza parlor?"

"Yes, hi Phil. What can I help you with?"

"Well, you asked me to check on Gloria's last name?"

"Oh, yes, that's right! Did you find anything?"

"Sure did. Her last name was Kaufman."

Candy turned to look back at Wanda. To Phil, she said, "Is that right? Are you sure?"

"It's all over her file," he confirmed.

"Well, thanks very much. I appreciate the call."

"Anytime. Glad to help."

"Who was that?" Wanda asked after the call had ended.

"Phil, over at the pizza parlor."

"What did he want?"

"He told me some very interesting news." Candy looked at Wanda with a thoughtful expression on her face. "So this trap you mentioned. You think we could pull something like that off?"

Wanda shrugged. "Piece of cake. Everyone in town is behind you on this thing. We'll call in the cavalry, get everyone to pitch in. Believe me, Julia von Fleming is no match for this group of villagers."

She just may be right, Candy thought hopefully. "But what exactly would we do?

What kind of trap would we set for her?"

They talked about it, and ten minutes later had a plan. After that, they both started making phone calls.

Forty-Seven

The original section of the Pruitt Public Library, located on the corner of School Street and River Road just a block north of downtown, opened its doors in 1891. Built in the same Colonial Revival style as the larger Pruitt Opera House on Ocean Avenue, it also shared a common benefactor — Horace Roberts Pruitt, who was responsible for a number of other buildings around town, including Pruitt Manor. Over the years, several wings had been added to the library to extend its offerings and services, but it remained one of the village's most distinctive buildings architecturally, with four white columns out front, a symmetrical facade, tall vertical windows with black shutters, dormer windows peeking out from the roofline, and a stately redbrick exterior.

Maggie Tremont knew the place well. She'd practically raised her daughter

Amanda there, as they'd attended weekly events while Amanda was growing up, and at one point Maggie had volunteered to help shelve books one night a week. Since she was also an avid reader, she was always stopping by to check out the latest bestsellers and discover new writers.

She had a favorite parking spot, off to the left of the library's entrance, but this afternoon the lot next to the building was full, so she was forced to park halfway up School Street and walk back. She checked her watch. She just hoped she wasn't late.

This was all happening so fast, and she wasn't completely sure she was ready for what she was about to do. The call had come from Candy just a little while ago, asking her for a favor. A *big* favor. Of course, Maggie had agreed instantly, but now that the time was growing close, she just hoped she could pull it off. She breathed deeply as she quickened her pace. They had one opportunity to get this right, and if she failed to be convincing, she could jeopardize the whole operation.

Still, despite the challenges ahead, she practically buzzed with anticipation, thinking of how she would act when the time came. She knew she had to be as natural as possible, so she decided it would probably be best just to let her instincts take over and avoid overacting or staging the scene too much.

As she hurried in through the library's front door, she just hoped everything was in place.

After waving hello to a few of the staff members behind the checkout counter on the main floor, she headed downstairs to a large meeting room in the library's basement, where events like author presentations, youth programs, and the semiannual book sale were held. Folding chairs had been set up in the center of the room, facing a low stage at the right side. Several nicer, plusher chairs sat empty on the stage, and a lectern and microphone had been set up as well. Against the wall on the opposite side of the room, a table covered with a white cloth held refreshments like coffee, tea, and baked items, provided by the Friends of the Library.

The place was buzzing. Many of the attendees had already found their seats, and the room was rapidly filling up. Maggie felt a sudden jolt of stage fright. She was going to have an audience! There were almost a hundred people here! She was about to give the performance of a lifetime, and everyone in town was going to know about it.

Depending on how well she did, she was either going to greatly improve or totally destroy her reputation in a matter of minutes.

That made her smile, for she wasn't sure she had much of a reputation to improve or destroy. But it made no matter — they had a murderer to catch, and she was willing to do her part to help with the effort.

As she entered the room she kept a low profile, waving to a few people she knew as she scanned the place to see who was there. She spotted Artie Groves off to one side and gave him a nod. Candy was nearby. Sally Ann was in her spot, holding a big black handbag. Maggie assumed Wanda was in her place as well.

She moved to her left, circled around the chairs, and found a quiet space along the wall close to the refreshment table. Checking her watch one last time, she folded her hands in front of her and waited.

It didn't take long.

After a few more minutes, a side door opened and several ladies and a gentleman stepped into the room. Maggie recognized the library director, Karla Kincaid, as well as assistant director Daniel Brewster and children's librarian Sharon Littlefield. Julia von Fleming was the last one through the door and the last to take the stage. Looking much like the popular author she was, she settled herself into one of the chairs, chatting with the staff members and waving to those she knew in the audience.

The place continued to buzz until Karla Kincaid stepped up to the microphone, switched it on, and began her comments.

"Hello, everyone. It's so good to see all of you here today. What a fantastic turnout! As you probably know, we have a wonderful program for you this afternoon. I hope you have your taste buds sharpened, because we're going to learn about all the wonderful traditional recipes from right here in the New England region. Our guest today is Julia von Fleming, author of *Homestyle New England Cooking,* and it's our honor and privilege to welcome her to the Pruitt Public Library!"

She led the applause as she turned to look back at Julia, then continued on, filling in some of Julia's background and discussing the popularity of her latest cookbook.

Maggie listened with only one ear, as part of her attention was turned toward the refreshment table on her left. She'd noticed Sally Ann inching toward it earlier from the other side, with careful glances in all directions. The two exchanged looks, and Sally

Ann gave her a subtle nod. Maggie nodded back, equally subtle.

"And now," Karla said into the microphone, her remarks concluded, "would you all please give a warm Cape Willington welcome to Ms. Julia von Fleming!"

Applause erupted again from the audience as Karla stepped aside. Julia rose from her chair with a broad smile and approached the mic. The two women shook hands, and Julia stepped up to the lectern while Karla returned to her seat.

"I cannot tell you," Julia began as the applause died away, "what a wonderful time I've had here in your village this weekend. I've met the warmest and friendliest people, and it's been a real treat for me to spend the weekend with all of you. Of course, this is also a beautiful time of the year to visit Maine, with the changes in color and brisk temperatures in the air. Much of the traditional New England diet, of course, changed with the seasons, so in my book, I break the recipes out in a seasonal fashion. For the winter, I've focused on soups, stews, and heartier fare, while the summer and fall recipes rely heavily on local produce like blueberries, strawberries, cranberries, squash, corn, pumpkins, and the like. Of course, I also devote a good portion of the book to seafood recipes, since the New England diet has always been tied to the ocean. A few years ago, I found this quite amazing recipe for authentic New England lobster rolls, which I got from a woman who used to manage a lighthouse with her husband. . . ."

Maggie caught a sudden movement out of the corner of her eye, and when she looked over, there it was. A jar of pickles from Sweet Pickle Deli had mysteriously materialized out of nowhere — although Maggie knew it had previously been sitting deep inside Sally Ann's handbag. The jar sat all by itself at one side of the refreshment table. Sally Ann was now moving away in the other direction, her handbag looking just a little lighter.

Maggie knew she had to move quickly, before anyone else spotted the jar.

"Oh, look!" she said in a voice loud enough to be heard by a few women around her. "Refreshments!"

As Julia continued on, talking about recipes for fish chowder, red beet eggs, cranberry applesauce, Boston baked beans, and oyster stuffing, Maggie wandered innocently over to the table, taking a look at all the items on display. On an impulse, she reached for the jar of pickles. "These look interesting," she said to no one in particular. "I've heard they're great."

Before anyone could intervene, she unscrewed the lid. The pickles inside were spears, not whole pickles like they'd been at the cook-off contest, and had a slight chill to them.

"Oh, scrumptious!" She plucked out one of the spears and bit into it. It had an average taste, and wasn't as crisp as she usually preferred, but it wasn't terrible. She ate it quickly and reached for another.

Several of the women nearby were watching her nervously now. Maggie smiled at them as she turned back toward the stage, still holding the pickle jar in one hand as she ate a spear with another.

"Of course," Julia von Fleming was saying, "you can't talk about New England cooking without mentioning pies! The cooks of New England make some of the best pies in the world, I can assure you of that! And no wonder, with all the local ingredients we have to choose from. In my cookbook, there's a wonderful recipe for wild blueberry pie that I learned from a woman who lives in Conway, New Hampshire. She got it from her grandmother, so you know it's authentic. The secret to the recipe is . . ."

Maggie was on her fourth pickle, and she was beginning to feel full, and even a little queasy. *I should eat another one or two,* she thought, but she couldn't, so with a slightly shaky hand, she set the jar back down on the table, clutched at her stomach, and belched. "I think I ate too much," she said, and groaned noticeably.

The ladies standing nearby looked at her with concern, and one of them came over and helped her into a chair. Maggie bent over at the waist as she sat, holding up a hand. "I'll be all right in a minute," she said. "I just ate too fast."

She groaned a little more and held a hand to her forehead. "Those pickles weren't what I thought," she said. "I'm not sure they were . . . good."

She threw back her head and rolled her eyes in their sockets. Her whole body seemed to shudder for a few moments. She let out an uncomfortable moan that now had some of the ladies visibly worried.

"She ate some of those pickles," one of them whispered, and another asked, "Should we call a doctor?"

Again Maggie held up a hand. "No, no, I'll be fine, I just need to . . ."

But she never finished. She shuddered several times before her whole body went limp, her eyes closed, and she slid from the chair to the tile floor with a dramatic *thump!*

FORTY-EIGHT

Julia von Fleming glanced down at her notes, though she knew the entire spiel by heart. She'd practiced it enough times over the past few years, honing it and getting it just right. She was dedicated to her new profession. She'd worked hard to get where she was. And so far the presentation was going fairly well. But she was ready for it to be over. She wanted to be done with this place. She was ready to leave it behind forever. Whatever had happened to her here, she felt it had been dealt with. The primary object of her wrath was gone. Residual damage had been done, beyond what she'd initially expected, for better or worse. She'd heard from the Pruitts through back channels. It appeared her scheme was going to work.

But she sensed she'd lingered here too long, and made a few slipups. Better to finish quickly and leave this state behind before they figured out what was going on.

She knew from the beginning that she'd probably have to face off against Candy Holliday at some point, and she'd been prepared for it. The goal from the beginning had been to leave no evidence, no clues, nothing that could be traced back to her. But she'd gotten careless. She'd debated leaving the tulip-patterned earrings and accessories at home, but in the end she'd decided no one would remember her fondness for them, since she hadn't been in town for years.

It appeared she'd been wrong.

It made no difference. It was all circumstantial evidence. Nothing could be traced to her directly — although she *was* concerned that she'd been spotted yesterday up in Old Town. By whom, she didn't know. But it had been someone driving a baby blue pickup truck; she was almost certain of that.

Making the trip to Old Town had been an impromptu move, after she'd seen Candy coming out of the general store yesterday afternoon and climbing into her Jeep. Julia had been out doing a little shopping, on her way back to the hotel after the book signing, and her instincts told her Candy was up to something. So she jumped in her VW and followed at a respectable distance, careful to make sure she wasn't spotted.

Just as she'd suspected, Candy had been on the trail of Maurice Soufflé, and had led her right to his place. She was stunned to learn he'd lived so close to them all these years, and none of them knew it. It had been a pleasant surprise for her, but a not-so-pleasant one for Maurice.

He got what he deserved, she thought as she shuffled through her notes. Mission accomplished — at least one part of it. The rest would take care of itself.

It was time to hurry this presentation along so she could leave, so she decided to skip the section on holiday recipes and jump right to the closer, New England desserts. She'd found some good ones in her travels, and ran over in her head the few she would discuss here today.

But as she looked up, about to continue her talk, she noticed a commotion at the other side of the room, where a table with refreshments had been set up. A woman appeared to be lying flat out on the floor. She wasn't moving. Perhaps she was even unconscious. What the heck was she doing? The silly thing was disrupting her presentation. Julia thought the woman looked vaguely familiar, though she couldn't remember her name.

Then she noticed something else that caused her heart to skip a beat.

Though she couldn't be certain, due to the distance, it looked suspiciously like a jar of pickles from the Sweet Pickle Deli. It sat on the refreshment table, right in the front corner.

Several women were hovering around the prone figure. "I think she's ill," one of them said loudly. "She ate too many of those pickles."

"They're the bad ones, aren't they?" asked a second woman.

"Is there a doctor in the house?" someone else called out.

A male voice from another part of the room spoke up in response. "Yes, right here! I'll take a look at her."

A distinguished-looking gentleman stepped forward, holding a medicine bag. His steel gray hair was combed straight back, and wire-rimmed glasses perched on his thin nose. He hurried to the fallen woman, knelt beside her, and somewhat awkwardly opened the bag and rummaged around inside. Eventually he pulled out a stethoscope and fiddled with it for a few moments before plugging the listening stalks into his ears. He looked up and around. "Give us some room, please!" he said, and motioned for everyone to step back.

Using the stethoscope, he checked the fallen woman's heartbeat, felt for a pulse, and pulled open her eyelids, one at a time, before shaking his head. "I'm afraid there's not much I can do."

A murmur of disbelief swirled around the room, and some of the women appeared visibly shaken. "It's those pickles again," one of them said, clearly stunned. "They've claimed another victim."

But no one was more shocked than Julia von Fleming.

Another jar? How could that be?

How did it get there? she wondered. *She* hadn't put it there. So where had it come from?

She felt her heart pounding. Could the jar on the refreshment table be *her* jar? Had she mixed things up and brought the wrong box into the building? She'd brought in several, including a box of her books and another one containing materials she might need for the presentation and an impromptu signing afterward. She liked to be prepared for every occasion. But had she been too careless this time, accidentally bringing in the box with the jars?

Karla Kincaid, the library's director, was already down off the stage headed toward the opposite side of the room. The other staff members on the stage were standing now, talking worriedly amongst themselves in low whispers.

I need to check it right now, Julia thought, fighting the rising panic, which threatened to swell inside her. *If someone else has died, the police will be suspicious of everyone here. They might even want to check our personal belongings and the cars out in the parking lot.* She didn't want to be caught red-handed with incriminating evidence. She should have ditched that box a day or two ago, but she held on to it, since she thought she might need it. But it had become a detriment, and potentially could get her thrown into jail.

She glanced around. Everyone's attention seemed to be aimed toward the back of the room. No one was looking in her direction at the moment. A perfect time to disappear for a few minutes.

She left her notes where they were. She would pick up the rest of her materials and her purse later. Right now, she had to move quickly, before things got out of hand.

Without saying a word, she bowed her head low and walked off the stage, around the side of the room, and out the door before anyone noticed what she was doing. Moving quickly, she climbed the carpeted stairs to the main floor and hurried out of the building, all the while wondering where that jar of pickles had come from.

Surely it couldn't be hers, could it? That seemed impossible. But she had to check. She had to make sure.

Had someone been digging through her stuff? Had someone broken into her car when it was parked out on the street and taken the box from the back without her knowledge?

If so, she had a pretty good idea who that person might be.

She chided herself. She'd been so careful. She couldn't imagine what had happened.

Outside the library, her head still bowed low to minimize the chance that someone might notice her, she walked briskly toward her white VW.

FORTY-NINE

Standing in a back corner behind the stage, arms crossed, trying to look as inconspicuous as possible, Candy watched as Julia von Fleming left the room in a rush. The cookbook author appeared visibly shaken. She looked as if she was desperate to get somewhere fast.

So far, so good, Candy thought. The plan was working. Now, if the rest of it played out as they'd hoped . . .

Once Julia left the room, several key members of their team signaled to each other, indicating that all was clear, and Artie Groves, who had been playing the role of the doctor, got the message. "Oops, false alarm," he said to those around him. "It appears I spoke too soon. I think she's going to be all right."

As if on cue, Maggie coughed several times, lifted a hand to her chest, and raised her head. "Those pickles were *much* too salty," she said, sputtering a little with her tongue, as if to rid herself of the taste. "Next time, I'll stop after the first one."

There were signs of visible relief around the room, and a few women even applauded, but Candy barely noticed. She had her phone out and was sending out a quick text message:

She's on the move. Parking lot, 5 mins.

Moments later she was on the move herself. But before she left, she located Karla Kincaid, tapped her on the shoulder, and whispered into her ear, "Keep everyone here for a few minutes, okay?"

Karla nodded back. "Will do. Good luck."

Candy crossed the room and climbed the stairs to the main floor. She headed to the front door, but before she exited, she stopped and peered out, scanning the parking lot.

She spotted Julia right away. She was just reaching her car, which was parked on the left-hand side of the lot near a wing of the building. She had a key fob clutched in her hand. She pressed it, and the VW's hatchback popped open.

She moved quickly, dipping her upper torso into the car's trunk space and rummaging around until she found what she wanted. She pulled out a small cardboard box, perhaps a foot square. She checked the contents quickly, shook her head, and then tucked it under her arm. Looking around, she spotted a Dumpster at the end of the library wing on her left. Without hesitation, she crossed to it in a dozen steps, peering surreptitiously in either direction as she approached it. Almost quicker than the eye, she raised the lid of the Dumpster and tossed in the box, then made a hasty retreat.

She scanned the lot as she returned to her car, but seemed assured no one had seen her. Candy remained out of sight just inside the main building.

Back at her car, Julia rearranged the boxes and then closed the hatchback. Palming the key fob, she pressed a button and locked up the car.

She appeared much more confident as she returned to the library — until she saw Candy, who had just stepped out the front door.

Julia stopped dead in her tracks, still halfway between her car and Candy. Her gaze narrowed and her jaw tightened. "You!" she said, her voice carrying across the lot.

"Yes, it's me again," Candy said as she started toward Julia. "I just thought I'd come out and get some air, see what's going on out here. Everything's kind of crazy inside."

Julia glared at her. "That was all your doing, wasn't it? I'll bet that was all an act designed to, what — throw me off my guard?"

"Something like that," Candy said as she got closer.

"That jar wasn't the real thing, was it?" Julia continued, still not moving. "It was a fake, a decoy? Where did you get it?"

"Actually," Candy said, glancing back over her shoulder at the library, "it *was* the real thing. It's one of Sally Ann's. She had only two jars left from the deli, but she emptied one out for us. Of course, she saved the original pickles for herself. Don't want to waste them on something like this. So we replaced them. The ones Maggie ate were store-bought. But," she continued, her gaze returning to Julia, "it was smart of you to double-check."

Julia was visibly angry. "You're saying you interrupted my presentation for that . . . that charade?"

"A small but necessary ruse. And it worked, didn't it? It caused enough doubt in your mind to make you come out here and get rid of that box you just tossed in the Dumpster."

Candy was only a short distance away now, and Julia crossed her arms, as if to strengthen her defense against an invading enemy. "I have no idea what you're talking about."

"Let me guess," Candy continued as she took a final few steps and stopped a few feet from Julia. "There are at least two jars inside that box. Because that would make sense, right? You had to be able to make good on the threat in that letter you wrote to the Pruitts, so you must have kept at least one jar nearby with the Sweet Pickle Deli label on it. I'm guessing the label on it looks fairly new, since you probably had it printed up just a few weeks ago — not like the one on the jar Sally Ann provided to us, one of the originals. You must have used either a local printer in New Hampshire or found someone online. I'm sure we could verify that easily enough. We'd just have to check your computer."

"You'll never get your hands on it. You can't prove anything."

"I'm getting to that," Candy said, "because it's the other jar that's the important one — the 'proof,' as you call it. That's the one piece missing in this whole puzzle — the jar Sally Ann Longfellow left out on her side porch Friday morning, the one Wanda was supposed to pick up and take to the cook-off contest. Someone switched those jars before Wanda got there, and whoever switched them left the jar from the Sweet Pickle deli in its place. But what happened to that jar of Sally Ann's pickles?"

"I'm sure I don't have a clue," Julia said.

Candy accepted that answer and moved on. "Trudy Watkins says you stopped in at the canning demonstration at the general store on Thursday night. That means you must have been in town Friday morning. Just out of curiosity, where *were* you at the time those jars were switched?"

Julia's face hardened. "Not that it's any of your business, but I'll tell you the same thing I told the police — I was in my hotel room, getting a little work done and preparing for the cook-off contest that afternoon. People saw me at the inn. I can prove I was there."

"Be that as it may, you could have found an hour or so to slip out, drive to Georgia McFee's place, and leave a jar in her mailbox, and then on the way back into town stop by Sally Ann's and make the switch. That's when Sally Ann's jar would have gone into that box in your trunk. And it's been there ever since, right?"

"That's crazy," Julia said. "I never heard

such an absurd accusation."

"You've probably been debating all weekend how long to hold on to those jars," Candy continued. "There's not much you could have done with them between Friday morning and today. You could have buried them somewhere, though I doubt you have a shovel with you, or dropped the box in a Dumpster, which you finally did. But you held on to them until now, because you thought they might come in handy at some point. That box wasn't in your hotel room this morning, as far as I could tell, so it had to be in the trunk of your car, right?"

Julia's eyes narrowed as she scrutinized her opponent. "You're fishing," she said.

"But then Maggie collapsed in there, and you thought your jar of poisoned pickles might have somehow made it onto that refreshment table today. That's what you came out here to check — and to get rid of the evidence once and for all. Because the truth is, those two jars, especially the one with Sally Ann's label on it, link you directly to the crime."

"It sounds like you've given this a lot of thought," Julia said, still standing with her arms crossed.

Candy shrugged. "Like I said, it's just common sense." She nodded toward the

Dumpster. "And it's easy enough to verify. We just have to check that box and see what's inside."

For a moment a look of fear flashed through Julia's eyes, but she fought it down, and instead gave Candy a defiant look. "Even if you're right, you still can't prove anything. My fingerprints aren't on those jars. Despite what you say, there's nothing to tie me to them. You might say you saw me toss them in the Dumpster, but it's my word against yours."

"Maybe so," Candy said, "so indulge me for a minute — since there's no one else around, and it's just your word against mine. I can figure most of this out. I take it this was partially about the money — the two hundred thousand mentioned in the extortion letter to the Pruitts — but it was also about you and Maurice Soufflé, wasn't it? That was the point of this whole thing from the beginning — to place the blame for the poisoned pickles on him. Possibly to ruin his reputation. And possibly — at least it's my guess — to try to flush him out of his lair, wherever that might be. Am I close?"

Julia studied Candy for a few long moments, and checked to make sure they were alone in the parking lot before she continued. "Close enough. You're certainly getting warm."

Candy took that as a signal to continue. "Yesterday when I was up at the Spruell place, Marcus told me that you wanted a cut of his deli business, and with good reason, since he used some of your family's recipes, didn't he? Your last name is Kaufman, isn't it? The original pickle recipe Maurice used was attributed to someone named Mabel Kaufman. A relative of yours? Your mother? Grandmother?"

Julia looked somewhat surprised. "How did you find out about that?" she wondered, her face drawn in thought. But then it dawned on her, and she held out a finger for emphasis. "Sapphire Vine, right? That's where you saw a copy of that original recipe. I gave it to her years ago, as evidence. I'm surprised she held on to it. It was my grandmother's recipe, of course. She's responsible for those pickles everyone loves, not Maurice. He stole it from me."

"So you had the recipe all along? But you said you've been trying to get it from him all this time."

Julia shrugged. "A fabrication. My goal was to nail that guy for what he'd done."

"So you were feeding Sapphire information about Maurice?"

"I was doing anything I could to try to

bring him down," Julia admitted, "but no one would listen to me. They were all too wrapped up in his pickles. Everyone kowtowed to that man. They kissed the ground he walked on, all because of their stomachs. No one had the courage to stand up to him — except one or two people, like Georgia McFee."

"So why leave a jar in her mailbox?" Candy asked.

"Because I figured she was smart enough to know what it was. I honestly didn't think she'd eat any of them. I thought she was too smart for that. Guess I was wrong. On the other hand, it helped point the finger toward Maurice in a pretty strong way. The stronger the evidence, the better. I wanted to destroy him in any way possible, from his reputation to, well, . . ." She let her voice trail off.

"So you followed me to Old Town yesterday and waited until I was gone to surprise him at his house, right?"

"I won't go into details, but it's safe to say I got the drop on him, yes. Of course, he was very surprised to see me, although at first he didn't know who I was, since I've changed my appearance since he last saw me. But he figured it out pretty quick."

"So why now?" Candy asked. "Why wait

so long to take your revenge if he cheated and betrayed you so many years ago?"

Julia's expression grew angry again. "Because of Maurice! Because of his greed and arrogance! He contacted me through my website a few months ago, and said he knew my true identity. Said he would expose me unless I split my book profits with him. Imagine that — he refused to share his profits from the deli with me, but demanded I share mine with him! So I had to fight back. I had to stop him, in any way possible."

Candy thought she had all she needed for the moment, but she had a final question. "There's one detail I can't quite figure out," she said, sensing that Julia was growing impatient and was ready to move on. "Why almost eat that pickle on Friday? Why put yourself in danger if you knew it was poisoned? Why not let someone else take the first bite, although if I remember correctly, you tried to get Herr Georg to do just that."

Julia gave her an indulgent look. "It's called deniability. It removed me as a suspect for most of your investigation, didn't it? That was the whole point."

"Were you actually going to eat it?"

Julia shook her head. "Not really. Maybe a

447

nibble or two — nothing that would be too damaging. I knew what I was doing. Now, if you'll excuse me, I believe they're expecting me back inside. I have a presentation to finish."

"I'm afraid you won't be doing that," Candy said, "because in a few minutes you're going to be placed under arrest."

Julia scoffed at this prediction. "You're not listening. I just told you — you have nothing you can pin on me. I'll deny everything I just told you. I'll tell the police you made the whole thing up to protect yourself after you killed Marcus Spruell. You have no evidence I did any of this. So, if you'll stand aside . . ."

With that, she tossed her head and started off toward the library, walking around Candy, who turned in a half circle, her eyes following the other woman. "Actually, I have much more evidence than you realize."

Julia stopped and looked back at her. "That box I just tossed away? I'll tell the police it's not mine. I'll tell them someone else must have put it there."

"You could, but I can prove you did it."

Julia looked at her quizzically, her mouth twisting a bit in disbelief. "How?"

"I have the whole thing on video," Candy said, and turning to her left, she waved an arm toward a nearby stand of tall bushes hugging the exterior wall of the library wing.

A moment later, the branches and leaves on the bushes shivered and began to part. Out stepped Wanda Boyle, dressed head to foot in camouflage, including a scarf around her neck and a camouflage hat, into which she'd tucked her red hair. She was carrying her phone, held out horizontally in front of her.

"Did you get all that?" Candy called to her.

Wanda waved a hand. "Got the entire conversation, boss. Also got video of her tossing the box into the Dumpster."

"How'd the sound come out?"

"It's a little faint because of the distance, but I could definitely make out every word she said. We got everything."

Candy looked back at Julia, a satisfied expression on her face. "See? Proof."

FIFTY

They both heard the sound of a siren then, cutting through the air. Candy turned and saw an approaching patrol car, which was just pulling into the library's parking lot. "Ah, the police have arrived, right on cue," she said.

Julia's entire body visibly stiffened, and she looked like she was going to make a run for it. Her head turned first in one direction, then the other, and before Candy knew what was happening, the cookbook author took off at a run, headed for the library building.

"Hey!" Candy called after her. "Julia, wait!"

There really weren't many places she could go, but Candy knew she had to follow. Out of the corner of her eye she saw the patrol car stop nearby. Both front doors popped open. Chief Durr got out on the left, while Tristan Pruitt emerged from the passenger seat. She motioned toward the library building "She's going back inside!" she called out, and headed after Julia at a run.

She heard voices shouting behind her but didn't stop. In seconds she reached the library's front door and raced inside. The ladies behind the front checkout counter looked at her as if they were in a daze, surprised by the sudden activity. "Which way did she go?" Candy asked.

One of the ladies pointed toward the left. "Into nonfiction."

"There's a back door on that side, though it's rigged with an alarm," another woman said. "Plus, there are stairs up to the second-floor reading room."

"There's another door and a balcony up there," a third woman added.

Candy nodded her thanks. "Let the chief know," she said, and disappeared under an archway that led her into the library's nonfiction section.

Stacks of books on metal shelves reached nearly to the ceiling. They stretched the entire way across the long room, from wall to wall. Candy remembered there were a couple of small private meeting rooms off to her left, and a staff room beyond the far wall. In the center of the stacks was a small reading area with tables and comfortable chairs.

Candy took a few steps forward and turned to her right, scanning the first aisle, its gray carpet looking bluish under fluorescent overhead lights.

No one there. She stepped forward again cautiously, checking the next aisle, and the next, moving quicker with each one.

She heard a shuffling sound somewhere off to her left, and turned into the next aisle, moving slower now, listening and keeping an eye out for Julia.

Too late she saw the large coffee table books spilling off the shelf to her left. They came crashing down onto her shoulder and back. One of them hit her solidly in her upper arm before she moved safely out of the way. "You're throwing *books* at me?" she called out to Julia, incredulously.

"Stay away," Julia called back. Candy could hear her footsteps retreating.

"You can't escape," Candy replied, still moving along the aisle. "The police are right behind me. It's over, Julia. Give yourself up."

She reached the end of the aisle and cautiously turned the corner, only to find a number of other heavy books being flung in her direction. She batted them away, grunting at the effort. But she had Julia in her sights now. The other woman was dashing along the row at the end of the aisles, heading for a door that led outside. In a few more steps she reached it and pushed on the bar. An alarm sounded instantly, but the door gave way, and Julia exited the building.

"She's going out the back!" Candy called to no one in particular, and rushed after Julia, heading along the row and out the door.

But by the time she got outside it was already over. Tristan was just coming around the side of the building and practically caught Julia in his arms. She struggled for a few moments, flailing at him, and managed to break free. But a second police car appeared then, also coming around the corner of the building. An officer jumped out and managed to corral Julia before she could go any further.

"Hold on to her. I'm on my way," Chief Durr said, coming up behind Candy as she sputtered to a stop. As he passed by her at a quick pace, he briefly slowed. "We'll take it from here, Ms. Holliday."

"You should check the Dumpster out by the parking lot," Candy told him, pointing with her arm. "You'll find a small box with two jars in it, including one belonging to

Sally Ann. Plus, Wanda has Julia's whole confession on video."

The chief nodded. "We're already taking care of the box, with Wanda's help. Nice job."

He gave her a tight smile before moving on to assist in the arrest of Julia von Fleming.

Candy bent over and placed her hands on her knees as Tristan approached her. "Are you all right?" he asked, sounding worried.

Candy nodded, taking a few breaths and brushing stray strands of hair out of her face.

"I got your text," he said. "We just finished up the paperwork."

"You get everything you need?" she asked.

He nodded. "It took some convincing — and of course the chief wasn't thrilled with your involvement in this whole thing — but he agreed with your conclusion and took appropriate action. We have a search warrant for her car but I'm not sure we'll need it now. It sounds like you've taken care of everything."

"I had lots of help," Candy said.

"You shouldn't have gone after her like that. You could have been hurt. Are you sure you're okay?"

"Just a few minor bruises," Candy admitted with a weak smile. "I never thought she would use books as weapons. I guess I felt the true power of the printed page."

FIFTY-ONE

Night was falling by the time she drove back into downtown.

It was after six on a Sunday evening, and most of the stores along Main Street and Ocean Avenue were closed, though a few places, like the pizza parlor, were still open. The sky was clear, with bright stars beginning to appear overhead, and there was a chill in the air, a typical early fall New England evening. The sea beyond the rocky coast was dark and silent.

Candy had spent the entire afternoon at the police station, along with Wanda, Tristan, Maggie, Artie, and Sally Ann, answering questions, making statements, and receiving stern lectures about involving themselves in an official police investigation.

"We keep having this conversation, Ms. Holliday," Chief Durr told her at one point, "but I'm not going to beat you up about it too much this time. I realize you were trying to clear your own name. It looks like you've been able to do that. I just wish you'd found another way. Still, it all worked out all right in the end, didn't it? Ms. von Fleming is now on her way to the county facility in Machias. She'll see the judge in the morning."

A little later, he said, "I think we have just about everything we need here," and finally released them, one by one.

But after hanging around the police station all afternoon, and listening to everyone else tell their sides of the story, she began to realize there were still a few pieces missing, and a few unanswered questions.

That's why, after leaving the station, she'd made her way back to Main Street, and parked outside Zeke's General Store.

She had other places she knew she should be. Earlier in the afternoon her father and the boys had dropped in at the station, to check on Candy and the others, and make sure everyone was okay. Even though she'd assured Doc she was fine, he had lingered, until she'd finally shooed him on home. "I'm sure they'll let us go shortly," she'd told him.

After more coaxing, he'd reluctantly left. "I'll be waiting for you," he said, giving her a kiss on the cheek. "Take care of yourself."

"I always do, Dad."

That had been a couple of hours ago, and she knew her father was back at the farm, anxiously awaiting her return, with a thousand questions in his mind about all that had happened that day.

Candy herself was feeling drained. It had been a long day. She'd attended the funeral of a goat, dodged an onslaught of heavy books, caught a criminal, and endured endless questioning from the police. She was sure there'd be more questions and more trips to the station before this whole case was laid to rest. But for now, she needed to relax, to eat, to clear her mind, to drink a cup of tea and put up her feet and unwind after a challenging day.

But there was still some unfinished business she had to take care of, and it couldn't wait.

So as the light leached from the sky, and another quiet evening settled over Cape Willington, Candy pulled up in front of the general store and shut off the engine. She sat silently for a few moments as the engine cooled and ticked, eyeing the store. She knew it would be closed by this time, but she hoped she still might find someone inside. The lights were still on. Perhaps someone was cleaning up.

Taking a deep breath, and feeling hesitant and uncertain about what might happen in the next few minutes, she climbed out of the Jeep, looked up and down the street, glanced at the general store again, and finally made her way across the sidewalk to the store's front door.

She jiggled the handle and pushed on the door. Locked, as she'd expected. She gazed in through the door's glass window, just as she had two nights ago, when she'd stood in this same spot, the rain pouring down on her. She thought she'd seen something moving inside the store that night, and now guessed that it had been Brian Jr., lurking in the shadows, apparently keeping an eye on her before following her out onto the street and spooking her.

She saw a similar movement inside the store tonight. Someone was back among the aisles, though she couldn't tell who it was.

She rapped loudly on the door. "Hello? Anyone still here? It's Candy Holliday."

Shadows moved inside, but no one appeared.

She knocked again, called out again, and waited.

It took some time, but finally a slim figure, wearing an apron with broom in hand, stepped hesitantly out from one of the side aisles near the middle of the store and looked in her direction. The figure studied her, as if trying to decide what to do.

Candy knocked again, more urgently this time. "Trudy, is that you? I need to talk to you. Can you let me in?"

The figure inside shook her head. "We're closed," Candy heard her say faintly through the heavy door. "Come back tomorrow."

"Tomorrow will be too late. Please unlock the door."

Candy couldn't tell whether she was recognized or not, because the figure moved away then, turning back into the store's shadows, moving toward the counter. She disappeared from view, and for a minute or two, Candy thought she was gone for good.

But then she reappeared, without the broom or apron, and approached the front door with slow steps, hands held together nervously in front of her. "Candy, what's going on?" Trudy asked through the door, her voice muted.

"We have to talk. Can I come in?"

Again, Trudy hesitated, but finally she relented and unlocked the door so Candy could slip inside. Then she relocked the door and turned toward the newcomer. "What are you doing here?" she asked.

"I'm sorry to interrupt you like this, when you're trying to clean up, but I have a few questions I'd like to ask you, if you have a few minutes. I suppose you heard what happened this afternoon?"

Trudy nodded. In a soft, almost breathless tone, she said, "They've arrested Julia von Fleming."

"They're charging her with the murders of Ned and Maurice," Candy confirmed. "I've been over at the police station all afternoon. We have Julia's confession on video. The police have pieced together most of the events that happened this weekend, but there are a few loose ends — things I haven't been able to figure out. I thought you might be able to help."

"Me?" Trudy said weakly. "I'm not quite sure how, but I suppose I could try."

Candy nodded. "That's all I can ask, because a few things still don't make sense. For instance, the last time you and I talked, you told me that Julia was at the canning demonstration in your store on Thursday night."

Trudy nodded her head in confirmation. "Yes, that's correct."

"You also said she'd driven over here that afternoon, from New Hampshire. You specifically said she was tired from the trip.

Do you remember that?"

"Yes, well, I suppose that's what I said."

"Because here's the confusing part," Candy went on. "On Friday, the Pruitt family received an extortion letter demanding two hundred thousand dollars, and threatening to harm more people with poisoned pickles if they didn't pay up. The letter was mailed to the Pruitts from Cape Willington last Tuesday."

"Uh-huh," Trudy said, listening attentively.

"Well, there's a problem," Candy said. "Julia wasn't here in town on Tuesday. She was still in New Hampshire. While I was at the police station, I checked her schedule on her website. She had an event at the library in Concord that evening, on Tuesday night, so she couldn't have mailed that letter to the Pruitts. Someone else must have mailed it — from here in town."

"Oh, I see," Trudy said, nodding, her face expressionless.

"Then there's the cook-off contest," Candy continued. "If I remember correctly, you said you went there to get a closer look at Julia, because she resembled Gloria. You said you didn't get a chance to talk to her, but you did talk to Marjorie Coffin. You told her there was a cardboard box on the hood

462

of her car."

Another faint nod. "Yes, that's correct. I remember that."

"There was a note on the box, saying there were several jars of pickled items inside. We've speculated — Marjorie and I — that the jar of poisoned pickles was in that box, and that's how it got into the gym. But here's the interesting part: Marjorie said the note on the box was handwritten, printed in block letters with a black felt-tip pen. She said the note was 'neatly done.' I saw Julia's handwriting at the book signing yesterday. It's legible but hardly what I'd call neat. However, I couldn't help noticing when I was in your store yesterday that you have very distinctive handwriting. I assume that little placard next to the pickled zucchinis was hand-printed by you, right, in those neat block letters?"

Trudy's voice was a little hoarse when she said, "Yes, it was."

Candy accepted this confirmation and moved on. "Then there's the issue of Sally Ann's jar of pickles, which was switched out for one with the tainted pickles in it. There's one question I've been asking myself over and over the past few hours, and so far I haven't been able to come up with an answer. Whoever switched those jars — and

463

we believe it was Julia — must have known Sally Ann was going to leave her jar of pickles out on the stoop for Wanda to pick up. But how would someone know she was going to do that? There's only one way — the person learned it from either Sally Ann or Wanda, of course, because it wasn't public information. Now, Sally Ann's not the chatty sort, so I doubt she told anyone she was leaving out that jar — other than Wanda, of course. On the other hand, Wanda tends to gab a lot. She was here Thursday night, in your store, during the canning demonstrations. You said so yourself — you said she was here the entire time, taking photos and conducting interviews. And Julia was here as well. Either Wanda and Julia talked to each other that night about that jar, which is certainly possible, or more likely there was a third party involved — someone who overheard Wanda mention it earlier in the evening, and then relayed the information to Julia when she was here."

When Trudy didn't respond to this, Candy came to her final points. "Another thing's been bothering me, and it's about the amount of money mentioned in the extortion letter sent to the Pruitts. Whoever sent that letter, from here in Cape Willington, demanded two hundred thousand dollars, or else. But why that exact amount? If you're going to ask for that much money, why not round it up to a quarter-million dollars — two hundred fifty thousand? That would be logical. Two hundred thousand seems like a somewhat random number — unless it was meant for two people, a hundred grand apiece. That would make sense, wouldn't it?"

She crossed her arms and waited for a response.

Trudy stared down at the floor and tossed her head a little. Finally, softly, she said, "Julia gave me the exact wording for that letter, you know. I typed it out on my computer, word for word, just like she said. Then I printed it out and sent it off. She even gave me the address to send it to. She said it had to be mailed from Cape Willington, and not New Hampshire."

"But why?" Candy asked, her brow furrowing. "Why get mixed up with her?"

Now Trudy looked up, her watery eyes focusing on Candy. "Because we had no choice — because we needed the money. And because Maurice Soufflé was the cause of it all. You know my husband Richard hasn't been feeling well. I told you he had leg problems. But it's much worse than that.

We haven't told many people about the extent of his health issues, but they go back to a stroke he had about five years ago — when Maurice was in town. Richard and Maurice — well, they didn't get along. They had a fight about something and Maurice got vindictive. He started spreading bad rumors about Richard and me and about our store. We started losing traffic. Our reputations were at stake. That's when Richard got so upset he had the stroke, and he's never fully recovered. He's tried to help out here in the store ever since, whenever he can, but I've run the place more or less by myself for the past few years, and it's honestly more than I can handle. Our profits have fallen off. We have trouble keeping up with the bills. We've even thought we might have to close or sell the place. . . ."

"But then Julia offered you a way out," Candy said, finally understanding.

"We've kept in touch all this time," Trudy admitted, "despite what I've led you to believe. I apologize for misleading you, but I had no choice. Julia and I bonded over tulips, but we also share a common hatred of Maurice Soufflé. When she found out she'd be coming here to judge the cook-off contest, she contacted me. She said she had come up with a way to get back at Maurice, and wanted to know if I'd help. Hopefully, she said, we could both make some money, and after thinking about it, I agreed. She assured me no one would get hurt — that the poison in the jars wouldn't kill anyone, that it would only cause queasiness or maybe vomiting. But, well, I guess she misled me. I think she said she used something like oleander leaves in the jars, and, well, maybe she used too many of them. When Ned died . . . well, I can't tell you how devastated I was. But by that time there wasn't much I could do about it. I had to keep quiet about what I knew."

Candy listened to all this, and when Trudy finished, she said, "I know this is hard for you, but I have one last question. How did the jar of poisoned pickles get from the box to the table at the cook-off contest on Friday? I presume you didn't put it there, or Julia, since your fingerprints would have been on it, which I'm sure you wanted to avoid."

"That's true," said Trudy. "We were very cautious, though I guess we weren't cautious enough. But to answer your question, Ned put it there, on the table."

"How did he know it was in the box?" Candy asked.

"Well, I suppose it's because I told him it

would be there."

"So you were the one spreading rumors about the jar on Friday?"

"Julia said we had to create a buzz about it. We had to get people looking for it, if we wanted the plan to work. I left the gym just as Marjorie was bringing in the box. She put it under the table with the pickled items, just as we expected, and shortly after Julia spotted Ned digging around in it. She saw him open the jar, take out a few pickles, and then put the jar on the table."

"So she must have been fairly certain he'd eat one or two of them, and she was just waiting for that to happen while she pretended to almost eat one herself," Candy concluded.

It all made sense now. There was silence for a few moments as the two women looked at each other, until Trudy said, "So I suppose I have to tell all this to the police now, don't I?"

Candy nodded. "Yes, unfortunately you do. But you don't have to do it alone. I'll go with you."

Trudy looked visibly worried. "But what will happen to us? What will happen to the store? Who will take care of it?"

Candy thought a moment. "Does Brian Jr. know about any of this? Was he involved in this scheme with you and Julia?"

Trudy shook her head, horrified. "Oh no, nothing like that. No one else knows about any of this. I haven't told a soul, especially Richard or Brian Jr. I didn't want either of them to get into trouble because of something I'd done."

"Then Brian Jr. can take care of the store for you," Candy said, "and others will pitch in. I'm sure Richard will help as best he can. And I'll help out behind the counter if I'm needed. You're going to have a lot on your mind over the next few weeks, so you shouldn't have to worry about the store. One way or another, we'll keep the place running for you, no matter what happens."

Trudy nodded gratefully. "You've always been a good friend, Candy," she said, and steeled herself. Finally she nodded firmly, as if accepting her fate. "So," she said in a long, winded breath, "I guess I'll go ahead and lock up the place, and we can head over to the police station. We might as well get this over with."

EPILOGUE

On Tuesday afternoon, Candy took off work
early. She was fairly certain she wouldn't be
missed in the office, and doubted anyone
would even notice her absence. The place
was humming along nicely. After her brush
with mortality, Wanda was back in the office
with a renewed sense of purpose, taking on
additional management responsibilities and
freeing up some time for Candy to focus on
writing and editing. The day before, Herr
Georg and Colin had dropped off their
judges' notes from the cook-off contest, and
the notes were complete enough so they'd
be able to put together a decent article for
the bicentennial issue. They'd decided to
exclude Julia von Fleming's comments and
choices, given the events of the weekend. Of
course, the cook-off contest would always
be marred by Ned's death and everything
that came after, but Candy and Wanda both
felt an obligation to the community and its

people to finish what they'd started. "Ned would have wanted it that way," Wanda assured her.

As she drove out to Sally Ann's place, Candy rolled down the driver's side window, letting in cool, fresh air. She was always amazed by how quickly the temperature changed during the month of September. It was as if someone had turned down a big thermostat in the sky by ten or twelve degrees, ushering in the autumn weather. It happened like clockwork every year, the inexorable shift from summer to fall in a matter of a few weeks, just like the changing of the leaves and the imminent arrival of winter.

She'd had a chat with Wanda that morning, and told her she'd been thinking of leaving the paper on a day-to-day basis. "I'd like to stay involved in some way," Candy had said, "but I don't want to come into the office every day. I have too many other things I'd like to do."

Wanda hadn't been totally surprised. "I knew something's been going on in that head of yours," she said. "I could tell you've been looking at greener pastures."

"I'm not sure what will happen with my position, should I decide to leave," Candy went on. "They might bring in a new editor, or they might promote from within. I'm going to recommend the latter."

Wanda's eyebrows had risen then in genuine surprise. "Any idea of potential candidates?"

"I'm looking at one this very moment."

Now, on her way along Gleason Street toward Sally Ann's place, Candy wasn't sure it was the most sensible decision to leave the paper right now — or ever, for that matter. It was a good job in a time when good jobs were hard to come by. But she felt it was the right one. She'd had a good run at the paper — she'd been there for five years now, starting out as the community columnist before working her way up to editor. She felt comfortable with her decision, which in her mind was almost final. It was time to get back to the farm. That's where her heart was. She'd neglected it for too long.

Still, she'd given herself plenty of time to think about it. "I'm not going to make any definite decisions for at least a month or so, until we see how everything settles," she'd told Wanda. "But I wanted to let you know, so you have a head start if the editor's position does open up sometime in the near future."

She pushed these thoughts away for now

as she pulled into Sally Ann's driveway. It was already occupied by an old red Saab station wagon, which had seen its share of winter wear. Candy heard a dog barking then, somewhere off behind the house, and a series of bleats.

"Random," Candy said to herself as she pulled to a stop and shut off the engine. "And the newest members of our community."

She brought her tote bag with her, so she could take a few photos and make a few notes, and headed back behind the house, where all the action was taking place.

It looked like a small petting zoo. And Sally Ann was in the middle of it all, beaming like a new mother.

With her was Neil Crawford, owner of Crawford's Berry Farm, located just outside Cape Willington out past Blueberry Acres. Neil was bearded and long-haired, a bit of a modern-day hippie, with an earthy demeanor and a gentle spirit. She'd met him a year earlier, when she'd helped him solve the mystery of his father's death. Neil had since inherited his father's berry farm, and for the past year he'd been splitting his time between here and his own farm in Vermont. But a few months ago he'd put the place in Vermont up for sale, realizing it was time to choose one or the other. He'd decided on Cape Willington. He was just returning from closing the sale on his farm in Vermont and taking care of last-minute details, including the dispersal of some of his farm animals.

At the moment, the objects of everyone's attention, especially Sally Ann's, were two sheep, which Neil had brought over with him from Vermont, apparently in the back of the Saab wagon. He'd had a much larger flock at his old place, but had sold most of the animals to a neighbor. However, he'd held on to two of the ewes, and brought them along with him. No doubt Random, his big shaggy dog, had occupied the front passenger seat on the way over. The dog was now keeping a watchful eye over the first meeting of Sally Ann, Guinevere, and the two new sheep.

"Do they have names?" Sally Ann asked.

Neil nodded. "This one's Bess, and this is Clara. They're yours if you want to keep them. I thought — well, Candy and I thought — that Guinevere could use a few companions . . . provided they get along, of course."

"Oh, I think they'll get along just fine!" Sally Ann said, beaming. She was happier than Candy had ever seen her. "I'll make sure they do. And thank you!" She seemed genuinely touched.

"You're going to need a grazing pen for the sheep, something bigger than you have now, but I can help you with that," Neil said, looking around her place.

"And others in town might pitch in too," Candy added. "I've been putting out the word. Before you know it, you'll have a whole army of people over here helping you build a new home for your flock."

"We know they can't take the place of Cleopatra," Neil told Sally Ann, "but consider this a new beginning for all of us. Plus, you can shear them in the spring and make a little extra money on the wool."

As Sally Ann fussed over her newest family members, Candy and Neil turned together to talk. "Everything go okay with the closing?" she asked.

"As smooth as possible. Looks like I'm a Mainer now."

"And a villager, that's true," Candy said, and she held out her hand. "Well, welcome to Cape Willington, Mr. Crawford."

He smiled, and they shook. "It seems like a nice community," he said. "I think I'm going to like it here. Of course, there's a lot of work to do out at the farm."

"Yours and mine both. Doc and I want to

put up a hoophouse behind the barn, and expand the back blueberry field, and maybe even set up a farm stand for a retail operation during picking and harvest season."

"Hmm, well," Neil said, nodding his approval, "those are ambitious plans. Maybe we can help each other out — work together."

Candy smiled broadly. "I'd like that."

"Me too," Neil said with a charming grin.

And as she turned back to Sally Ann and the animals, full of ideas for the future, Candy knew she'd made the right decision.

RECIPES

HELEN ILGENFRITZ BOLTZ'S PICKLED RED BEET EGGS
This recipe is from my
great grandmother Helen.

Put in a Large Jar or Crock:
1 can sliced red beets with juice, or 1 red
beet cooked, plus the cooking liquid.
4-6 hard-boiled eggs, shelled, left whole
(depending on jar size).

Mix 1 part white vinegar to 2 parts water
and add a little sugar until mixture is to
your taste. Not too sour, not too sweet.
  The liquid mixture must be enough to
cover the eggs and beets. Amount depending on the size of the jar.
  Cover the jar and let sit in the refrigerator
at least one day until the eggs are red and
pickled. This does not need any boiling
water bath. The jar of pickled red beet eggs

will keep for one week (or not, if you eat them quickly!).

DOC'S FAVORITE HARVEST COOKIES

1 cup butter
3/4 cup sugar
3/4 cup light brown sugar
2 eggs
1 teaspoon vanilla
2 tablespoons milk
1 1/2 cups flour
1 teaspoon baking soda
1 teaspoon cinnamon
3 cups uncooked quick oatmeal
1 cup white chocolate chips
3/4 cup dried wild blueberries
3/4 cup dried cranberries

Dried apricot can also be used as a substitute, or in addition to the other fruits.

Preheat the oven to 350 degrees.

In a large mixing bowl, mix the butter and sugars together until it is creamy.

Add the eggs, vanilla, and milk. Mix until it is smooth.

Add the flour, baking soda, and cinnamon and mix well.

Add the oatmeal and mix well.

Add the white chips, dried wild blueberries, and dried cranberries. Mix.

Drop by full teaspoon or by tablespoon amounts of dough onto ungreased cookie sheets.

Bake in the 350-degree oven for about 10 minutes or until cookies are a golden brown.

This recipe makes about four dozen cookies. Eat them before Doc finds out you have them!

FROZEN CUCUMBER SALAD
Recipe courtesy of Aunt Mary-Helen Thorne, St. Albans, Maine.

2 quarts sliced, unpeeled, small cucumbers
2 medium onions, sliced
1 tablespoon salt
1 cup vinegar
1 1/4 cups sugar

Combine cucumbers, onions, and salt. Let mixture soak for 3 hours.

In a saucepan, warm vinegar and sugar, stirring to dissolve sugar.

Drain cucumbers and add to vinegar-sugar mixture.

Ladle into freezer containers and freeze.

When ready to use, take out of freezer and

let thaw.

Serve chilled.

Yield: 1 1/2 quarts

DUFFY'S DINER
CRANBERRY APPLESAUCE

6 cups unsweetened apple cider or apple
  juice
20 apples (about) or 5 lbs. These should be
  cored and quartered
One pinch of salt
One 12 oz. bag of fresh cranberries, rinsed
1 cup of sugar
Pint-sized canning jars
Boiling water bath canning pot

In a large pot on medium high heat, bring
the cider or juice to a boil, turn it down to
a simmer, and reduce by half, so half the
liquid is left. This can take 20 minutes to
half an hour.

Add the apple quarters, cranberries, and
the salt and sugar.

Bring back to a boil, then turn heat down
to a simmer.

Stir occasionally for about 1 hour, or until
you have a thick puree.

Duffy puts in only one cup of sugar. If
you like it very sweet, add more to your
taste.

Set a sieve over a large bowl or pot. Ladle the cranberry applesauce into the sieve. Push sauce through the sieve with the back of a spoon into the bowl or pot. This gets rid of any chunks or skin and leaves a smooth puree.

Ladle the cranberry applesauce into thoroughly clean pint-sized canning jars. Leave 1/2 inch of headroom. Put sterilized lids on the jars.

Process the jars of cranberry applesauce in a boiling water bath canner for 10 minutes.

Let the jars cool completely; check to make sure all the lids have sealed properly.

Store in a cool, dry place.

This recipe yields about 5 pints of cranberry applesauce.

THE BASICS OF CANNING AND PICKLING

BY CANDY HOLLIDAY
INTERIM MANAGING EDITOR,
THE *Cape Crier*
PUTTINGFOODBYCAPEWILLINGTON.COM

The process of canning and pickling food for preservation, or "putting food by," goes back ten thousand years. Today, it is not as necessary to can, but preserving fresh food and seeing all the jars filled with pickles, jams, and fruits on your pantry shelf is very satisfying.

First in the process is to make sure you do the canning safely. There are two basic methods for canning. One is the boiling water bath method, and the other is to use a pressure canner. The boiling water bath process is when the jars are immersed in boiling water in a boiling water canner for a certain period of time, depending on altitude. This seals the jars and preserves the food in them. The pressure canner heats the jars to a temperature above the boiling point, sealing and preserving the food that way.

The boiling water bath is for foods that are high in acidity, including fruits, pickled products, and tomatoes. Tomatoes today are not as acidic as they used to be, so lemon juice needs to be added to be able to use the boiling water method. The pressure canner is for all other foods, meats, and foods that are not going to be pickled.

My favorite method, and favorite foods, are pickled using the boiling water bath method. For this method of canning, you'll need the following basic equipment:

CANNING JARS. Jars commonly come in half-pint, pint, and quart sizes. You can reuse the jars as long as they are clean and free of cracks or chips in the glass.

CANNING LIDS. These two-part lids include the band and the lid itself. The lids are for one-time use only. Food safety cannot be guaranteed if they are used more than once.

A BOILING WATER CANNER, or large pot deep enough to cover the jars with one to two inches of water. The canner includes a rack to put the jars in to keep them raised off the bottom of the pot.

AN 8- OR 10-QUART POT. You'll use this for cooking the fruits and vinegars. Some tend to boil over, so a larger pot is better. (I learned this the hard way!)

CHEESECLOTH, MEASURING SPOONS, CLEAN DISH TOWELS, and a **TIMER.**

A JAR LIFTER. This usually comes with the canner and is used to remove the hot jars from the pot.

LABELS. To label and date the food after it is canned.

Prepare the jars for canning by washing them in hot water and then sterilizing them in boiling water for 10 minutes. Leave them in the hot water until ready for use.

Repeat the process with the lids and bands.

Prepare your favorite recipe, fill the jars, and process them in the canner for the amount of time stated on the recipe, or adjust for altitude.

Remove them from the canning bath.

Then you have the "popability" test, as we call it. Makes sure all of the jars make a popping sound, which indicates the lid has sealed. You can test this by pressing on the lid with your thumb. If there is an indentation, and the lid doesn't pop back, it is sealed.

Now you can preserve your harvest and enjoy fresh food all year long!

CPSIA information can be obtained
at www.ICGtesting.com
Printed in the USA
FFOW05n1615310715